A note to n

I'd like to share a conversation ~~~~~~~~ one of my children about regret.

I don't currently choose to waste any time on it.

It's not that I've never made a mistake or that all of my choices have been good ones, but somewhere in my twenties I decided to make every decision with the most loving heart I could and it freed me from regret.

I accept that I am a fallible human being and that those around me are the same.

I choose to start each day with the mindset that I can and will do better than I did the day before.

I'll be kinder.

Stronger.

More forgiving.

A better listener.

More present in the lives of those I love.

Humbler in the face of the wonder of the world.

And when I falter, I do my best to make amends. Not every apology is accepted, but I've made myself okay with that as well. The only person I have control over is myself.

Regret is a friend I choose to ban from my heart and my house. It brings nothing of worth and instigates trouble wherever it goes.

It's close friends with bitterness and envy.

I've seen it hang out with spite a few times.

It invites depression over on a regular basis.

None of them are welcome in my life.

If you're carrying the weight of every mistake you've ever made, release it into the universe.

Trust me, ban regret from your home and heart.

You'll not only feel better, but you'll bring more joy to those around you.

He Said Forever

The Lost Corisis

Book 4

Ruth Cardello

Author Contact

website: RuthCardello.com

email: ruthcardello@gmail.com

Facebook: Author Ruth Cardello

Twitter: RuthieCardello

Goodreads

goodreads.com/author/show/4820876.Ruth_Cardello

Bookbub

bookbub.com/authors/ruth-cardello

Copyright

CHAPTER ONE

Jared

O F COURSE SHE'S *beautiful.*

Another man might have been pleased that the woman who'd stepped out a blue sedan had legs that went on forever and curves ample enough to strain the top buttons of her sundress. Some might have appreciated the way the wind flattened what otherwise would have been loose clothing in the most deliciously revealing way.

Michawn Courter was sheer perfection, but I wouldn't have expected less from Hamilton. He had excellent taste in women. Long dark brown hair with caramel highlights bounced and was loosely tied back from her face. Her eyes were dark and stunning but it was the smile she shot me that was nearly my undoing.

This one would be hard to pass on.

As a rule, I didn't so much as flirt with any of the women Hamilton sent me. Mostly because I had no issues when it came to finding willing sex partners on my own, but also because Hamilton had a bad habit of telling women I was ready to settle down.

I wasn't.

Far from it.

After what could only be called a late-life crisis, Hamilton had reshuffled his priorities and retired, selling his multibillion-dollar company to me. His reasoning for changing his mind regarding the importance of having a partner was understandable. Two of his friends had died and he was feeling his mortality.

The same man who'd spent the last decade warning me to not let a woman distract me from success had made one woman the center of his universe. Not that Fara wasn't amazing. She made Hamilton happy and anything beyond that wasn't any of my business.

A recent back surgery for an old injury had her recovering at an exclusive rehab center with Hamilton at her side. My reason for being at his home in Newton was to facilitate his surprise for her and ensure its completion before their return.

There were very few people I would cancel meetings for and even fewer who would dare to ask me to. When it came to Hamilton I didn't say no because I owed him more than I could ever repay.

But agreeing to marry simply because Hamilton was indulging in a late-life crisis?

That crossed the line of what I was willing to do for anyone.

Normally knowing the women Hamilton threw my way

came with expectations I had no desire to entertain was enough to nullify any attraction I may have felt for them.

This woman was different and I didn't like it.

Sporting a huge smile, she stood in the driveway with a piece of luggage beside her as if expecting me to rush over to assist her. I folded my arms across my chest.

Seemingly unbothered by my stance she bent to pick up her luggage and I sucked in a harsh breath. I'd always considered myself an ass man, but the kind of cleavage she flashed would have turned my best friend Calvin's head and probably his husband's as well.

Damn.

When she straightened, she brought her luggage in front of her, holding it with both hands and my mouth dropped open. Right there in Hamilton's driveway I found a way to end wars. Governments simply needed to have this woman walk across a battlefield in that dress holding her luggage so her breasts pushed out and upward so high they promised to spill out. There wasn't a man alive who could think about killing with that view and all his blood heading south.

World peace—done.

Holy shit.

She closed the distance between us, placed her luggage at my feet, and held out her hand in greeting. "Jared Seacrest?"

I nodded once in acknowledgement.

"I'm Michawn Courter," she added.

I've never been a man who struggled to express himself.

Confidence was the backbone of my success. It had been my swagger that had caught Hamilton's attention nearly a decade ago. I'd survived an unsavory childhood by grit alone and achieved more than I'd ever dared think possible by never being intimidated by a situation or a person.

Still, something about the smile she beamed me left me temporarily speechless. I stood there, arms folded, glaring at her because what I wanted to do had nothing to do with giving her a tour of Hamilton's homes and everything to do with getting her out of that dress. "You're late," I said gruffly.

"I am." Her smile didn't waver. "But I'm here."

I leaned ever so slightly toward her. The air sizzled between us. "I won't be for long. I cleared my schedule for this tour. Considering how late it is, it'll be brief."

She glanced down at the watch on her wrist then pursed her lips. "I would have been here an hour ago, but . . .traffic. If there's somewhere you need to be, don't let me hold you here. Mr. Wenham said both homes have staff. I already have a pretty good idea of what I'll be designing so I don't mind who shows me around."

Not used to being so easily dismissed, I frowned. "That won't be necessary since I'm already here."

She tipped her head to the side. "Are you having a bad day or are you just irritated that I'm late?"

I lowered my arms and growled. "Neither."

Her smile returned. "Then why don't you show me

where I can put my things?" There was a twinkle in her eyes that confused me. "If you have time."

She glanced down at her luggage then at me.

I considered letting her carry it again, remembered the damage that view had done to my ability to concentrate, then picked it up. Something needed to be said upfront. "Whatever Hamilton told you about me was likely inaccurate."

"All he said was that you'd be here to give a quick tour."

I doubted that. "And nothing more?"

She raised and lowered her bare shoulders, a move that had me instantly imagining kissing my way over both. "Not that I can remember. We talked a lot about his son Gavin discovering his wife is pregnant with twins. Mr. Wenham said he'd recently married a woman he wished he'd met earlier and that she might have some mobility issues when she returned home. My goal is to not only bring the magic, but also ensure it's all accessible."

"The magic," I scoffed.

Her hands went to her hips as the wind once again plastered her dress to her intimately. "Have you seen any of my work?"

"I have not."

"Do you have any children, Mr. Seacrest?"

She knew the answer to that already, but I was willing to play along. "None I'm aware of."

"Well, either way, I've worked with many families to

create spaces in their homes that spark their children's imagination. Childhood is supposed to be fun and fanciful. That's what I offer."

Hamilton had chosen well this time. This one was not only a beauty, but she lit up as she talked about her work. Tempting. I didn't like how effortlessly she held my attention. "Everyone has to make a living, I suppose."

Her nose wrinkled. "You're not an easy one to impress, are you? That's okay. You wouldn't be the first to start off doubting the impact my spaces can bring to a family. I'll win you over."

Leaning closer, I warned, "Don't." Decreasing the space between us had been a mistake I instantly recognized. The light scent of her perfume tickled my senses as my blood headed south.

Her eyes rounded. "Don't what?"

"Think we'll see each other again after today. I agreed to meet you once, that's all."

After opening and closing her mouth, she frowned. "Hamilton gave me your contact information. It was my understanding that I'll be sending the project proposal to you."

I straightened and frowned because she was sounding so sensible. "Will there actually be one?"

She looked around before saying, "Yes? Did I miss something?"

With a growl, I let some of my frustration show. "You're

good, but I know what you're doing here."

"Sorry?"

Watching her expression closely, I laid my cards on the table. "Hamilton means well. He had a life-altering experience and it changed his priorities. It did not, however, change mine."

She blinked a few times quickly. "I don't understand."

"Quit the pretense. Like I said, Hamilton thinks he's helping by sending every single woman he meets my way, but I'm perfectly happy with my life the way it is. So, don't bother pretending to take room measurements if you're really here just to meet me. I'm not saying I wouldn't fuck you. What I'm saying is I don't have the time or the interest for more than that."

After a pause, she said, "Whew, I'm glad we got that out of the way because I'm happily engaged and this could have gotten awkward fast." Her tone was light. "Although I appreciate the compliment, however crudely it was delivered, I can assure you there is only one reason I'm here, and that's to get the measurements of the rooms I'll renovate for Mr. Wenham."

I looked her over from head to toe, this time paying special attention to her bare left hand. "Engaged? You expect me to believe that?" Was she hoping that the idea of her with another man would add a thrill to the chase? Perhaps set her apart from the others I'd turned away?

She brought a delicate hand up between us. "The stone

was loose in my ring so it's with the jeweler." Her gaze met mine. "You'll just have to take my word for it."

"What's his name? This man you're engaged to."

"Teddy. His actual name is Theodore, but he's a big teddy bear so that's his nickname."

I turned and started walking again. It bothered me how much I didn't like the idea of her with another man. Was Teddy real? A lie? Both possibilities were equally distasteful.

She followed me. Without speaking, we made our way up the four steps to the front door of the mansion. I held the door open for her. As she walked past me, she paused and searched my face. "I hope I didn't embarrass you. Obviously you and Mr. Wenham are going back and forth about something, but he was fully aware that I'm engaged. I'm not part of his plot to change your marital status. Mr. Wenham simply liked my work enough to hire me."

"Did he?" Two things could be true at once. Hamilton could want his homes renovated and play matchmaker. Since none of his earlier attempts had worked, it was possible Hamilton had told this woman she'd need to play hard to get to catch my attention.

She held my gaze, though, like someone who had nothing to hide. "This is an incredible opportunity for me. Doing both homes will bring in the funds to not only pay for my wedding, but hopefully have enough extra to cover the pro bono projects I have on the calendar."

"Pro bono projects?"

"I also design playgrounds for low-income communities. Some of my ideas are expensive and fundraising only goes so far. My friends joke that I'll never have a designer purse if I keep channeling my profits into pirate ships with slides or multilevel spaceship climbers, but I'm not really the designer purse kind of person. I'm not into material things unless they're able to warm the heart of my inner child. Everyone's inner child, really. I love that what I do brings joy to so many people, regardless of where they live."

She was laying it on far too thick to be believable. "So, you pay for playgrounds in poor neighborhoods because you want to bring joy to everyone."

"Not entirely. I only pay for whatever the grants and fundraising don't cover." Our gaze held and I could have sworn I saw a flicker of desire in her eyes.

God, she was beautiful.

I leaned closer, so close my lips hovered above hers and her breath tickled mine. "And you didn't come here to meet me."

Her tongue darted across her lower lip. "Exactly."

"Because you're engaged," I challenged.

She inhaled audibly and stepped away from me, looking totally and deliciously flustered. "I am. Happily. Very happily."

CHAPTER TWO

Michawn

T HAT DIDN'T JUST happen.

I love Teddy.

Loving someone makes it impossible to find another person attractive, doesn't it?

If so, what were those licks of heat that just seared through me?

I have never, would never, cheat.

Not even in my head. Teddy was my soulmate. We were getting married, and every fiber of my being was happy about that.

Like touching the handle of a pan that was unexpectedly hot, I'd recoiled as soon as I became aware of the burn.

Nope. I reject whatever that is.

Teddy and I hadn't had sex in a couple of weeks, which was unusual for us, but I'd been busy and then he'd broken his leg. That had to be it. Beneath everything else, people were mammals. My body was obviously craving sex.

I relaxed.

Oh, my God, when Teddy feels better this story will make

him laugh and keep him hopping in the bedroom. Not that we had a problem with that. Teddy and I fit together like peanut butter and jelly. Everything was simply better when we were together.

I raised my eyes to look over the man I'd made the mistake of standing too close to. He was as tall as Teddy, which put him well over six feet. Polished. Muscular.

Tense.

Angry.

Impatient.

All the things Teddy never was.

Our eyes met and held; I sensed a sadness deep in him that tugged at my heart. I didn't know much about him, but his impeccable haircut and suit that looked tailored to fit his wide shoulders told me a lot about him. So did his Italian shoes that likely cost more than my car. Money and status were important to this man. My guess was he'd made his own fortune. Trust fund children didn't have the dangerous edge he exuded. His nose was slightly bent as if it had been broken and there were small scars on his chin, eyebrow, and neck. This was a man who could hold his own in a fight—even if he didn't always win.

What had put the shadow in his eyes?

And what would it take to convince him I wasn't flirting with him? Sure, I'd smiled at him, but I liked people. And, in general, they liked me. Not everything had to be sexual.

Except this time I likely was giving off the wrong signal.

All he had to do was lean in and I had trouble breathing. I glanced down at the cleavage the top of the sundress revealed and groaned. I'd put on a little weight recently and the top was tighter than the last time I'd worn it. I wished I'd worn something big and baggy. When my gaze rose to Jared's again, I saw a hunger that made everything about being alone with him feel wrong.

I was being ridiculous. He was an attractive man in the prime of his life and he found me attractive. Of course that made me feel good. As long as I didn't act on it there wasn't a problem.

He wasn't the first man to be attracted to me despite knowing I was with Teddy. In high school I'd fended off my brother's drooling friends. Later, when they'd partnered up with others, it became something we even laughed about. In college some professors had paid more attention to my breasts than my answers, but that hadn't stopped me from graduating in the top of my class and winning award after award for my designs.

I squared my shoulders and forced a smile back to my lips. *I can fix this. All I have to do is push past the initial awkward phase.* "How about we start over? I'm excited to be here and I'm sorry I was late. I'm engaged to my childhood sweetheart, am living my best life, and I appreciate that you put aside time to give me a tour. Unless I hear differently from Mr. Wenham, I'm here to take measurements and get inspired. So as you show me around, I'd love if you'd tell me anything you think would help me match my vision with their lifestyle."

Jared's eyes narrowed but we were interrupted by a man in a suit before he had time to say anything. The man asked if he could take my luggage and offered to show me to my room.

"Thank you. If you put the bag in my room I'll be back in a little while. Mr. Seacrest was about to start my tour."

The man offered to have a meal prepared for me when I returned as well as address anything else I might need. I thanked him. House staff might not exist in my world back home, but many of my clients had them.

"Will you be staying as well, Mr. Seacrest?" the man asked.

Looking irritated with the question, Jared answered abruptly, "No."

The man appeared to wait for Jared to say more, then when he didn't, turned and left. I lost a little respect for Jared in that moment. Kindness and manners cost nothing.

As if he could hear my thoughts, he growled, "What?"

"I didn't say anything."

"But you wanted to."

Without giving myself time to consider if it was a wise thing to say, I blurted, "How a person treats staff says a lot about them."

His nostrils flared as he pinned me with a glare. "You think you know me?"

I didn't like how my body came alive beneath his gaze. I swallowed hard. The wisest course of action would have been to apologize again, but he was beginning to irk me. "Only what you've shown me."

There it was—the sizzle of mutual attraction that was undeniable. My hands fisted at my sides and my chin rose. Teddy was just as good-looking. He'd admitted to me that women flirted with him. I'd never wondered if he'd been attracted to any of them, but it wasn't inconceivable. What mattered was he'd never acted on it.

Being someone's partner was a commitment—a promise. One we'd both kept.

Meeting Jared might prove to be a good experience for me. It's easy to be faithful when one is never tempted. But discovering there was another person who could rev my engines? Didn't that make my decision to be faithful even more meaningful?

There had to be a way to diffuse the situation. "Teddy says I can be too blunt, and sometimes he's right."

"I don't give a fuck about Teddy."

My mouth dropped open as my mind raced. Everything I said seemed to be making the situation worse. Still, I felt compelled to defend Teddy. "That's a shame because he's a very nice man. If you met him, you'd like him."

"I highly doubt that."

"And he'd like you. He's the type who sees good in everyone."

"Of course he does."

I took a deep breath and held my tongue. This was going bad fast and, as he'd said, we didn't have to see each other again after that day.

His face remained tight and for so long I thought he might tell me to leave, but then he let out a breath and ran a hand through his hair. In a harsh tone, he demanded, "Do you have what you need to take notes?"

In a relieved scramble I retrieved my phone from my purse. "Yes. Lead on."

It wasn't an easy feat to focus when he looked like a dark-haired Thor striding ahead of me into the house Hamilton had purchased for his son Gavin.

Do not look at his ass.

Do not look at his back.

Keep your eyes off those thighs.

Once inside he turned, and when our eyes met again I shuddered from the intensity of his gaze. *Note to self, also don't look him in the eye.*

Focus on why you're here.

Thankfully the starkness of the entryway was distracting. Like the rooms that flanked it, it was white on white, devoid of warmth or character—the perfect blank pallet. "This is Hamilton's son's home, correct?"

"Yes."

"I can see why a family would be uncomfortable here."

Jared looked around and shrugged. "It looks fine to me."

He turned on his heel and crossed the foyer to open a set of tall double doors. "This is the home office."

A clear glass desk that resembled something out of a villain's ice lair commanded the center of the enormous room. "Charming."

"Gavin and Riley's main residence is in Back Bay. Hamilton is hoping to lure them out of the city at least for the weekends by making this home more child friendly." He nodded toward the window. "It already has a playground."

I followed his gaze to the white swing set surrounded by flower beds. Decorative, but I doubted a child had ever touched it. "I see that."

He waved a hand at the fifteen-foot bare walls of the office. "I can't imagine there's much you'll need to change in here so we'll move along to the next room."

"Wait." I stood in the middle of the space and let it speak to me. High ceilings. Solid structure. Huge windows. Twin children. A new father who would need a place for himself but would want his family to love being in this home. A new mother who would want her physically-challenged mother to visit often and feel comfortable.

The room transformed in my mind. "With the view of an outdoor playground, this is the heart of the house. It shouldn't be an office. It could be an amazing multi-level family room/library." I pointed to the bare expanse of one wall. "I see a pillowed loft closed off enough to be safe for the little ones with books in low shelves that allow for some toys as well. Soundproof padding on the floor with a ladder. Possibly an elevator to make it accessible for all ages. Definitely a slide, but one large enough for older children and adults to use. Nature-based green, blue, and purple to soothe and inspire. Below the loft I see a comfortable place with tables and overstuffed chairs. Imagine a park vibe, but with more comfortable seating. It'd be the place the family would read, relax, and refresh together. Computer desks of different heights over there, partially hidden by fake bushes. The ceiling is so high and the space so large this room could have a giant tree right in the middle."

"A tree? You're serious?"

"Very." He wasn't the first to doubt my ideas, but I didn't have to advertise to find new clients because my work held up over time and didn't disappoint. If I was confident about what I did, it was because I'd worked hard to earn the right. So, a little doubt in the beginning never bothered me. I continued to share my vision as much for myself as for him . . . outside of watching children enjoy my designs, the initial vision was my favorite part of the process. "A fake tree. This one would be climbable, with a swing or two. And some of the higher branches would be thick enough for a teen to sit on to read so I'd design those branches for comfort as well as safety. Like a cat tree, but for kids. The floor around it would need carpeting that looks like grass with enough padding to soften a fall but also be easy to clean. The children could be . . . children." Yes, I could see it all clearly and it was beautiful. No notes necessary when the image was so vivid, but I used a laser pen to take measurements of the room and jotted those stats down. "The ceiling needs twinkling lights to simulate stars at night. Peaceful. Playful. This would be a place the whole family would enjoy for years."

"Gavin designed the Terraanum Building. Have you heard of it?"

"Yes." It was well-known to local architects.

"Does he seem like someone who'd want a tree in the middle of his office?"

Although, there was some merit to Jared's question, I said, "It wouldn't be his office anymore, and I've read about the modifications that have been made to the Terraanum recently—community gardens, play areas inside and outside. Love and marriage tend to change a person's view of what's essential."

Jared looked unconvinced. "You're out of touch with reality if you think a man would give up an office like this for what you described. Kids or no kids."

I took a few photos of the room with my phone, happy to have something besides Jared to focus on. "I'll sketch a mock-up of my plans and forward them to you. You can contact me with Mr. Wenham's decision, but I believe he'll love my ideas. People don't come to me looking for the ordinary. Mr. Wenham wants to make this house a magical place for his grandchildren and I'm confident his son will be happy with a smaller office when he sees how much his whole family can enjoy this space."

He gave me a long look. "God, you're convincing."

"I believe the word you're looking for is talented." Yeah, I said it, but he was so arrogant it was practically my duty to take him down a notch or two.

His mouth curled in a half smile. "That too, I'm sure."

My cheeks warmed, but I refused to take that bait. Instead, I said, "I'd love to see the next room."

He didn't move at first, then nodded. "Sure. Dining room? Kitchen? Or one of the bedrooms?"

I tripped at the last suggestion. He caught me by an arm and steadied me. The touch of a man other than the one I was about to marry shouldn't feel as good as his did. I yanked my arm free. "Thank you, but all I need to see is the first floor. I'll be upstairs later . . ." I almost added *alone* but was glad I stopped before uttering it.

"Of course, then follow me."

I did, kicking myself mentally the whole way. By allowing myself to get flustered, I was giving off the exact opposite message I needed to be sending. I wasn't interested in flirting or anything beyond the tour. Although I'd already clearly stated my reason for being there, it was difficult to stop blushing every time he looked at me.

The dining room was, shocking, all white with a long glass table that could seat an entire football team. I couldn't imagine a family, even a large one, relaxing enough in that room to enjoy it. I made a quick note of small changes to fix that.

Arms folded across his chest, Jared asked, "Let me guess, you suggest they ditch the table and install a slip and slide?"

I gave him a side look. "That would be funny if it wasn't delivered like an insult."

He frowned but kept his next thought to himself.

Seriously, had no one ever checked this man? I had two brothers who were known to sometimes cross lines when it came to pranks or jokes. Surviving them had only been possible by establishing clear, healthy boundaries. It was why, as adults, we were still close. Sometimes things needed to be stated clearly. "You can mock what I do, but it won't change how much I love it. I enjoy every part of the process. There isn't much you could say about me or my life choices that would bother me, because I'm where I want to be, living the life I've always dreamed of having, supporting myself by doing what I'm proud of."

He gave me a long look I wasn't sure how to decipher. I believed that most things worked out for the best, though, so if standing up for myself cost me the job . . . well, it wasn't meant to be. I'd find another client and things would work out. They always did.

In a tight voice, he ground out, "Who are you?"

It was an odd question that took me off guard. "Exactly who I said I am. Nothing more. Nothing less."

"All the shit you just said is true?"

"Why wouldn't it be?" My mouth rounded as I paired what he was saying to what he'd shared about Hamilton Wenham earlier. "When I say this, it's in the kindest way possible, but I really didn't come here to meet you." On my phone I pulled up a photo of me with Teddy laughing a week earlier. We'd been at my parents' house by the pool and posed for the picture, but just as my mother had raised her phone to take the photo, our dog, Piper, had jumped out of the pool and rushed in front of us to shake off. I loved the image because it had captured how easy loving Teddy was. We were best friends as well as lovers and all of that showed through in the photo.

When I turned my phone so Jared could see it, he rocked back on his heels. "You're really engaged."

Without hesitation, I said, "I am. Teddy and I have been together forever. We bought a house before getting married, but we're now ready for the next stage." I took a deep breath. "Before long, I hope to be designing rooms for my own children."

He stepped back from me. "I'm happy for you."

There it was—that hint of pain in his eyes that I'd sensed earlier, and it pulled on my heartstrings. Had I been free to, I might have hugged him in that moment, but instead I replaced my phone into my purse. "Thank you. I don't take any of it for granted. I found the love of my life early, our families get along, we have all the same friends, and we're getting married. I know how lucky I am to have that."

He made a sound deep in his chest then turned on his heel. I followed because I needed to see the rest of the house, but kept my gaze safely glued to the back of his calves. Whatever had happened to him, I sent up a little prayer that he would find peace with it and someone who could help him heal.

CHAPTER THREE

Jared

IF I WERE the type who allowed myself to leave a situation because it was uncomfortable, I would have left Michawn standing there and headed back to my office. Everything about her, as well as the life she described, was pissing me off.

I have a life that anyone would envy. I could sell my two companies and live in luxury without ever having to work another day in my life. People tread lightly around me in the business world because I was at a level of success and influence that meant I often won merely by showing up.

In every area of my life, I was winning.

Who was she to look at me like I was a rescue animal in need of saving?

Sure, she was hot enough to get my dick's attention, but the more she talked about love and marriage, the closer I came to vomiting in my mouth. *Seriously, no one is as fucking happy as she wants me to believe she is.*

Thankfully her state of mind was of no consequence to me. Her family, her fiancé, their fucking dog . . . none of it mattered. I was done.

We went from room to room and then over to Hamilton's house with a minimal amount of speaking. When she started to share ideas she had for Hamilton's backyard, I raised a hand and said, "Save it for Hamilton. He'll want to see the designs before any work is started. I can't pretend to be interested."

Sure, it was a dick thing to say, but I'd started the day in a foul mood and meeting her hadn't helped to improve it.

"Okay," she said quietly and remained reserved as we made our way through the final rooms. Good. I led the way because the less I looked at her, the better. Even that wasn't enough, though, to calm my erection. She smelled like some damn flower I didn't know the name of, but that didn't stop it from becoming my favorite scent. I was painfully aware of every swish of her dress against her legs as she walked. Each time she craned her neck upward to check out the ceiling molding, I imagined kissing my way down that long neck as I hiked up her decadently sheer sundress.

It was bad.

Thankfully, every torture session comes to an end. We were in the driveway again when I told her to send me the designs, the contract proposal, as well as the information regarding who she'd be subcontracting to do the work. I'd forward everything to Hamilton and get back to her with approval and payment.

She nodded then stood there looking at me. I could have

handled it if the look in her eyes had reflected what I was feeling, but instead there was only compassion and it made me want to punch her teddy bear fiancé.

I wasn't the jealous type, and certainly had no right to feel that way, but I let myself imagine releasing my temper on the man who was only guilty of making her his.

"Thank you for showing me around," she said softly.

"It was nothing." Her gratitude annoyed me. I'd been an ass the whole time. She should have been telling me off. Had she looked at all intimidated by me, I would have felt awful, but she was definitely not impressed.

Her phone buzzed. She checked quickly, typed something, then said, "I have to go, but I should have everything I need. I'll double check the measurements tomorrow morning before I head out. If I have any questions should I email you or Mr. Wenham?"

"Me. I'm your point of contact until Hamilton returns."

She scrolled through her phone then smiled. "Phone number. Email. I have it all. My full proposal should be ready in about a week."

"I'll watch for your email." There really wasn't much else to say.

She stepped forward and shocked me by placing a hand on my forearm. The connection jolted me and I would have pulled away had I not spent so much of my life planting my feet and holding my ground. "Don't give up," she said softly.

Muscles tightening from head to foot, I growled, "On

what?"

"Whatever you've been through, whoever hurt you, you need to know that you deserve to be happy just as much as anyone else does. I know you didn't enjoy our time together today, but I hope I didn't add to whatever you're going through."

I straightened and looked down at her with anger welling inside me. Why did she have to be so damn nice? It was screwing with my plan to forget her as soon as this tour concluded. My voice was tight as I said, "You didn't and thanks for the pep talk, but I assure you, it's not necessary."

She dropped her hand. "You went out of your way to put down what I do. Do you know who does that? Unhappy people."

Yes, she was an unwelcome, off-limits temptation, but she wasn't wrong. I was still off-kilter from the text I'd received that morning. "Today started as a shit day. I shouldn't have taken that out on you."

"It happens." A small smile returned to her face. "I figured it was something like that. Mr. Wenham was such a nice man, I guessed this didn't represent who you are." She stepped away and toward the house. "I wish I could say it was a pleasure to meet you, Mr. Seacrest, but . . ." The wink she gave floored me. "I hope you have a better day tomorrow."

Watching as she turned and walked away was nowhere as easy as it should have been. She stopped at the top of the steps and met my gaze. "Everything will be okay. You've got this."

We stood frozen like two actors after a director suddenly called, "Cut." If she weren't engaged I would have closed the distance and kissed her then, but she was not only in love with someone else, he sounded like he could make her happy.

She had her sights set on settling down and starting a family.

All I could offer her was a weekend or two of sex.

It was better to let her go.

She held my gaze and said, "When you see how I transform this place you'll understand why I love what I do."

I pocketed my hands and strove to appear unaffected even though my heart was racing. "I'm sure I will." She opened the door and was halfway through it when I blurted, "Your fiancé is a lucky man." I hadn't planned to say that and wasn't happy I had.

Why did I? Maybe I felt bad about dismissing what she did for a living. Maybe it was just a painful truth I couldn't contain.

"I tell him that every day." The smile she shot me was so full of happiness it gutted me and stayed with me long after she disappeared through the door.

Fuck.

As soon as she was out of sight, I hopped into my car and headed back to Boston. From my office I called Calvin and told him I needed a sparring session to clear my head. Calvin was the only person from my childhood I'd stayed in contact with. He was one of the few people who knew Seacrest wasn't the name I'd been born with. We'd met when we'd been placed with the same foster family and removed for the same reason. We both had hot tempers and fast fists.

He'd gone on to be placed with a family who introduced him to martial arts while I, an offender with more strikes on my record, was sent to a behavioral center. Most foster kids lose track of each other as they move around, but Calvin and I found ways to stay in touch. When I regained enough freedom to see him again, he convinced his foster family to take a chance on me and that's how Calvin and I became family. Loyalty is a stronger tie than blood. Although I appreciated the roof and bed that foster home had given me, they had issues of their own. The year after Calvin and I aged out of the program, they divorced and went their separate ways.

Calvin and I got an apartment together, worked whatever jobs we could find, and plotted our futures. I was determined to prove myself in the business world and that meant getting an education. Needing a fresh start, I changed my last name and applied to schools with a fabricated backstory. Neither of us had anyone to call for business advice, but determination is a capable teacher. I chose my path, researched the hell out of how to pay for it, and made it happen. Sure, most of the documents I sent the schools were fabricated, but the risk had paid off. Had I not gone to a mid-level college, I would have never met Hamilton.

Calvin's dream had been to own a mixed martial arts gym. He honed his fighting skill in illegal cage fights and took me along for the ride. Eventually he came out of the shadows and won a UFC championship, a win that brought in enough money for him to open his first gym.

Learning martial arts taught me discipline and unauthorized cage fighting gave me an outlet for my anger as well as money for school. When things were going well in my life I chose opponents at my level. When I couldn't get the demons in me to silence, I set up a cage fight with someone I knew I'd lose to.

More than once, that lack of good judgement had landed me in the hospital with a fractured . . . everything. Did I mention that my mouth could get me in as much trouble as my hands ever had?

I'd made an effort to find better indulgences than sparring with Calvin since meeting Hamilton because the violent side of me was something Hamilton couldn't understand.

Don't worry, Calvin didn't go easy on me. I joked he'd missed the memo that gay people were supposed to be nonviolent. He assured me that my misconception was based on not knowing enough gays.

Comments like that were usually followed by a beating that left me wincing for days.

Bradley, Calvin's husband, lamented that Calvin and I

were the product of a failing foster home system and seriously fucked up families. He wasn't wrong.

Yet, somehow, we'd both pulled ourselves out of that life. Calvin had grown one gym into a lucrative national chain and, later, when I had the cash flow, I invested in his business, which allowed him to take his dream international.

No matter how much success I achieved, there were times I needed the release of giving or receiving a good punch. It was the rush of the adrenaline, possibly the revisiting of a time when I hadn't been able to protect myself, and the powerful feeling that I'd never be that vulnerable again.

I wouldn't suggest no holds barred MMA as therapy for everyone, but it was sometimes the only way to reset my head when it started to fill with unproductive thoughts. I refused to let my past infringe on the life I'd made for myself, and if that required scrambling my brain matter from time to time, so be it.

After the day I'd had, I needed to get into a ring with Calvin or I'd never be able to focus on work. I called him and asked if he had time to meet me that evening.

"Absolutely," Calvin said. "My Upton gym at six?"

"I'll be there."

"It's Bradley's night to cook and he always makes more than either of us should eat. I'll tell him you'll be joining us."

"Not tonight."

"Yes tonight, or I'll be fending questions from Bradley

about what's bothering you and you know I hate that. Are you having a bad day?"

"Yes."

"Will sparring make you feel better?"

"Yes."

"That's all I care about, but Bradley will want the details."

"You couldn't have married a man who doesn't like me? Even Hamilton doesn't grill me as much as Bradley does."

"He does it because he cares. I'll ask him to make the cake you love. Will that make it easier?"

"I do love his cooking."

"It's up to you, but if you don't come for dinner, you know he'll call you. Especially if I don't have the answers to most of what he'll ask."

"My father sent me a text this morning. He's out of jail and wants to see me."

"Oh, shit."

"I didn't respond. I have no interest in ever seeing him again and no idea how he got my number."

"Yeah, I can see how that would put you in a bad mood. He reached out to you last year, didn't he?"

"Yes, and I changed my number. I have zero interest in anything he has to say."

"Understandable. Can you do four o'clock instead? I have a feeling I'm going to need to sit in an ice bath before dinner."

I laughed without humor. "I'll go easy on you."

"I was going to do the same, but now I have to kick your ass."

"Whatever. I'll see you at four. Thanks."

CHAPTER FOUR

Michawn

I KICKED OFF my sandals as I entered my bedroom at Gavin and Riley Wenham's house and marveled at the lack of creativity of the previous owners. How had that conversation gone? What should we go with for carpeting? White. The walls? White. Furniture? Bedding? Accent pieces? Fuck it, make it all white.

I hope I don't cut myself on anything or drop a crumb of food. No wonder Hamilton reached out to me.

I thought about what Jared had said about the downstairs office. Could he actually not see that the space lacked everything that made a house a home? I changed out of my dress into shorts and a T-shirt. Outside was hot, but my room had cooled enough that I grabbed a blanket as I carried my laptop to the couch.

I opened my messages and reread the last one from Teddy. He'd wanted to make sure I'd arrived okay and said he couldn't wait to see my designs. I'd just finished talking to Jared so I told him I'd call him as soon as I got to my room.

He'd answered that he had a headache and was going to

lie down, but if he missed my call he'd call me back as soon as he woke. The surgery to his broken leg had been extensive and the rest would do him good.

I paused as I remembered getting the call from his father telling me to meet them at the hospital because Teddy was hurt. There was nothing funny about a broken leg, or at least it was too early to make a joke about it, but it was difficult to believe he could get hurt by delivering cookies to his niece's second-grade classroom for a party. Someone had left a pile of books in the hallway next to a set of stairs. He'd tripped over the books and taken a tumble.

Totally Teddy. He was sweet enough to deliver cookies for a child and clumsy enough to nearly kill himself doing it. I smiled. No, not funny, but adorably Teddy. It would make a good story to tell our children.

The trip to the Wenham's had been scheduled before Teddy had gotten hurt and I hadn't wanted to leave his side, but his mother had offered to stay with him. Teddy understood working with Wenham was a huge opportunity that would bring in a whole new level of clients. We needed the money for our wedding, and if I did an impressive job, we might be able to pay off a large chunk of our mortgage.

That didn't make it easier to be away from him.

Rather than calling Teddy directly, I called his mother, Fran. She answered in a hushed tone. "Theodore is finally sleeping. I can wake him, but he said his leg is really bothering him so it might be best to let him rest."

I'd wanted to hear his voice, but I understood. "That's why I called you instead. He said he had a headache and might lie down. How is he?"

"Less fussy than expected, which means he really is feeling crummy. He has always been a tough one to get to slow down, but this seems to have wiped him out. Piper hasn't left his side."

"Aww, Piper loves him." I sighed. "I should be there."

"Michawn, don't you dare start feeling guilty. He wanted you to go. Do you know how proud he is of you? I don't think there is a doctor or nurse at the hospital that he hasn't told about you and your work."

I wiped at the corner of my eyes. "You raised a good one, Fran. I believe I'm going to keep him."

"You'd better. I want grandchildren. Theodore said you two plan to start trying right after the wedding."

"We do. We've been together forever . . . waiting seems silly. I hope we don't have to push the wedding back because of this injury, but I've made myself okay with the possibility. What's important to me is that he'll enjoy the day as much as I will."

"He said almost exactly those words to me earlier. You're two peas in a pod."

I chuckled. "We are." After a pause, I said more seriously, "This is the first time I've seen him in pain. It's killing me."

"I know, love, but he'll heal fast. In the blink of an eye

this will be an easy-to-forget speed bump on your way to making a family together."

"Fran, you always know what to say to make me feel better."

"You know you can call me Mom."

She'd told me that before, but I'd always held back. "I know, but Teddy and I live together already. Not too much will change when we marry, so I want to keep that for then. It'll make it even more special."

"Okay, but you know you've been one of mine since you kids were in elementary school and you practically moved in."

"My parents say the same about Teddy." Jared flashed in my thoughts as did the moment I'd realized it was possible to be attracted to someone beyond my future husband. Attraction, though, didn't matter. It was a hollow offering when compared to what Teddy and I shared. "Tonight I'm sleeping at one of Wenham's homes. I plan to stay in, get inspired, take a few more measurements tomorrow morning, then fly home. If Teddy wakes up have him call me."

"I will, love. Don't forget to text us the info for your flight."

"I won't." On impulse, I said, "Fran, thank you for being such an amazing future mother-in-law. People tell horror stories about in-laws so I know it's not always this wonderful."

"Oh, poo. Any mother would be grateful to have you

marry their son. You've always been good for Theodore. He used to get bullied before he met you. We had a hard time getting him to go to school. Then we moved, he met you . . . and you brought out the best in him. He knows it. We all do. The two of you were meant to be."

I snuggled into the couch and smiled. *Meant to be.* That's what Teddy and I were to each other.

"Good night, Fran."

She chuckled. "Good night, love."

An hour or so later I was still sketching my vision digitally when my phone rang with a video call. *Tracy.* She was not only my best friend, but my maid of honor as well.

With her hair piled wildly on top of her head and a huge smile, she jumped right in with, "Tell me if you're busy, but if you're not, tell me everything. I'm totally living vicariously through you. Oh yes, and I brought Teddy ice cream this afternoon. His mother was fawning all over him, fluffing his pillows and bringing him drinks. Don't let him guilt you about not being there."

I smiled at the image I was certain was true. Fran was that kind of mother. I had a good mother, a great one actually, but Teddy had the kind who would still fold his underwear for him if we let her. "I just got off the phone with Fran. Honestly, knowing she'd be there with him was the only thing that made being away okay."

"Be prepared to have to retrain him completely when you return. She got him a bell."

"She didn't."

"Oh, yeah. And he uses it."

I laughed. "Oh, boy. Yeah, we'll work on that when I get back."

In a more serious tone, she said, "He's uncomfortable, but in pretty good spirits. Of course he misses you. We all do. When do you get back?"

"Tomorrow around noon."

"You're staying in one of the mansions?"

"I am."

"Is it fancy? Do you have staff waiting on you constantly?"

"I do. It's . . ." I looked around the stark room. "Nice. In fact, in a little bit someone will be delivering a sandwich to my room."

"You need an assistant on these trips. I have to see these places."

I laughed again. "It's not really all that glamourous. Today I arrived, took a tour of both homes I'll be working on, and now I'm sitting in a room alone, recording my ideas. You're always welcome to come, but I'm not sure what you'd do."

"Meet a rich, single man willing to sweep me out of this town and away to somewhere exotic on his jet." She made a sound in her throat. "They're all married, though, right? You meet mostly couples."

"Usually. The man who showed me around today was

single. I think. The owner wasn't able to meet me so he had a friend of his give me the tour."

"A friend of his? Was he a hundred years old?"

"No, actually, he was probably in his late twenties."

"Butt ugly."

"Above average in the looks department."

"Gay?"

"I don't think so, but I didn't ask."

"And you didn't call me? You met my dream man and didn't think to fly me there immediately? Tell me you at least got his number for me."

The thought of Tracy with Jared struck an odd chord in me. Weird. Nothing had happened between us. Nothing ever would. Why couldn't I picture Tracy with him? "I don't know that he would have given me his number if he had a choice. He was . . . moody."

"Hot and rich? I would have dropped to my knees to help him with that."

Tracy was all talk. She absolutely wouldn't have, but oddly I didn't like the image that her comment put in my head.

She tilted her head to one side. "Don't give me that look. You're not allowed to be marrying Teddy and want to keep all the rich guys you meet."

My mouth rounded. "I don't know what look you're referring to, but I'm happy with Teddy. He's all I need."

Tracy's eyes narrowed. "You say that like we haven't

been friends since preschool. Remember in middle school when your mother would send you with fruit and Teddy's mom would send him with brownies that he would hand over to you? I'd ask you for a bite of that brownie and you would give me that same look. So don't try lying to me."

I did love brownies.

"I always shared them with you," I protested.

"But it took you a minute. Now spill."

I sighed. "If I tell you something it has to be in the vault. I mean deep, deep in the vault."

"You know you can tell me anything."

I could, which was the only reason I was considering saying anything at all. "Until this trip I thought Teddy was the only man I could find attractive. And honestly, I feel a little guilty . . ."

"You fucked the rich guy."

"No." I burst out laughing. "No."

"Kissed him?"

"Not even close."

"Flirted outrageously but remembered Teddy at the last minute."

"Tracy, be serious. Can you imagine me doing that?"

"So, what *did* you do?"

"Nothing. My heart raced a little. I may have imagined him naked."

She cackled. "Oh, my God. I do that constantly, probably with every man I meet. My mailman. My dentist. Teddy a few times over the years. Even your dad once . . ."

"Ewwww, stop."

"Hey, it was the summer your father was working out and he looked good shirtless."

"No. Hard no." I wiped a hand down my face. "So, it's not a big deal. Everyone has those thoughts."

"Absolutely. I don't know what married people are like, but I'm in my sexual prime and getting no action. I've been very careful to keep my number of partners down to what I can count on one hand, but the older I get, the more I think being a whore might be better. Maybe I should put out on the first date. Hell, that's when they're the most interesting anyway."

I groaned. "You'll meet someone, Tracy. Probably when you least expect it."

"Not in this town. You're taking me with you on your next job. I have to expand my dating pool."

"Deal."

After a moment, Tracy said, "So, tell me about this guy who made your heart race."

I shook my head. "I don't know what it was about him. Certainly not his personality. He didn't want to be here. Of course, that didn't stop him from saying he was willing to have sex with me but nothing more. Men sure don't know how to sell sex, do they? I mean, really, what woman would jump for that?"

"How rich is he?"

"He looked well off. Wenham is extremely wealthy and the man who met me seemed to be a peer rather than an employee."

"How good-looking? On a scale of one to ten?"

"Eleven?"

"Name. I need his name."

"Jared Seacrest."

She propped her phone up so I could still see her grab a tablet to look him up. After scanning whatever she found, she whistled. "You weren't kidding. He's hot. And loaded. Yeah, that line works for him all the time. In fact, he's probably scratching his head wondering why it didn't with you."

"I told him about Teddy and that we're engaged."

"Smart move. You're a good fiancée. How did he react?"

"He didn't love hearing about him."

"I can imagine." Tracy put her tablet down and wagged a finger at me. "What were you wearing?"

I rolled my eyes. "My yellow flowered sundress."

She slapped one of her cheeks. "You know that dress barely fits you, right?"

"It's comfortable and it's almost a hundred degrees here today. I wasn't about to wear slacks."

"That poor man. He's out there, somewhere, wondering what he did wrong and pining for a night between your ladies."

"You're an idiot. I'm sure he forgot me as quickly as I

intend to forget him."

"Not likely. That yellow dress is practically see-through."

"It is not."

"It is."

I growled. "If that's true, why wouldn't my best friend tell me that?"

"I just figured you were wearing it for Teddy."

"Right," I said with a laugh. "The dress isn't as bad as you're making it out to be."

"Best friends don't lie."

I covered my eyes briefly with a hand then lowered it. "Well, now I understand why he was confused about my reason for meeting him. Do I have any other outfits I should leave at home?"

"Your green cut-off jeans. Your ass hangs out the back of them."

"Great. Duly noted."

"And that off-white and blue bathing suit. Your nipples show through that when it's wet."

"Seriously? You need to tell me shit like that."

"I didn't know you wanted to know, but from now on I'll say something."

After taking a few deep breaths, I tentatively asked, "My wedding dress . . . you know, the one you helped me choose . . ."

"Is stunning and perfect."

"Well, that's a relief. From now on, though, if I have

anything hanging out, say something. I can't believe Teddy never told me."

"Teddy would never say boo to you. He knows he has a good thing. You love his parents. You're the reason he has friends. You're gorgeous. Trust me, you could walk all over that man and he'd ask you if you wanted to do it again."

"That's not true and it's not something I'd ever do."

"Teddy's always had it bad for you."

"Because we were meant to be."

"I don't remember you feeling that way at first, but he won you over. Absolute adoration will do that."

"Stop."

"I'm not saying Teddy isn't perfect for you. I know you'll be happy and raise the best kids together. All I'm saying is I bet it was fun to have a guy not agree with everything you say. Did he really outright tell you he'd have sex with you but that's all? How did you say no to that kind of challenge?"

"Um, Teddy?"

"He would have forgiven you."

I laughed. Best friends knew just what to say to put things into perspective. I was being ridiculous and that's why it was easy to joke about it going anywhere. "Good night. I fly back in the morning. Will I see you tomorrow?"

"I'll drop by. Oh, and try to have some freaking clothes on when I do."

We both laughed and ended the call.

CHAPTER FIVE

Jared

CALVIN AND I limped into his home like two kids who knew they'd gone too far but had done their best to clean up and cover the evidence. I touched my face just below my split lower lip and winced. We might be sore, but we were showered and changed because Bradley had a rule about the smell of the gym staying out of their home.

I didn't mind Bradley's rules. He'd brought a calm to Calvin that not even a knockout fight with me had ever been able to achieve. The kiss they exchanged was followed by a wrinkle of Bradley's nose. "Some people would send their friends to therapy, Cal, not beat them bloody."

Calvin placed his arm around Bradley and gave his cheek a nuzzle. "You know I can't say no when he needs me."

I winced again as I moved my shoulders. "I gave as good as I got."

Looking completely unimpressed, Bradley looked me over. "I would offer you both ice packs but I refuse to encourage this."

Truthfully, we should have stopped before the last

round. There was a tipping point, even when fighting a friend, when the past and present blurred and I stopped holding back. It was always painfully obvious when Calvin crossed the same line. "I do feel better." I groaned and touched what was definitely a bruised rib. "And worse."

Calvin clapped the back of his hand cruelly on that very spot. "You're welcome."

Shaking his head Bradley thumbed toward the hall bathroom. "Go wash your hands. Dinner is already waiting on the table."

"Yes, Mom," I joked.

Bradley arched an eyebrow. "And it's getting cold. If it's not as delicious as it normally is, you'd better not push me, Jared. If I ever do snap, you'll wish it was Calvin beating you down."

I smiled an apology and glanced at Calvin.

He laughed and raised his hands in surrender. "Just thank him and go wash your hands. That's what I'd do."

I met Bradley's gaze. Through Calvin, he'd become a permanent fixture in my life and it wasn't a bad thing. "Thank you." Out of respect for the work he'd put into the meal I didn't waste time getting to the table.

When we were all seated, wine poured and plates full, I let out a long breath. I might not have the traditional, picture-perfect life Michawn seemed to have, but I had people who understood and accepted me. This was the only family I required. And the Wenham clan, although I didn't expose them to the darker corners of my life.

After taking a sip of wine, Bradley said, "It's been a year since you two scrapped like this. Want to talk about it, Jared?"

I downed a good portion of my wine before answering. "Not particularly, but I will."

Bradley smiled and gave Calvin's arm a pat. "See, he wants to *talk*. You should try that next time instead of throwing hands."

Calvin exchanged a look with me. "What do I know? I've only known him most of my life." He softened his comment with a smile.

"No one eats before I hear what's going on," Bradley said in a firm voice when Calvin picked up his fork. The ease with which my previously short-tempered friend lowered his utensil spoke to how much he cared for Bradley.

That didn't mean I couldn't eat. "Shouldn't we dig in first? You know, so it doesn't get cold?" I raised my fork hopefully.

Bradley sighed. "I want the whole story before dessert."

I nodded and dug into the best beef stroganoff I'd ever tasted. I had a private chef and ate at five-star restaurants on a regular basis, but there was something non-replicable about a homemade meal. Bradley made comfort food better than anyone else I knew.

It's a miracle Calvin isn't overweight.

We were well into our third glass of wine, finished with

the main course, and were caught up on everything that didn't matter when I pushed my plate back, rubbed my hands over my face, and rested my elbows on the table. "I hate when my father contacts me. I don't want to look back. I don't even use the rearview mirror in my fucking car. I care what's ahead. The past is dead to me."

In a gentle tone, Bradley asked, "Do you know what he wants?"

I lowered my hands and growled. "No, and I don't care."

Bradley added, "He might just want to talk, Jared. Probably apologize for not being there for you and your mother. He's done his time, had a lot of time to think . . ."

"And wants a handout," Calvin said with disgust.

"That'll never happen," I added without missing a beat.

Calvin shook his head. "Not everything is about money. He might just want to make amends."

I snapped, "There is no way to make amends for what he did."

"I didn't say there was," Bradley said slowly. "All I'm suggesting is—"

"No." My refusal was unwavering, but when I heard the harshness in my tone, I softened. "Sorry. I don't expect you to understand. When I see a message from him—"

"It all comes back," Calvin finished for me.

I nodded. "Yes."

"The nightmares."

Calvin knew me too well. "Always."

"The guilt."

I confirmed it with one abrupt nod.

Calvin took Bradley's hand in his. "I remember when the memories were so bad the only way to get them out of my head was to inflict the same kind of pain on someone else. I might still be doing that if it weren't for Jared . . . and you." He looked across at me. "I revisited that place today for you, but it's not healthy for either of us."

None of us spoke for several minutes. I crumpled one of the napkins in my hand. "I didn't know it took a toll on you. I always was more fucked-up than you were."

Calvin shook his head. "What we went through sucked. I'll never be normal, if that's even a thing, but when I lose control like I did today, it doesn't feel good anymore. I don't need the release the way I used to. You delivered some strikes tonight like you wanted me dead. And although I understand that it wasn't me you were hitting, when you're in that place and I join you, I'm not the man I want to be." He met Bradley's gaze. "Not the man you'd want to be with."

Bradley nodded in quiet understanding.

Calvin continued, "It's too easy to pass the abuse on, Jared. It has to stop with us. And I say this as your brother from another mother, you can't let yourself go to that place anymore." He cleared his throat. "Don't let your father turn you into him."

Bradley stood, walked around the table, and hugged me so tightly my eyes shone with emotion. He'd been raised by a sweet heterosexual couple who still called him every day to make sure he'd slept well and was eating right. I was grateful Calvin had found someone like that for himself.

"You're both going to be okay," Bradley said softly.

I gave his arm a pat and nodded.

Bradley straightened and started clearing away the plates. "So, how about dessert?"

"Sounds good," I answered in a gruff voice.

I smiled at the large piece of chocolate cake Bradley handed me. When Calvin retook his seat he gave me a sympathetic look similar to the one Michawn had and I didn't like it. I didn't like that I couldn't get her out of my head either.

It's beyond me why I filled the silence with, "I met someone today—"

"You *met* someone?" Calvin cut in with a voice that was an octave higher.

"Not like that," I corrected quickly. "Hamilton is having his house renovated. He asked me to give the architect a tour." When I stopped there, Bradley rolled one hand through the air requesting I continue. "She was beautiful."

"Oooooh," Bradley said.

Calvin gave me a long look. "But?"

"She's engaged." The words were thick in my throat.

Calvin made a face. "Engaged isn't married. What the hell are you doing here?"

Stabbing the cake with my fork, I admitted, "Happily

engaged. She's fucking ecstatically engaged."

Bradley added, "That sucks. Sounds like you really liked her."

I pushed my cake back. "She went on and on and fucking on about how wonderful her life is. How fantastic her fiancé is. Her life is perfect and it made me—"

"Angry that yours wasn't?" Bradley asked softly.

"No," I growled. "Maybe. I don't know. I'm in a really good place in my life. I have everything I've ever wanted. Why would a conversation with one woman I don't care if I ever see again leave me feeling so shitty?"

"Because you're still a little messed up?" Calvin offered.

Bradley smacked his arm. "Because you don't have everything you've ever wanted. Sure you're successful, but you want what Calvin and I have."

"I'm not like Calvin," I said hotly.

"Black?" Calvin asked.

I rolled my eyes.

"Gay?" he pressed just to be an ass.

"Interested in getting married and spending the rest of my life fucking the same person every night." When both of Bradley's eyebrows rose, I added, "No offense, Bradley."

"Only a little taken," Bradley said with a sigh. "Mostly because I know when you're talking out your ass and that's what you're doing. You would love to have someone to come home to. It won't happen for you, though, until you believe you deserve that."

That wasn't true or what I wanted to hear. "She's probably not even as happy as she pretends." I pulled out my phone and did a social media search for her name. When I saw a photo that looked like her, I opened the profile and then her feed. It was full of photos of her laughing with people her age as well as romantic poses with a tall, beefy man with a mop of curls who in every single fucking photo and video looked at her like she was his world. I tossed my phone down.

Bradley picked it up. His nose wrinkled. "Yeah, you're not breaking these two up."

"I wouldn't even try," I said and meant it. "That's never been me. But, I also don't want to be someone who looks at photos like that and can't be happy for them. She was a nice enough woman. Really nice. She uses money from her work projects to fund playgrounds for low-income neighborhoods—that fucking nice. Of course she has someone in her life."

Bradley scrolled through her feed on my phone again then showed a few photos to Calvin. "Talented and beautiful." He lowered the phone. "But there are others out there like her."

I took my phone back and pocketed it. "This isn't about *her*. What's bothering me is how angry it makes me that she's happy. What the fuck is wrong with me?"

"I got this one," Calvin said with a raised hand. "Everything is changing around you and you don't like change.

Bradley and I married. Gavin found Riley and tied the knot. Hamilton retired and married Fara. We're all pairing up and you're worried that you'll be left behind. Add your father's message to that and you feel like you deserve to be."

Bradley brought a hand to his chest. "That is really insightful, Cal."

Calvin smiled. "I do know him."

Some of what he said reflected how I felt, but not all of it. "I'm glad you found each other. This isn't about feeling left behind. I'm reasonably certain you two will name your first child after me and expect me to change diapers and babysit. I know you're not going anywhere."

"Hear that, Calvin? We've already scored a babysitter." Bradley put a hand on Calvin's arm.

Calvin smiled. "We'll talk later. This is about Jared."

After turning his attention back to me, Bradley sighed. "You can be happy for someone and still wish you had the same for yourself. That doesn't make you a bad person. It makes you human."

I mulled that around in my head. There was something I wanted, but struggled to articulate it. "I wish you'd met her and heard the way she described what she does. She said she creates spaces so magical they make a person's inner child smile. For just a moment, I saw the world through her eyes and it wasn't an ugly, twisted place. I wanted to believe in her . . . and have her believe in me." I groaned at how much the wine had loosened my tongue.

Bradley clasped his hands to his chest again. "Now that's romantic."

"Except the part about her already belonging to someone else."

"Well," Calvin said gently, "at least you know what you're looking for now."

I picked up my fork again. "Yeah."

CHAPTER SIX

Michawn

AFTER A RESTLESS night, I woke early and checked my phone for a message from Teddy but told myself not to be disappointed when there wasn't one. He wasn't feeling well and was probably sleeping more because of the painkillers.

I almost texted him, but decided to shower first instead. If he was still sleeping I didn't want to wake him. *I'm worried about nothing.*

It's not like he's alone.

Or angry with me.

Unless Tracy told him what I'd confessed to her last night.

No, she'd never do that.

And I have nothing to feel guilty about because nothing happened.

I'm being an idiot.

Even if I confessed to Teddy what would I say? And would he even care? I certainly don't want to know every time he looks at another woman and feels a tingle.

Some things are better left unsaid.

As I dressed after my shower, I thought: *I wish I hadn't said anything to Tracy. I gave importance and life to something that I should have shrugged off and forgotten.*

Now it'll always be there—something I can't deny I felt because I shared it.

I finished repacking the bag I'd barely touched and sat down on the edge of my bed with my cell phone. Even though it was still early, Fran would be awake for sure. She said her favorite time of day was the quiet of a sunrise.

She didn't answer on the first ring or the second and I reassured myself there were endless reasons why she might not be able to. She might be in the bathroom, outside with Piper, or helping Teddy in or out of bed.

I laid the phone on the bed, telling myself the sense of dread I felt was irrational. Any minute Fran would call back with a reason for not answering. She'd tell me Teddy was up and able to talk. I'd tease him about actually using the bell she'd bought him.

Nothing was wrong.

I don't know how much time passed before her ringtone broke the silence. I grabbed for my phone. "Fran." A lack of immediate response from her sent a chill through me. "Fran?"

"He's gone, Michawn."

"Who? Piper? Did he get out of the fencing again? If so, he doesn't go far."

"Theodore," she answered in a thick voice then let out a

wail I knew would haunt me until my last breath.

"What are you saying, Fran? Where would Teddy go?" That wasn't like him. He wouldn't leave without telling me or his mother where he was going. And where would he go with a broken leg? Our friends were pranksters, but they'd never do anything to upset a sweetheart like Fran.

Time suspended when Teddy's father came on the phone. "Michawn, Theodore died in his sleep last night. The EMTs couldn't say what it was from, but the hospital will do an autopsy. Your brother is here because we couldn't get your dog off Theodore. Piper tried to bite Fran then me and the EMTs couldn't get near Theodore to help him. I told you that dog needed to be trained."

No. This isn't right. Teddy can't be dead. "I don't understand what happened."

Sounding angry with me, Teddy's father said, "I don't expect you to. While you were off gallivanting with those rich people you're always trying to impress, my son was in bed, dying—alone. If you'd been here—"

My brother Christopher's voice cut in. "That's enough. Michawn, there was nothing anyone could have done for Teddy. The EMTs took his body to UMass where he was pronounced dead, but they said he died sometime during the night. Tom and Megan are on their way to you."

"Died? No. That's not right," I choked out.

"I'm sorry."

No. There had to be a mistake. Teddy had always been

healthy. He'd died in his sleep? "I should have been there."

"It wouldn't have mattered, Mich. He went peacefully. You probably wouldn't have even known. There's nothing you could have done."

The room around me blurred as tears filled my eyes and bile rose in my throat. "No." Beginning to hyperventilate, I asked desperately, "Why didn't anyone call me?"

"We were in the thick of it until just a few minutes ago. No one wanted you to get the news while you were alone."

"If you're done," Teddy's father said harshly in the background, "I'd like my phone back."

Tearfully, Fran added, "No one is angry with you, Michawn. It just doesn't make sense. He was fine yesterday. I checked in on him." Her breathing sounded as heavy and labored as mine was. "I thought he was sleeping. I never checked to see if he was breathing. He looked so peaceful . . ."

I wrapped my arms around my waist and bent over, the pain of loss so excruciating I didn't know if it was survivable. I threw up on the carpet between my feet and didn't care about the mess or that some had gotten on my bare legs.

Teddy was gone.

Gone along with every reason I had to be happy.

I threw up again and closed my eyes. *Teddy, how could you leave me?*

It's always been us.

I don't want to be me without you.

Cold washed over me in waves. I heard voices coming from my phone but I was too numb to care what they were saying. I lay down on the bed and curled up into a tight ball. Hours later that was how my siblings found me. They cleaned me up, tried to say things to soothe me, and drove me to my parents' house.

That night, Piper at my side, I lay awake on the couch at our house. I couldn't bear to go into the bedroom. My family had offered to stay with me, but I'd lied and told them I needed to sleep. I doubted I'd ever sleep again.

On and off throughout the night, I cried into Piper's neck. He seemed to understand how much I needed his quiet comfort. "You were there when he died, Piper. Would I have known? Could I have saved him?"

Piper didn't answer, but I didn't expect him to. He whined and laid his head on my stomach. Anyone who thought animals don't feel loss would have changed their mind had they seen Piper mourning Teddy. He ached as deeply as I did.

Sniffing, I pet the side of his face and said, "You shouldn't have tried to bite Fran. She was always on your side."

Piper whimpered as if in explanation.

I hugged him close and nodded. "I know. Today, I'm allowed to go to the morgue to see his body. I'm afraid to. What if I don't want to leave him and start trying to bite people too?" It wasn't a funny joke, which might have been the reason it concluded with me bursting into tears again.

CHAPTER SEVEN

Jared

Two Weeks Later

LATE ONE EVENING, after everyone else had gone home, I sat in the quiet of my Boston office and turned off my computer. I hadn't expected to hear from Michawn before she left Hamilton's, but that hadn't stopped me from checking for a message from her.

I was a man who went after what I wanted, but not when it was to the detriment of others. Hamilton and I had always agreed on that. Rising waters raise all boats. The only acceptable casualties in life were those who brought the fight and left me with no other choice.

There'd been a few of those in business, but not many.

Most of my adversaries eventually understood that I made a better friend than I did an enemy. There was strength in collaboration and paying a favor forward was never a waste of time. Hamilton had taught me that by not only rewarding my hard work at his company with promotions, but by helping me start my own business when he'd thought Gavin was ready to take over for him.

Integrity and loyalty mattered. They were why he'd sold me his company when Gavin had made it clear that he didn't want to follow in his father's footsteps.

A person was defined by the promises they kept and the decisions they made.

I wouldn't have been able to look Hamilton or myself in the eye again had I gone after another man's woman. Especially since, as far as I could tell, he was good to her.

I didn't check to see if she made it home the next day. I did force myself to have dinner with a woman I'd been interested in before meeting Michawn, but it was a wasted evening that ended early. She didn't light up the room the way Michawn did when she smiled.

She didn't talk with the same passion Michawn had.

Afterward, I accepted an invitation to a party I normally would have refused, simply to prove to myself that women like Michawn were common enough. The problem was they weren't. Some were taller, shorter, thinner, rounder . . . but none were her.

When the second week had started with no communication from Michawn, I sent her an email. She didn't respond. I double-checked the address and sent a more forceful request for an update.

Nothing.

She hadn't seemed upset when we'd parted. Sure, some people hid how they felt, but she didn't seem the type. Even when I'd essentially propositioned her, her response had been as direct as they come.

Not rude, just firm.

If it wasn't my responsibility to handle this first step of the renovations for Hamilton, I wouldn't have contacted Michawn again. My frustration grew, however, when my texts as well as messages on her phone weren't responded to.

Who the fuck did she think she was? If she didn't want to move forward with the project, the professional thing to do would have been to say so.

Had she been anyone else, if I hadn't lost sleep remembering her laugh and that damn sundress of hers, I would have flown to wherever she was and demanded a response. I didn't seek her out, though. The last thing I needed was to see how happy she was with someone else.

She wasn't the only reason I'd lost sleep over the past two weeks. What Calvin had said about our last sparring session had gutted me. His opinion carried weight because when everyone else had given up on me, he hadn't. He'd risked the first good placement he'd had for me and was very likely the reason I wasn't in jail like my father.

It was a debt I could never repay, but one I'd prided myself on trying to. Yet, there I'd been, selfishly dragging him right back to the brutality we'd known as children. And he'd gone there without complaint, again and again for me, even when it put his new safe place at risk.

He was right—it wasn't healthy.

I wasn't healthy. Something had to change. He deserved

better from me.

Hamilton did as well. I'd avoided calling him about Michawn long enough.

"Jared," Hamilton said cheerfully when he answered my call. "How are you?"

"Good. How's Fara doing?" Hamilton had given me text updates, but I'd been waiting to have something to share from Michawn before I called him. How had two weeks passed so quickly?

"Better every day. She's ready for company now. We were remaining in Boston for all of her rehab, but we've decided to return to Newton where it's quieter. We'd love to see you."

"I'm in. Just say when."

"How about tomorrow for dinner in Newton? Fara is looking forward to regaining some normalcy. Gavin and Riley will be there. We were all recently talking about how we want to see more of you. Don't get too busy for us."

"Never. Tomorrow sounds perfect." I cleared my throat. "About the surprise you were planning for Fara, although it sounds like you've already told her, I have some bad news. The woman you hired for the renovations has completely ghosted me. I wouldn't suggest using her. If you'd like, I'll check out another architect."

"Oh, shit. I should have called you. I figured you'd been contacted as well. That project is on hold, possibly for a long time. I really liked her work, but I understand why she needs to take some time for herself."

"Did something happen?" I tensed.

"The poor thing. Her fiancé died while she was at our home in Newton. A blood clot was the confirmed cause. Heartbreaking. Her parents called to tell me she wouldn't be able to move forward with the project. We sent flowers."

I ran a hand through my hair while I processed the news. I'd hated the thought of her with another man. If I'd heard they'd broken up I might have fist-bumped the universe, but to lose him like that? No.

I knew what it was like to lose people I loved, people I thought would always be there to take care of me. I hated that she'd been introduced to that feeling. If I could have turned back the clock and protected her from that loss, I would have.

"That sucks," I said simply because her loss affected me beyond what I knew how to express. I remembered the photos she'd shown me, how she'd glowed as she'd talked about the life she'd have with him. All that was lost to her now.

"I'm sorry. I hope you didn't waste much time trying to contact her."

I cleared my throat. "No, not really. And you've had a lot on your mind, so don't put another thought into this."

Fuck. I wish I could do the same.

"You okay?" Hamilton asked. "You sound . . . affected by this news."

"I'm fine." I paused. Hamilton ranked high on my short list of people I trusted. Although I was certain he'd done a background check on me before hiring me, I'd never really spoken to him about my life before I'd changed my name. "I have some things weighing on my mind and if you have a few minutes, I need someone to talk them out with."

"Of course. Do you want to come here or is over the phone okay?"

I inhaled deeply before answering. "This works. I'm not good at talking about stuff like this, but you've always brought out the best in me . . . and I need to know what that would be right now."

It wasn't easy to tell him about why I'd changed my name or how angry I became whenever my past nipped at my heels. Hamilton didn't suggest I give my father a chance to apologize. Hamilton was a big believer of people needing to accept the natural consequences of their actions.

He was concerned, though, when I talked to him about how I'd used cage fighting as a release and what Calvin had recently said about it. It wasn't an easy admission to make, not even to myself, but there was something freeing about it as well. There was still a lot of shame and guilt attached to my old life. Hamilton often said he considered me his second son. I didn't have a good track record when it came to father figures, but like Calvin, Hamilton had stood by me.

He was quiet for several minutes after I said I needed to make some changes, but I didn't know where to start or if I was even capable of being more than I already was.

I didn't share how angry I was that the universe had just side-swiped Michawn or that I was convinced if someone like her didn't deserve happiness, there was no fucking chance for me.

When Hamilton spoke, it was with the same quiet strength and confidence he'd employed when he'd told the fresh-from-college me that I had what it took to one day run my own company. "Jared, you are more than just a survivor. I've never known anyone with as much drive and dedication as you have. You hold yourself to a high standard, but you need to also be kind to yourself. No one is as good as they appear or evil to the core. We all have regrets. All you can do is wake up each day determined to be a better version of yourself. Thank you for trusting me with the truth about the boy you once were and how angry you are. Now I want to hear about the man you want to become. Tell me about him."

"I'm still figuring that out," I admitted. "All I know is I can't bring more pain to the people who care about me."

"From what you said, your thoughts calm when you push your body. You need to find release in a healthier place. You enjoy working out, don't you? Get your ass in the gym and ask Calvin to join you. This is no different than what you learned with Gavin. You and he would be unstoppable if you figured out how to get on the same side of the fight."

When I finally left my office, rather than going home, I

called Calvin and met him at one of his gyms, but this time to work out together rather than spar. After I told him what had happened to Michawn's fiancé, we lifted free weights until our arms were spent, then ran on treadmills long past when either of us enjoyed it. I needed to quiet my thoughts and couldn't stop until I did.

As Calvin was locking up, I said, "I never meant to drag you down. I'm sorry."

He took a weak swing at my arm, missed, and groaned. "I'd accept your apology, but I'm not sure I'll be able to move tomorrow. Do you think, maybe, we could get together sometime and practice a little thing called moderation?"

I laughed. "Yeah, we could try that."

CHAPTER EIGHT

Michawn

Two years later

FROM THE HOME office in my rented two-bedroom condo I double-checked the accuracy of the technical drawing I'd been sent by a local architect. Subcontracting for several companies rather than taking a job at one allowed me to work remotely and on my schedule. After selling the home I'd bought with Teddy, to preserve what little was left of my sanity, Piper and I had moved to a neighboring state.

Alone.

Although I'd appreciated everyone's concern in the beginning, the constant attention had become suffocating. I didn't need my family moving their schedules around so one of them was always with me. I quickly began to resent being asked, "How are you?"

How am I?

How would anyone be after losing not only the man they loved but the future they'd dreamed of spending with them?

Angry. Sad. Tired.

Defeated.

And trapped in that place.

In an attempt to cheer me, my parents had often spoken in terms of "When you're back to feeling like yourself . . ."

That's when they thought I should live on my own again.

It was when they imagined I'd stop avoiding my friends.

As soon as I'm back to feeling like myself . . .

I couldn't stay in a town where I had so many memories of Teddy. I didn't have the energy to lie to our mutual friends and say I was okay. I got physically sick whenever talking about the wedding, the money we'd lost on it, my suddenly rocky relationship with Teddy's parents, or why I wasn't looking for my next creative project.

So I moved.

In the beginning there'd been endless calls and texts from concerned friends and family. I'd rallied for a while and tried to sound upbeat, then began letting their calls go to voicemail. And the texts? Every few weeks I'd delete them—unread.

Piper and I were fine.

I had a roof over my head, a job that paid the bills, and food in the fridge. I didn't want or need more than that and I was tired, so tired . . .

After a year of not returning most calls, only my family and Tracy still left messages. Every once in a while I'd text them back with a photo of Piper and reassurance that I was fine. Tracy had recently asked me to call her. She said she had news she wanted to share.

I wanted to return her call. I really did.

I don't know why I didn't. One day slid into the next and before I knew it a week had gone by without responding to her text. It felt too late, too lame, to answer her then.

So I didn't.

A knock on my door startled me. No one dropped in anymore. I pushed loose hair out of my eyes and shuffled to the door's peephole.

Tracy.

I rubbed a hand over my face. Shit. Had I known she was coming I might have showered and changed out of my sweatpants. Or maybe not. I'd stopped caring what I looked like.

I groaned and mustered a smile as well as an apology as I opened the door. "Tracy. I was just about to call you."

She looked me over and shook her head as she walked past me. "Of course you were."

Piper romped over with an excited whine and a wildly wagging tail. Tracy bent and gave Piper a few good scratches as Piper wound around her legs. "At least someone is happy to see me."

I closed the door slowly. "I'm happy to see you." It was impossible to look her in the eye as I lied. We'd always been honest with each other. How could I tell her that seeing her often left me feeling worse rather than better?

"I took the day off from work to come down to see you.

Let's go somewhere for lunch."

"I can't."

That wasn't true. I just didn't want to.

I wanted to want to go. If I could flip a switch in me that would change how much I now resented the presence of other people, I would flip it in a heartbeat. To appease my parents, I'd gone through more than one therapist. They all essentially said the same thing: Mourning takes time . . .

Apparently, I needed to be patient.

I needed to forgive Teddy as well as myself.

They made it sound so easy.

Yes, I'll get right on that.

Right after the nightmares end and I no longer force myself to eat every day only because I don't want Piper to lose me as well.

As soon as I wake up and don't roll over to place my hand on Piper's chest to make sure he's still breathing . . . yeah, that's the day I'll start doling out forgiveness.

I'm still angry.

Sorry if that's inconvenient for anyone. I'm doing my best to spare you all from having to deal with it.

Tracy's lips pressed together as if she were taking her time to choose her words carefully. "You work from home, right?"

"Correct."

"Then we could order in. I don't mind eating here."

A lump of emotion rose in my throat. She was a good

friend, a better one than I deserved. God, I wanted to do better . . . to be better. "I appreciate that you drove down here."

"I love you, Michawn."

Her words gutted me. I blinked several times and sniffed. "You know I feel the same."

She straightened and hugged her large purse to her stomach. "It's been two years, Mich. I should be able to drop in on my best friend."

I looked away. "You're always welcome."

"I should be able to tell you I'm engaged without feeling guilty."

My eyes sought hers and I felt like the worst person on the planet because I couldn't remember the name of the man she'd told me she was dating. "Congratulations, Tracy."

Tears filled her eyes and her voice deepened. "Do you remember the night you told me Teddy had proposed to you? I couldn't stop hugging you and you couldn't stop smiling?"

Yes, the memory was painfully vivid. I told my feet to move toward her. She deserved that from me. When I remained rooted where I was, I said, "I'm sorry."

She folded her arms across her chest. "So am I. I'm getting married and I want to share this experience with my best friend. Where is she?"

I raised and lowered my shoulders. Honestly, I didn't know. "Anything you need . . ." My voice trailed away because I didn't know what I could promise. More than anything else, I didn't want to disappoint her. I cleared my throat. "Your parents must be thrilled."

"They are."

Neither of us said anything for a long moment. "Did you pick a date?"

"We're working on that, but I wanted to make sure that it's one that will work for you."

"For me?" I swallowed hard.

"I can't get married without you there. Michawn, you're my heart sister. What do you need? What's holding you back? Talk to me. Whatever you're going through, you're not alone. I'm right here. Tell me what to do to help you."

My guilt was so tangible I could almost taste it. Stomach churning, I took several deep breaths to calm myself. Would she choose the same church Teddy and I were going to? We had all the same friends. Everyone who would be at her wedding would have been at mine. "I—I . . ."

"It's been two years, Michawn."

"I didn't realize there was a time limit to mourning." I closed my eyes briefly at the unintentional bite in my tone. I hated that I didn't recognize myself anymore. Where was the person who would have thrown her arms around Tracy and bounced up and down with her gleefully? Would she ever be back?

"That's not what I'm saying." Her voice softened. "I'm worried about you." She looked around. "This place looks like you just moved in. No pictures. No decorations . . ."

"I put it all away." I'd thought boxing up the memories of Teddy and stashing them in a closet would help, but it hadn't.

"Not just that." She waved a hand around the room. "There's no . . ." She didn't have to finish for me to know that her next word would have been *magic*. As far back as when my parents had allowed me to decorate my own bedroom I'd added things designed to make people smile. Bright colors. Fun decorations. Unique comfortable chairs. Swings. Slides. I'd always said life was too short to worry if things matched.

Some had accused me of being too much but I'd always taken that as a compliment. I didn't have to glance around to know the beige walls of my living room were still bare. The only personal items in the room were Piper's bed and toys. "I don't own the condo so anything I put up will only need to be taken down when I move."

"You've been here over a year."

I sighed. "I don't want to have this conversation, Tracy."

"And I want you to be my maid of honor."

Bile rose in my throat.

She lowered her arms. "I understand, Michawn. My heart hurts for you. You're afraid that being part of my wedding will be torture."

Yes.

"And that you'll disappoint me."

In a whisper, I admitted, "Exactly."

"I'm sorry. I refuse to take no for an answer. You and I are family. We're supposed to be there for all the big moments of each other's lives. Weddings. Funerals. Baby showers. The good. The bad. The ugly. We ride them out together. Remember how we promised to be there for each other when we deliver our babies just in case our husbands are clueless . . ."

She stopped at my harshly inhaled breath. There'd be no babies in my future. Not anymore. "About the wedding—"

"Don't say it. If you say you don't want to be part of it, it'll change things. Tell me you'll think about it."

That was a promise I could make easily since I wouldn't be able to do much else after she left. "I'll think about it."

We fell into another long silence.

She broke it first. "It's going to be okay, Michawn. I'll figure this out."

Heart thudding in my chest, I said, "I do love you, Tracy. I just . . ."

She hugged me, then straightened and sniffed. "I should let you get back to work."

I stepped back and nodded toward my computer. "I do have a lot to get through today." There was nothing I couldn't have put off but the tension between us was uncomfortable.

She walked to the door then turned. "You don't have to agree to plan parties or be festive. I just need to know that you'll be there at my side."

I nodded, didn't promise anything, and hated myself for it.

She left without saying another word.

I let her go and stood there long after she'd gone.

I understood why she'd threatened that things would change between us if I couldn't be there for her wedding. We'd grown up dreaming of sharing that day with each other.

When someone imagined the future often and with such detail that it already felt real—changes to that vision felt like a death. I knew because mourning Teddy had included mourning all our future moments. Our wedding, our children, the fights we would have worked our way through. All of it.

I didn't want to let Tracy down, but what if, during the ceremony, I burst out crying?

I couldn't ruin one of the happiest days of her life. She deserved better than I could promise.

Tracy thought she wanted me there, but what she really wanted was for me to be the person I used to be.

I wanted that too, but she was gone.

Two years.

When do I stop feeling like I died with Teddy?

CHAPTER NINE

Jared

"DON'T SAY YOU'RE not coming," Hamilton said as a member of his house staff refilled my glass of water. "Fara, tell him the twins don't turn fifteen months every day. We're celebrating on Wednesday."

I glanced across the table at Gavin and joked, "At what age do we stop having these monthly birth celebrations for your spawn?"

Gavin's wife, Riley, laughed. "You say that like you don't eat more of the sweets than they do."

"Exactly." I leaned down and picked up one of the twins as he and his sister, Marina, paused their toddler sprint around the table beside my chair. "Are you trying to make me fat?"

Hunter gave my flat stomach a pat and said, "Fat."

"Thanks, kid," I said with a groan. He clung to my neck when I went to return him to the floor.

Marina pulled on the sleeve of my jacket. "Up, Jarry. Up."

"Wouldn't you rather sit on your mother?" I asked as I

tried to loosen Hunter's stranglehold.

"They love their Uncle Jarry," Gavin said with a smile.

Facing toward the table, I settled Marina onto one of my legs just in time to catch the more daring Hunter as he'd begun to climb me like a tree. His little hands clasped my face and pinched. "I love you, Jarry," he said.

"Love you too, little guy." That made him smile. With a wiggle he spun to sit on my other leg facing the table as well. Unfortunately, while both of my hands were full, four of theirs were free and my glass of water tumbled forward.

Fara caught my drink with the speed of a woman who'd raised twins herself. It was great to see her feeling good enough to lunge forward without worrying about physical limitations. Riley swooped in from the other side to remove the utensils and my plate of food.

I bounced my legs lightly which had both toddlers giggling and holding on to the table rather than reaching for everything on it. Prior to these particular two I wouldn't have said I had a great fondness for children. They were growing on me, though. So was the more relaxed side of Gavin that Riley and the kids were bringing out.

I'd never seen Gavin as comfortable in his own skin as he was since he left his father's company and started living his life on his terms. I could say the same about Hamilton since he'd retired. Both of their lives had undergone drastic changes, but none either of them seemed to regret. "I'll be there on Wednesday."

"Would you like me to take one before they pull the tablecloth onto your lap?" Hamilton asked, holding his arms toward his grandchildren.

"Do I look like an amateur uncle?" I asked, pushing my chair slightly back as I continued to bounce them.

Riley rested her chin on one hand and smiled. "No, you're a pro. I always knew you had it in you."

"That's why you're almost their favorite uncle," Gavin said.

"Almost?" I echoed in mock outrage. "I'd like a recount on that vote."

Fara laughed. "They love all of their uncles equally."

Hamilton coughed. "Riley, don't tell Dominic that or you'll end up with a barn full of ponies."

"That'll probably happen anyway," Gavin said lightly. "We've repeatedly said our little celebrations are about getting everyone together and not about presents, but he doesn't listen."

Riley brought a hand to one of her cheeks. "My brother doing what he wants? I can't imagine that. I warned him he's going to spoil them. My twin isn't any better. He brings them presents every single time he sees them."

Hamilton made a goofy face at the children and they both laughed. "Children need to be spoiled now and then. Don't you?"

"*Who are you?*" Gavin asked and nodded toward me. "Do you recognize him? That is not the man who raised me."

I chuckled and chose to stay out of that one.

Hamilton continued cooing to his grandchildren while addressing his son. "I don't have to lay down the law with these two cuties, you do. I get to say yes, fall asleep before they do when I read stories to them, and help Dominic pick out their toys. Grampie can afford to spoil you too. Who wants their own company? You?" He tickled Marina's belly. "Grampie will get you one."

Marina laughed. "Company."

"We're in trouble," Riley said to Gavin.

He put an arm around her. "We'll just keep having children and hope he goes broke before he can ruin them all."

"I *would* like more," Riley said with a sweet smile that made me hope they got that huge family they were both wishing for.

"Down," Marina ordered. "Down, Jarry."

"Yes, ma'am." I lowered her to the floor. She toddled to Hamilton and climbed onto his lap. Hunter turned and gave my cheek a sticky pat. "Oh, that's delightful."

"They're breaking you in for when your friends start a family. How are Calvin and Bradley?"

I dunked a napkin in my water and wiped down Hunter's hands. "Same. Haven't seen too much of them, but I've been busy."

"Because you choose to be," Hamilton said around Marina as she removed his glasses to inspect them. "I made that choice once. I hope you wake up earlier than I did."

"It's possible to run a business and have a life," Gavin interjected.

"I run *two* now, remember?" I sighed, unsure of why I'd even gone there. These were the people who'd supported every step of my transition from poverty to wealth. They knew exactly what I had and what was required to maintain it. Also, their loyalty to me was above question. Still, that didn't make the conversation any easier. "Listen, I know where this is going so let me clarify from the start—I enjoy working as much as I do. I never imagined I'd achieve the level of success I have, I'm grateful for all you've done, and everything is good." I sniffed. "Except, possibly whatever's in Hunter's diaper. That smells like a problem I don't want to deal with."

"Oh," Riley said in a rush as she swooped Hunter out of my arms. "No one wants that. Gavin, could you get the diaper bag and meet me in the other room?"

Gavin stood. "Absolutely. Dad, you and Fara are in charge."

I wasn't offended in the least, especially since a second dirty diaper was quite likely impending.

Fara lifted Marina and snuggled her to her chest. "We've got this. Marina give Grampie back his glasses."

"No," Marina said.

Fara gave the little one a firm look that I would have expected from Hamilton and Marina reluctantly held out the glasses to Hamilton. I hid a smile behind my hand. I remembered clearly how easily Hamilton had commanded a room full of even the world's most wealthy. He'd always held himself as well as everyone around him to a nearly impossible-to-maintain high standard. Yet, there he was, unable to get his glasses back from a child. If he hadn't been glowing with pride at Marina as well as Fara, I would have wondered if he'd lost his mind. Instead, I decided, this was simply how happy looked on him.

"Hamilton," Fara said while settling Marina onto her lap. "Have you told Jared?"

He touched his wife's arm gently. "I haven't."

"You should."

I straightened in my chair. It sounded serious.

Riley returned to the room with a smile. "False alarm, but it's getting late so we'll probably head next door to give them baths and put them down for the night."

Fara rose and handed Marina to her. "Need help?"

"Thanks, Mom, but you should stay and visit with Jared. We'll be over early for breakfast before we head back to the city."

Hamilton waved for Riley to come to him. "Before you go, I'd like a moment with all of you. There's something I need to tell Jared."

My concern that it might have been something about Fara's health faded. "Hamilton," I said, "just say it."

Riley raised a hand. "I'll be right back with Gavin."

Never one to be rushed or pushed, Hamilton waited

until we were all in the same room again before he said, "Gavin and Riley if you don't mind staying another few minutes . . ."

"Of course," they said in unison.

We all retook our seats, Gavin with Hunter in his arms and Riley holding Marina. They looked as clueless regarding what Hamilton was about to say as I was. Hamilton said, "I received a call from a woman who had a most interesting request and one that I was hesitant to grant."

Fara linked her hand with Hamilton's as the rest of us collectively held our breaths. "Hamilton allowed me to listen in. It was a beautiful conversation. You could hear how much this woman loves her friend."

"Who? And how do they have anything to do with me?" I demanded. A horrible thought came to me that enraged me. If my father had found someone with the nerve to involve Hamilton—

"Do you remember the architect we hired to renovate these houses?" Hamilton asked.

That reverberated through me. Remembering Michawn was easy. Forgetting her was something I still struggled with. "Sure."

Hamilton continued, "She took the loss of her fiancé hard. She moved away from her family and friends, gave up creating play spaces, and now lives alone with her dog in Rhode Island."

My gut twisted painfully but I was careful not to let my

feelings show on my face. "That's a shame." It was. I hated to hear she was still suffering. "I hope she gets some help."

"Help, yes, well, her friend said she's tried that route. She also said Michawn has a lot of people who care about her, but she's withdrawn from all of them." Hamilton cleared his throat. "The woman—Tracy is her name—said Michawn confessed to having felt a . . . ahem . . . spark of something when you two met. She thinks Michawn might be feeling guilty about that and it could be part of why she can't move on. She wondered if you would consider going to see her."

A flash of pleasure at the idea that she'd felt something toward me rushed in and departed just as quickly. "Hard no. I'm the last person she'd want to see."

"You don't know that," Riley said. "If you did have a connection, maybe seeing you again . . ."

"Right," I said with sarcasm. "I'll knock on her door and when she opens it say, "Hey, remember me? I'm the guy who came on to you the night your fiancé died. It's been two years and a month. What do you think? Want to give this a go?"

Gavin frowned. "That does sound like a bad idea."

Hamilton sighed. "It did to me as well, at least at first. Tracy was quite persuasive though. She wasn't suggesting that Michawn would be ready for a relationship or that you were the one for her. She's hoping that seeing you, talking to you, will jolt her friend out of a dark place."

I shook my head. "I'm no one's happiness guru." I pointed to each of them. "Anyone at this table would be more qualified to deal with this. Most days I can't even"—I almost swore but held it back because the little ones were listening intently—"stand myself. I have my own issues."

Fara nodded. "You're right." She waved a hand through the air as if to erase her words. "Not about any of us being more qualified, but right to honor your own struggles. I used to question my worth, at least as far as relationships went. I'd made mistakes and part of me believed I didn't deserve to have someone of my own. It's not easy to help others when you're not in a good place yourself. It took Hamilton to show me that love doesn't require perfection."

Her sincerity touched me. I said, "You've shown him the same. He's lucky to have you."

"You could be that for this woman," Fara said softly.

I leaned over and gave her hand a squeeze. "I love you for believing that, but that's not how the world works. I was attracted to her, she felt the same, that's not the same as what you and Hamilton have."

"Yet," Hamilton said. "For anything to work you have to give it a chance. Where's the man who told me he'd be running my company one day? He gave one hundred ten percent of himself to everything I threw his way and that's why he always won."

"This isn't about winning. That woman is obviously struggling."

Gavin leaned back in his chair as Hunter played with his

tie. "You feel something for this woman, don't you? This wasn't someone you met and forgot. I can see it in your eyes."

"She was very nice. I hope meeting me didn't make losing her fiancé harder than it had to be." In response to Gavin's eyebrows rising, I added, "Nothing happened, but there was a connection."

Riley cuddled her daughter closer. "And then she lost her fiancé. She probably blamed herself . . ."

"How could she? She wasn't there."

"Exactly," Hamilton said. "She was with you. Guilt doesn't require justification. You know that as well as I do."

I did. It was something I'd slowly begun to face these past two years. Adult me knew that my mother's drinking and the lack of care she'd given me was the reason I'd been taken from her and put into foster care. Young me had blamed myself for telling the teachers there was no food in my house and my mother left me alone for days at a time. I didn't put alcohol in her hands. I wasn't the one who'd hurt my mother by staying, then hurt her more by leaving. Both of my parents had paid for their own bad decisions but I still hated that my father had taken his temper out on her and I'd never been able to stop him, hated that part of me had been happy when he'd been put in prison.

It had weighed on me to the point where I'd changed even my last name. So, yeah, I understood that starting over was sometimes necessary.

Who was I to tell Michawn she shouldn't? "She left. That's a sign that she wants to be left alone."

"Or did and now she's just lost. You could be the spark that reminds her she has a lot left to live for," Fara said as she exchanged a look with Hamilton.

"Go see her," Hamilton said firmly. "If she looks well-adjusted, walk away. But if you think she needs a friend . . . be that for her."

I made a sound. "Friendship wasn't where that spark was headed."

Hamilton leaned in, his face serious and his tone one I knew well from when he'd shown me the ways of running a business. "Then do better."

"I agree with my father." Gavin chimed in, "A few years ago I wouldn't have imagined I'd be loving the life I have." He took Riley's hand. "The life we're making together. Riley sold me on happily ever afters."

Hamilton met my gaze. "You're in a much healthier place now than you were when you met her. Take some of what you've learned and share it with her."

"Thank you, but it's a bad idea." I stood. "I'll see you all Wednesday."

Fara added, "She's only an hour or so away. You could easily drive down to see her and still be back for the celebration."

I gave her a quick kiss on the cheek. "I could but I won't."

"You should," Hamilton said.

"He will," Gavin added.

Riley hugged her husband as they each still held a child. "Did you mean what you said about happily ever afters?"

He bent to kiss her. "I did. Let's get these kids to bed."

I walked out with them, got into my car alone, and drove back to my apartment where I stripped and plopped down onto my bed—alone. Going to see Michawn was a horrible idea.

That's what I told myself throughout that long and restless night.

It's what I told myself the next morning when I couldn't concentrate at any of my meetings.

I hadn't changed my mind even when I cleared my afternoon schedule and decided that a drive might help me clear my head.

CHAPTER TEN

Michawn

"NO MORE," I told Piper when he dropped his ball at my feet for what felt like the hundredth time. He sat, wagged his tail, and whined with his tongue flopping out of one side of his mouth. I caved and bent to pick up the ball. He started dancing in excited circles as soon as he knew he'd won. "That's the last one, then we need to go."

Not at all concerned with how little work I'd gotten done since speaking to Tracy, Piper happily chased the ball across the empty dog park. He and I frequently chose this hidden gem of a place because few others did. It allowed me to exercise Piper without the distraction of other people.

Breathing heavily, Piper plopped at my feet. Deciding to let him rest before heading back, I poured some water into his portable bowl and took a seat on one of the benches. I had several designs on deadline, but I couldn't concentrate.

I leaned forward, propped my elbows on my knees and buried my face in my hands. I hadn't called or texted Tracy since she'd come by and the weight of that guilt was making sleep impossible. She'd always been a good friend to me. I needed to just call her and tell her . . . what? That was the part that held me back. Two years. How was everything still this hard?

"Michawn?" a deep male voice asked from close enough that it startled me. Normally Piper would have alerted me to the presence of someone, but when I lowered my hands he was lying at my feet wagging his tail.

My gaze riveted to the stranger and I froze as I realized I remembered that strong jaw. It wasn't the first time I'd looked into those dark eyes. His suit was similar to the one he'd worn the day we'd met and his hair was cut short in a conservative style, but he seemed broader and more muscular than I remembered.

This time, however, there was no spark of attraction. All I felt was sick that I might have been talking to him as Teddy died alone. I shook my head.

"Jared Seacrest. You're not Michawn Courter?"

I stood. "No. Sorry." What was he doing there? Had he been walking by and spotted me in the park? Thanks, universe, but I don't really need another reason to hate myself this week.

He bent and offered a hand toward Piper for a sniff. "Hi, Piper."

Piper's whole body wagged in greeting.

"How do you know my dog's name?"

"You told me, remember? You said you wanted to be as happy as your dog when you ask him if he wants to go for a walk."

Piper spun and barked at his favorite word. I called him to my side. I did remember, but didn't want to.

"Mind if I sit here?" he asked.

"I do."

He sat anyway. "This is a nice little park."

I clipped Piper's leash back on his collar and held it tight. "You're welcome to stay and enjoy it." I took a step away.

"Don't go. It wasn't easy to find you."

"Find me?" My voice rose an octave. "Why would you want to?"

He ran his hands down his thighs and eased back against the bench. "To make sure you're okay."

Every muscle in me tensed. We were little more than strangers. Why would he care? Between clenched teeth I muttered, "Thank you for your concern, but it's unnecessary."

"So, you're doing fine."

It might have been the doubt in his voice or the fact that I felt cornered but I glared at him rather than answering.

His eyebrows rose and fell. "I was sorry to hear about your fiancé."

I wanted to tell him to keep any mention of Teddy out of his mouth, but that would have required engaging with him more than I had any intention of. I took another step back, pulling Piper with me. "Thank you."

His gaze held mine. "I regret the way I spoke to you the

day we met."

"It doesn't matter." He hadn't been the one in a solid, loving relationship. No, that had been me.

"It matters to me. If I said anything that made you feel—"

"You didn't."

"I don't want to be the reason you're—"

Something inside me snapped. "Did you kill my fiancé? No? Then you're not the reason for anything." I told myself to go but I stood there gasping for air.

He cleared his throat. "You're beautiful and I took a shot. It was incredibly poor timing and I hate that I might have added another layer to what happened to you."

Another layer? Did he actually believe anything we'd said to each other hadn't paled out of existence as soon as I'd heard about Teddy? The anger swirling within me was beyond what I could contain.

He'd sought me out. Why? Because he'd thought I was beautiful? I wanted to punch his perfectly sculpted face. "I don't know what you're doing here, but I have no interest in prolonging this conversation or ever seeing you again."

He met my glare without speaking so I added, "Read the room. When you see a woman in sweatpants, a sweatshirt, old sneakers, with her hair pulled back and not a stitch of makeup . . . that woman is not looking to meet anyone."

He frowned. "I'm not coming on to you."

For some inexplicable reason that stung. "It wouldn't

matter if you were. I'm here with my dog during the least busy part of the day because I want to be alone."

He nodded slowly. "I heard you were still struggling."

"Heard? From whom?" Who the hell had he been talking to?

"You do seem different. I want you to know though that if you felt a spark of attraction to me it's nothing to feel guilty about."

Fury rose in me. "Oh, my God. I don't know what spark you're talking about but you need to stay away from me."

He rose to his feet. "I'm not good with this kind of stuff, but I needed to see how you're doing."

Throat tight, I lashed out. "Why? We are no one to each other. Please go."

He gave me a long look, rubbed his hand over his chin then turned to walk away. I let out a breath of relief, but tensed when he turned on his heel to face me again.

"Michawn Courter?" he asked as if he'd just stumbled upon me.

"What are you doing?" I asked impatiently.

"Plan B: Starting this conversation over."

"You had a plan B for meeting me?"

"Yes. I like to be prepared."

"And it includes pretending I didn't just tell you to leave? It relies on me having the memory of Dory from Nemo?"

He pocketed his hands and was quiet for a moment. "This is a beautiful park. I can see why you come here."

My hands fisted at my sides. "If you won't leave, I will."

"That'll only initiate my plan C."

"Plan C?"

"I don't have one yet, but I care enough to come up with one if I have to."

I shook my head wildly. "You care enough? About me? Because we met once?"

"Let's go somewhere where we can talk," he said calmly. "Coffee?"

I rolled my eyes skyward. He was insane. Or I was. Either way, this was a bad idea. "No." I pulled Piper closer. "Come on, Piper. We're leaving." I began to back away while facing him.

"Meet me here tomorrow at eleven o'clock. I'll bring lunch."

"Not going to happen."

"No pressure. No expectations. Just food and conversation."

"That's your plan C?"

"No, we're still on plan B. See you tomorrow."

"You won't."

"I will."

I shook my head as I turned away, lengthening my stride so I quickly put distance between us. Clumsily I opened the fence gate and scurried through it with Piper. When I glanced back, Jared wasn't in pursuit. He'd sat back down on the bench.

I half walked, half ran all the way back to my apartment then locked the door behind me. What had just happened?

Piper sloppily drank from his water bowl then lay on the floor in front of the couch. I hugged my arms around myself as I paced my living room. Why would a man seek me out two years after we exchanged what could at most be described as a few heated glances?

He'd said he'd heard I wasn't doing well. Who would have told him that? We didn't move in the same circles. The only connection we had was Hamilton Wenham. Had he spoken with my parents again? They'd said he'd called a few times that first year to see if I was interested in finishing the project I'd started for him.

Was that what was behind Jared seeking me out? Hamilton wanted work done? There were easier ways to contact me than hunting me down at a dog park. Did rich people do things like that? I wasn't the only person capable of designing indoor play areas.

Jared was a businessman, a successful one. Gorgeous, even though that was no longer enough to make my heart flutter. Still, it meant he would have many other opportunities to occupy his time. There was no way he'd actually go to the park the next day with sandwiches and wait for me to show up.

I forced myself to get some work done, but kept restlessly standing up and walking from room to room. I hunted for old emails or texts from him but I'd purged them. If I'd found a way, I would have told him to not waste his money buying food I wouldn't eat because I had no intention of meeting him.

Confused.

Irritated.

Panicking a little, I would have called Tracy if we were on better terms. It didn't feel right to lay an issue at her door when I hadn't yet given her the answer she was waiting for.

So, instead, I puttered around my apartment, made myself some soup that I left mostly untouched, then napped on the couch with the sound of television playing in the background.

I checked and double-checked that I'd locked the door of my apartment, even though I didn't believe Jared meant any harm. His sudden appearance had me feeling unsettled, uncertain, and more than a little angry at the intrusion.

Halfway through the night I gave up on sleep and went to stand in front of a mirror. Beautiful? Not anymore. My hair had outgrown any styling. Tanned skin didn't conceal the dark circles under my eyes. I'd lost weight, but not in a way that made a person more attractive. I looked gaunt, drained . . . fragile.

I wasn't the woman he'd met. Not on the inside or the outside.

Was he disappointed when he came face-to-face with the new me?

Why did I care?

Padding back to the couch, I wrapped myself in a thick blanket, closed my eyes and tried to hold back the painful memories seeing Jared again brought back. I relived receiving the news about Teddy and the surreal weeks that had followed. Too vividly, I remembered how he'd looked at the morgue and then in his casket.

Was Teddy watching from the other side and upset that Jared had sought me out? Angry with me for being confused that he had?

Did Teddy even exist anymore? Maybe there was nothing for any of us after we died.

I used to believe there was.

I used to believe a lot of things I didn't anymore.

Eventually I fell into a light sleep that I woke from too early. A shower followed by an attempt at work didn't make me feel any better. I paused at 10:45 and wondered if Jared was sitting on the bench at the dog park.

At 11:00 I told myself I was glad I hadn't gone.

How long would someone like Jared wait before giving up?

At 11:30, I once again dressed in sweats and an oversized sweatshirt, leashed up Piper, and headed off to the park. I was certain he'd be gone, if he'd been there at all.

I froze a distance away from the park when I spotted Jared's large frame seated on the bench. I stood there, undecided if I should retreat or advance, when Piper barked in welcome and Jared waved.

I began to walk toward him mostly because Piper was pulling me along. Jared stood and smiled at me. Gone was his suit and tie. In its place was a loose pair of sweatpants and sweatshirt that were similar enough to mine that I wasn't sure if he was mocking me—right down to the well-worn sneakers.

He didn't stand as I approached the bench. I came to a stop a few feet away and said, "You're still here." I released Piper and he bounded off.

"I knew you'd come."

"That's presumptuous."

"Or confident. Women find me hard to resist."

My mouth rounded. "You're serious?"

He shrugged his broad shoulders and a hint of a smile stretched his lips. Was his intention to make me smile? Very little did that lately. "You're onto something with your choice of clothing. It sends a message. I could use this. Like a cloak."

There was a spark of humor in his eyes, but also something else. I struggled to understand his intent. "Are you mocking me?"

"No. This attire is genius. It does make a person appear unapproachable."

"And you like that because otherwise you're so good-looking women can't resist you?"

"You said it, not me."

"Actually, you said it first."

"Oh, well, then, I'll take it as a compliment that you agreed."

"I didn't—"

"I brought you a sandwich and a water."

I wasn't hungry, nor was I ready to accept anything from him.

He leaned over and placed the bag a few feet away from him on the bench. "I'll put them right here. You know, for when you're brave enough to take food from me."

"I'm not a squirrel you can lure closer with food."

"But you *are* afraid of me?"

"Not at all." I wasn't. My heart was racing and my senses were on high alert, but not because I thought he'd hurt me.

"Then sit down."

I moved the paper bag aside and sat gingerly on the part of the bench farthest from Jared.

After a pause, he said, "You're thinner than I remember."

"Thanks?"

"No appetite?"

His question was a sucker punch I wasn't expecting. "Don't." I gripped the bench on both sides of me.

"If you need someone to talk to—"

"Been there, done that. All I want now is to be left alone."

Not looking a bit offended, he asked, "Are you still an architect?"

What the hell? "Yes."

"Still creating play spaces?"

I shifted and tensed. "Does it matter?"

His dark eyes were impossible to look away from. "It does to me."

Why? What was he doing, asking about me like he cared? I considered lying to him and I wasn't sure why I didn't. The truth wasn't something I was proud of. "I've moved on to other things."

"Such as?"

Pinned by his intense gaze, I admitted a little more. "I freelance as a consultant for companies now."

"Doing?"

"I double check the accuracy of technical drawings."

"Why?"

"Because people are often careless with their calculations."

"No, why did you stop creating your own designs?"

I looked away. It wasn't the first time I'd faced that question. Each therapist I'd spoken to had eventually asked some version of it. Two years and the reason hadn't changed. "I no longer see images in my mind." I raised a hand between us. "Before you tell me that it'll come back and that everything I'm going through is normal, I need you to know that I don't give a shit what you think of me. People have handled loss better than I have. Good for them. I don't care."

The corner of his mouth twitched. "Try the sandwich. According to the young man behind the counter, the tomatoes are grown locally and therefore it'll taste better."

"I'm not hungry."

"Did you eat breakfast?"

I frowned. "Why do you think that's any of your business?"

"Eat the damn sandwich," he said in a low tone.

It was such a strong command I laughed in surprise and picked up the bag but stopped myself before opening it. "Did you put something in it?"

"Like what?"

I shrugged. "I don't know. People don't usually walk up to me on the street and demand I eat something."

"You caught me. I stalk women at dog parks and force-feed them. Please don't turn me in."

"You're a bit of an asshole."

"You currently have the social skills of a porcupine/skunk/love child."

I blinked and almost smiled as I imagined how such a creature would appear. The look we exchanged turned heated so quickly it took me by surprise. Wait, I remembered that feeling.

No. No. No. Not happening.

Nervously, I pulled my attention from Jared to the paper bag on my lap. "What kind of sandwich is it?"

"Chicken salad."

"Safe choice."

"I don't know you well enough to know how adventurous you are . . ."

There it was again . . . a rise in my body temperature. I hadn't thought myself capable of feeling that way anymore. I inhaled sharply.

He continued, "Food-wise."

I let out a shaky breath. My body remembered wanting this man and that sent conflicting emotions through me. The last time I'd felt this way I'd lost everything.

Tears filled my eyes. To give myself something to do I unwrapped the sandwich. It looked delicious, and if offered up under other circumstances, I might have scarfed it down.

Piper rested his head on my knee and whined but not for the food. I rewrapped the sandwich, stuffed it back in the bag and put it aside. Piper stayed as he was, his attention on me. I pet his head gently.

I know you get upset when I do, Piper. I'm sorry.

Was that why Jared was there? Because he felt guilty that he'd come on to me the night Teddy died? I straightened my shoulders and cleared my throat. "Thank you for the sandwich and for coming to check that I'm okay. As you can see, I'm fine. Whoever told you I wasn't, doesn't know how well I've settled in here. You can go back and assure them I'm good."

"Michawn, look at me."

No, I wasn't ready to do that. I kept my eyes firmly glued on the grass at Piper's feet. "I don't want to do this."

"This?"

"Whatever this is."

"It is something, isn't it? I feel it too."

My hand tightened on Piper's leash. "I feel nothing."

"That's a lie."

It was, but that was the last thing I was ready to admit. "Is that what you tell yourself whenever a woman turns you down?"

"Impossible to turn down what I didn't offer."

My temper flared and my eyes flew to his. "Are you here to make me feel worse?"

"I thought you felt nothing."

That was far from true anymore. Guilt. Anger. Frustration . . . desire. It was all swirling within me. Each time I tried to rise above the waves he pulled me under again. "There was a spark, okay? I hate that there was. It cost me everything."

My words hung in the air.

When he didn't say anything, I snapped. "Go ahead, say it. Tell me that Teddy dying had nothing to do with that one moment of weakness. Tell me nothing happened between us and therefore I have nothing to feel guilty about. Tell me time heals all wounds and I'll be fine." I bent forward and hugged myself as nausea assailed me. My breathing quickened until I was gasping for air. "Say it."

"Do you prefer beef or chicken tacos?" he asked.

Shaking from head to toe with emotion, I paused to process his question. "What?"

"Mild, medium, or hot sauce?"

I fought to normalize my breathing. Why was he talking about food when I was falling apart? "I don't know."

"I'm a meat and cheese man. Simple. But a good hot sauce gives it the kick I crave."

Slowly sitting back up, I succeeded in composing myself somewhat. Tacos were a much safer topic. The adrenaline rushing through me began to subside. "As far as sauce goes, the hotter the better."

His eyes dilated with a desire that brought heat to my cheeks. It wasn't supposed to be this easy.

"I'll bring you one tomorrow. Same time. Same place."

I shook my head. "Don't. I won't meet you." After a pause, I added, "I know I said that yesterday, but this time I mean it."

"That's your choice, but I'll be here."

Confused, I stood. "What are you hoping for? That I'll have sex with you? You already told me women can't resist you. Go feed one of them."

His grin was easy and disarming. "I'll bring a Milk-Bone for Piper." He rose as well and stepped closer. For just a moment I thought he might kiss me and had no idea what I'd do if he did.

I waited for Piper to growl as he sometimes did when strangers approached me, but he didn't. He sat at my side, tongue lolling out, wagging his tail so much one would think Jared had already given him a treat. Jared raised a hand and gently caressed my cheek. My senses went into overload but I wouldn't raise my eyes above the neckline of his sweatshirt. "This isn't about sex, although I'm definitely attracted to you."

"I don't understand."

"That's okay, I'm only beginning to." He picked up the bagged sandwich and handed it to me. "Eat it or don't, but take it with you."

I accepted it and raised my gaze to meet his. The air between us was charged with both attraction and intense emotion. In his eyes I saw the pain I'd sensed the first time we'd met. It called to my own. He wasn't telling everything would be okay because he knew it wouldn't be. He was just as broken. The realization shook me.

Was he hoping I could heal him? I couldn't even heal myself. Clutching both the paper bag and Piper's leash, I took a few steps back. "Don't come here tomorrow."

"I have to, but I'll go for now." He nodded toward Piper. "I'm sure Piper wants to run around." He walked out of the gated area. Only when he was a good distance did I begin to breathe normally. Piper started sprinting around me in circles, but my attention didn't waver from the back of the man who only stopped and turned when he reached his car. He smiled.

I almost smiled back but turned away instead.

After he drove away, I sat on the bench and replayed our conversation. *What am I doing?*

CHAPTER ELEVEN

Jared

TWO DAYS LATER I sought a moment of peace on the patio of the house Hamilton had purchased for Gavin and Riley. Everyone else was down on the lawn with the children as they played on the variety of bounce houses Hamilton had rented for the day.

Not much had been done to renovate either home since I'd shown Michawn around. Hamilton had said he'd looked into other designers, but none had compared to her. Her spaces had that non-replicable extra something that had her former clients still raving about years later.

Hamilton said he'd rather keep both houses the same than settle for less. I understood that feeling when it came to Michawn—and that explained why no woman stayed in my life very long. I was far from celibate, but none of them plagued my thoughts in the middle of the night.

Only Michawn did that.

Wanting to see her again was clouding my judgment. Until she'd failed to show the next day, I'd felt like I was making progress. Her friend had been right about Michawn feeling guilty about the first time we'd met.

Even though she hadn't done anything, she'd felt something.

I'd felt it too.

The difference between her then and now was stark, but it didn't make her less beautiful. She'd become fragile. Uncertain. Nothing like the confident woman who'd challenged me to treat her better as she described how wonderful her life was.

Was that woman gone forever? I hated to think so.

Deep in thought, I didn't notice Riley until she'd joined me on the patio. "So this is where you're hiding."

"Not hiding, just taking a moment." I turned so I was facing her.

"I want to ask you something, but you can tell me it's none of my business," she said as a smile spread across her face. I'd never had a sister, but she was quickly becoming one.

"It's none of your business," I said without missing a beat.

She laughed. "You don't even know what the question is."

I did. I hadn't said anything about my trip to Rhode Island because I was still working out how I felt about it. I rubbed a hand over my face. "I went to see her."

"That's awesome." Her voice rose in excitement. "So?"

"She didn't want anything to do with me."

"Oh." Riley stepped closer. "I'm sorry."

"Don't be. I knew going was a bad idea."

After a moment, Riley asked, "Is she okay? How was she?"

Despite Michawn's request to say she was fine, I shared the truth with Riley. "Not good."

"That makes me so sad."

"What makes you sad?" Dominic Corisi demanded from behind Riley.

Perfect. What my already awkward conversation with Riley needed was her volatile brother's contributions. When Gavin had first told me who Riley's brother was, I'd been concerned. Dominic was a powerful man with a shady past and a ruthless reputation. How shady? He'd made so many enemies his security team was its own militia. How powerful? Those who went up against him didn't twice—even at the highest levels of government. There were suicides, disappearances, and rumors.

The Corisis were not a family I thought Gavin should associate with until I saw Dominic with Riley and her mother. When I dug deeper into his past, I gained some respect for him. We'd both survived abusive, shitty fathers and gone on to succeed despite them.

Where we differed was in the ego department. Dominic had a bit of a God complex that I had difficulty tolerating for any amount of time. He was far too accustomed to intimidating people for me not to want to knock him on his ass.

Still, he was Riley's brother so I did my best to play nice when it came to him.

When Riley looked at me as if asking if she could include Dominic in the conversation, I shook my head. She pressed her lips together then nodded in agreement.

Aggression flashed in Dominic's eyes. "I don't like secrets."

And I didn't like his tone. "This has nothing to do with you, Dominic."

"Careful, Seacrest. When it comes to my family, everything is my business."

Riley put a hand on his arm. "Dom, it's nothing. Really."

"Careful?" I leaned toward him then glanced around. "No bodyguard tonight? *You're* the one who should be careful." Sure I was tweaking the lion's tail, but old habits died hard and I'd sat with tacos for two hours waiting for a woman who'd never shown.

"Who do you think you're talking to?" Dominic growled.

"Someone I'd wipe the floor with if he took a swing." The past two years of hitting the weights instead of Calvin had given me a build that made most men think twice before confronting me.

Riley planted herself between us and rolled her eyes. "Seriously, the two of you need to take it down several notches. It's not cute and it doesn't belong at a family gathering. Dominic, although I appreciate that you watch out for me, you don't always have to. Boundaries, remember?"

Dominic frowned.

Riley continued, "I was asking Jared about a woman he was hoping to help and hearing that he hadn't been able to was what made me sad. Jared has always been amazing to me."

Dominic rolled his shoulders back. "Oh."

Riley turned to me. "And don't think I'm happier with *you*. That's my brother you just threatened to deck. He doesn't need a bodyguard—he has me. And you should both be careful because I throw hands like a ninja." By the end of her lecture, there was some humor in her eyes, but steel as well.

Message received.

"He started it," I muttered, aiming to defuse the tension with a joke.

Dominic nodded slowly. "I did," he said, then flashed a smile. "I hope I never have to kill you, Seacrest."

"I hope you never throw out your back trying."

He let out a deep laugh. "Sometimes I almost like you."

I smiled because the storm had passed and we'd gathered to celebrate family, not indulge in a brawl because we were both more comfortable fighting than talking.

To my surprise, Dominic's demeanor softened and he nodded toward me. "Who's this woman you couldn't help?"

Riley gave me a pained look and mouthed, "Sorry."

I shrugged. Really, it didn't matter what Dominic knew. "Someone I met a couple of years ago."

"Years?" Dominic asked. "That's playing the long game."

"It's not like that," Riley said.

I pocketed my hands and took a deep breath. "She was engaged."

"Was," Dominic said as if weighing the word.

"He died," Riley added quietly.

Dominic arched an eyebrow.

I shook my head.

He shrugged as if the idea of me removing someone's fiancé from the planet had been a real possibility and not one he completely disapproved of. I wasn't about to correct him. Let him wonder when it came to me.

"Is she in some kind of trouble?" Dominic asked in a tone that made me wonder if he was genuinely interested.

"No." I leaned a hip against the railing of the patio. "I wouldn't be here if she were."

Riley added, "It's such a sad story. Her fiancé died the night she met Jared."

This time both of Dominic's eyebrows rose and he looked like he was holding back a comment.

I pinched the bridge of my nose. "He was recovering from breaking his leg and died from a blood clot."

"A blood clot?" Dominic didn't sound convinced.

"It's more common than I knew. Still, just heartbreaking." Riley glanced at her brother. "Hamilton had hired her to renovate his new house as well as ours. She is so talented. Even though it's been our weekend getaway for over two years, I still feel like I'm staying in a hotel when I'm here. I wish I knew what changes she'd imagined."

Michawn's vision for the room facing the playground came back to me so I described it, quoting the description with as much detail as I could remember: the fake tree with limbs sturdy enough for a teenager to lounge and read on, the swing, the pillowed loft with a slide, the padded floor all with the feel of being in a park even while indoors.

Riley's face lit up. "That sounds amazing. We've added outdoor play spaces at the Terraanum but nothing anywhere near that magical."

Magical. Yes, that was how Michawn had once described her work. When I added how Michawn had also planned to ensure it was all accessible with an elevator, Riley teared up.

"For my mother," she said as she wiped at the corners of her eyes. "What a beautiful soul. I need something good to happen for this woman."

Me too.

Dominic nodded.

From the lawn below, Gavin called out to Riley. She told him she was on her way then gave us a firm look. "I need to help Gavin, but I'm trusting the two of you to get along."

Neither of us uttered a promise, but I wasn't looking to start trouble and Dominic seemed to be of the same mindset.

A few minutes passed without either of us speaking or making a move to leave.

Eventually, Dominic cleared his throat and said, "I don't normally get involved—"

"Thank you."

"But I do have some advice—"

Shit. "I'm all set."

"You need to ask yourself if this woman is the right one or the right-now one."

"She's neither."

"If whatever you feel for her is temporary, you should step back and let someone else help her."

I folded my arms across my chest. "You know nothing about me, her, or the situation."

He looked me straight in the eye and said, "Let's cut the pretense, shall we? What is it you think I don't know about you . . . *Mr. Smith?* Because I wouldn't bet your life there's anything my people have missed."

I sucked in a harsh breath. "Are you threatening me?"

"No." He turned to look out over the lawn. "I'm clarifying the situation. You're here because I allow you to be."

"*Allow* me to be?" Were we still engaging in a pissing contest?

He straightened and turned to face me. "So, now that you know how little tolerance I have for bullshit, why don't you tell me what you could have done better when you went to Rhode Island."

"How do you know I went to Rhode Island?"

He sighed. "We went over this. There's nothing I don't know when it comes to people in my circle."

"I'm not in your circle."

"You're here, aren't you?"

I couldn't deny that one. "What do you want, Dominic? What is this?"

His stance relaxed a bit. "I want to help you."

"Help me?"

He nodded and looked toward his family below. "I'm the happiest I've ever been and it has to do with my family."

I followed his gaze to where his wife was sharing a joke with their twenty-year-old daughter, Judy, and their adolescent son, Leonardo. Rumors circulated of how Dominic had met the former teacher, but she appeared as happy as he claimed to be. Their children weren't like any I'd ever known, but that was expected, considering how they'd been raised. The very first time I'd met them had been the day Gavin had proposed to Riley at a private carnival Dominic had arranged for the event.

After learning who I was, Judy had asked for permission to test the security systems at my companies. I declined the offer with humor at first, thinking she'd been joking, then more firmly when I realized there was a real possibility that she would attempt it.

Leonardo was equally intense but in a different way. He'd cross-examined me to determine my intelligence level then debated the ethicality of my business philosophies. Apparently, I passed the test because the kid sought me out on a regular basis at family gatherings. I'm not ashamed to say that he was the reason I remained up to date on news from around the world. Talking to him felt like a college pop quiz on current events. I liked it, but I couldn't imagine he had many friends.

"Congratulations?"

Dominic continued, "I was like you before I met Abby. Angry. Stuck in the past."

"I'm neither," I said even though that wasn't necessarily true. I'd made progress, but many days were still a struggle.

"I didn't realize how much better my life could be. It's because of Abby that I'm a good husband, a good father, and I'd like to think a good friend."

I shot him a side glance. Half of me expected him to crack a joke and say he was messing with me. Half wondered if he'd been drinking despite there being no other hint that he had been. I opened my mouth to say something, was still at a loss, so snapped my teeth together again.

"When I heard about you and your little decorator—"

"Creative Space Engineer."

"Whatever. When I heard about why you'd gone down to see her, I didn't expect you to be here today."

"I promised I would come."

"And you botched it with your designer."

Lowering my arms, I took a deep breath and reminded

myself that he was Riley's brother and therefore someone I had to at least attempt to get along with. "Thank you for this . . . interesting conversation, Dominic, but it's time for me to rejoin everyone else."

"I didn't take you for a coward."

I froze. "What did you say?"

"Hamilton described you as a self-made powerhouse he entrusted with his legacy company because you don't back down from a challenge. I don't see it."

My eyes narrowed and my hands clenched at my sides.

He continued, "I'll let you in on a secret, though. You haven't failed until you give up."

"What the hell are you talking about?"

"It's not shocking that following her to a dog park and bringing her a sandwich didn't work."

"I didn't follow her there, I . . ." I stopped when what I'd done didn't sound any better in my head. "She's been through a lot. I respect that."

"Respect is important, but women don't want weak men."

That had me standing taller. "Excuse me?"

"You didn't answer my question earlier. What is this woman to you?"

I defaulted to the easiest answer. "Nothing."

Dominic smiled. "Then there's nothing further you should do. She doesn't matter. Don't give her or her situation another thought."

"I'm not going to because she essentially told me to leave her alone."

He shrugged. "I know some good men who are at the stage in their lives where they want to settle down. I might start sending some her way."

Anger rose within me. "I know what you're doing."

"Calling you on your bullshit?"

"No, you're trying to goad me into a fight."

"With Abby down there watching? I'd never hear the end of it."

"Then tell me, Dominic, what the fuck *is* your goal?"

He frowned. "I already told you. I want to help you help this woman—unless she really doesn't matter to you."

"I don't need your help."

He glanced around. "Is she here? Did your plan work?"

"Fuck you."

He laughed. "The first thing you need to do is lure her away from Rhode Island."

"Lure. Sure, that doesn't sound sinister."

His expression turned serious. "Pain and anger can become a comfortable addiction. No one chooses either, but when too much time is spent with negative habits, a person becomes trapped in that place and those habits. For me, anger had me obsessively trying to avenge what I thought my father had done. My dark goals became all I focused on, and that only made me more miserable. The cycle wasn't broken until I met Abby. She shook me free of a prison of my own making—one I'd become resigned to live in because I didn't understand I had the choice to leave it. You, my friend, remind me too much of my old self. We both know those marks on your face are from your own addiction. What is it?"

Not what *was* it. He knew. These past two years, I'd been careful to indulge in only underground fights when I'd have time to heal before seeing anyone. "MMA cage fighting."

Dominic didn't look surprised. "Win or lose it's what you need."

In a hoarse voice, I said, "Sometimes."

"Whatever your father did to you, he's not the one punishing you now—that's you."

I didn't respond to that one because it cut too deep.

He pocketed his hands and sighed. "I've been there."

I believed him.

He gave me a long look. "You're not too fucked up to be able to help her."

My answer was a slight incline of my head.

"Have you considered that your damage might also be your strength? Who better to show a person the way out of hell than someone who knows the place well?"

Feeling cornered, I snapped, "Beautiful, but unrealistic. Sorry if I don't buy into the idea that love heals all."

"Good, because it doesn't. I'm the same man I was before Abby and the kids. The difference is that I no longer allow my demons to control me. I would never raise a hand to my children or my voice to my wife. Every single day I hold to a promise I made to myself to be the man they deserve."

I glanced down at his family. Abby looked up and waved. Dominic waved back. Impulsively, I asked, "How did you know she was the one?"

He took a moment to answer. "Being with her felt a whole lot better than being without her. Jared, when it's right, you won't need to punish yourself to quiet the chaos in your head. She'll bring you that kind of peace."

Tempting as that sounded, I couldn't imagine being married with kids. "I'll keep that in mind."

"This woman . . ."

"Michawn Courter."

"She matters."

"She matters," I muttered in agreement.

"Then you know what you need to do."

Crazy as it had sounded when he'd first said it, his plan was gaining appeal. "Lure her away from Rhode Island."

He nodded in approval.

I let out a disgusted sound. When he cocked his head slightly in question, I said, "I can't believe I'm taking advice from you."

"I can't believe you'll want me to be your best man at your wedding. Especially considering how close you've always been to Gavin."

What? "I'm not looking to get married."

Dominic clapped a hand on my shoulder. "When the time comes, find a way to break the news to Gavin gently." Then he turned and made his way down the steps to rejoin his family.

I hung back, my thoughts racing.

Gavin had told me that beneath Dominic's brash exterior there was a good man who wanted the best for his family. I'd found that assessment difficult to believe until just then.

What Dominic had said about feeling trapped in a prison of his own making had resonated with me. Changing my name hadn't freed me. Success and power hadn't either.

Hamilton had suggested that helping Michawn would help me let my guilt go. He'd meant well, but there was a side of me he'd never understand. Dominic got me. I was still losing battles to my demons.

But could they be my strength?

Could I use them to shake Michawn free of her prison?

I gripped the railing of the patio with both hands. *I can if I free myself first. I've been running from my father because I thought he had the power to make me feel shitty about myself, but I've been doing that job for him.*

And it's time to stop.

Michawn, I do have what it takes to save you.

And make you mine.

CHAPTER TWELVE

Jared

I CUT THE engine of my car in the driveway of a modest, middle-class home at the end of a cul-de-sac in a Massachusetts town that hadn't been on my radar until I'd asked Hamilton where Michawn's family lived. My hands were clammy. I took a deep breath.

The lawn looked freshly cut. Flowers framed a path that led to a wooden porch lined with hanging flowering plants. It was picture-perfect . . . nothing like where I'd grown up nor the world I'd fought my way into.

A tall man with a mop of dark hair bounded down the steps of the house and approached the car. I got out to meet him. We took a moment to size each other up.

"So, you're Jared Seacrest," he said as he looked me over. He was about my height and built like a tank. The hand he offered in greeting was calloused and delivered a crushing grip that almost made me smile.

I returned the favor with as much force as I could deliver while attempting to make it look effortless. "You must be Christopher. Tracy told me you're the one who'll kick my ass if I step out of line."

His eyebrows rose, then he smiled and released my hand. "I'm glad we understand each other. Just to be clear, I don't agree with Tracy when it comes to you. We don't know you. Michawn has made it clear she doesn't want to. I don't see the point of you wanting to meet us."

Before I had a chance to respond, a leaner version of him joined us. His smile was easy, his handshake light but firm. "Hey. I'm Thomas. It's a pleasure to meet you. I spent a good portion of last night reading about you—impressive stuff."

"Thank you." Looking into me was understandable. I'd done my homework when it came to them as well. Janice and Charles Courter were both locals who'd married straight out of high school and raised four children. She was a stay at home mom. He was a truck driver. Their oldest, Christopher, had followed in his father's footsteps. Next was Megan, an IT manager for a bank. Thomas, the youngest, taught literature at a state college. They were a hardworking, well-respected family whose roots were generations deep in this area.

Christopher folded his arms across his chest. "Funny thing is, no matter how much digging Thomas did he couldn't find anything about you before college. Nothing on social media. Like you didn't exist."

A woman I recognized from photos as Megan stepped into the conversation. "I couldn't find anything either, and

I'm pretty good at stalking people online." She stood next to Christopher, mirroring his stance. "For someone as high profile as you are now, there is starkly nothing about you as a child or with your family."

If it weren't for Michawn I would have ended the conversation right then. As a rule I didn't talk about my early life, but this wasn't exactly a normal situation. With my thumb I traced one of the scars on my chin. "I had a rough childhood, went through foster care and a juvenile detention center. My biological family isn't one I want anything to do with, so when I got my shit together, I changed my name and started over."

Megan lowered her arms and her expression softened. "What was your previous last name?"

"Smith. I was Jared Smith. My father's name is Dennis Smith. I've had nothing to do with him since he was convicted of murder and put in prison."

Her mouth rounded.

Christopher's eyes narrowed.

Thomas lifted a splayed hand. "That's what I call an inspirational story. Knowing where you came from makes what you've achieved even more impressive."

"I'm not here to impress anyone," I said.

"What are you here for?" Christopher demanded.

"I'm going to kidnap your sister," I said as if that were the most natural thing in the world. "Your family has been through a lot and I want to make sure I do it in a way that doesn't cause more pain for any of you."

"Did you say *kidnap*?" Christopher growled, leaning in.

Thomas laughed. "I don't think he did. People don't just say that."

"Christopher heard him right." Megan gave me another once-over and took a defensive pose again. "Tracy said you had an idea that might help Michawn. Did you mention that part to her?"

A female voice called out from the door of the home. "I did not make a nice meal so your father and I could eat alone. Would you all please come inside?"

"In a minute, Mom," Christopher answered.

"Christopher John Courter, you do not 'in a minute, Mom' me. Dinner is on the table. All four of you need to come inside, wash your hands, and sit your butts at the table. Your father is about to say grace without you." A smile replaced her frown. "Jared, I made meat loaf and mash potatoes. Are you hungry?"

I gave the wall of siblings a quick look, then said, "Starving."

"Fantastic," she beamed. "Come on in."

Christopher bent closer and in a low tone said, "Eat up, it'll be your last meal if I don't like your definition of kidnapping."

"He's not joking," Megan said before turning to lead the way to the house.

Christopher followed suit.

Thomas stayed behind and waited until they were out of earshot. "Listen, Jared, I give you credit for coming here. Tracy has built you up as someone who really cares about Michawn. I hope that's true. We're all worried about her. If things get heated in there, keep that in mind. If you're really here because you want to help Michawn, every single person in that house will love you for it." He stood a little taller. "But if you hurt her, I'll help them bury your body." With that, he clapped a hand on my back and smiled.

"Okay, then."

As I followed him into the house, I thought *I could like this family.*

CHAPTER THIRTEEN

Michawn

ONE WEEK, TWO days, and four hours had passed since I'd left Jared sitting on a bench in the dog park waiting for me. I'd told myself it was for the best, but that wasn't how it felt.

My apartment looked like a tornado had hit it because I'd dug out every photo I had of Teddy, every bit of memorabilia, and spent the last week lost in memories of our time together.

I'd missed more than one work deadline.

Gotten drunk a few times.

Piper was wired since his only exercise had been short walks to relieve himself. I couldn't bear to go back to the dog park in case Jared was there . . . or worse, wasn't. At least I'd finally showered; that it was somewhat of an achievement didn't speak well of my mental state.

For the first time since Teddy had died, I wondered if I should call my parents for help and have myself committed somewhere. Having photos of Teddy everywhere was sheer torture, but I couldn't bring myself to put them away again.

I hated myself every time I thought about Jared and hated Teddy more than ever for leaving me.

Everyone says I should move on.

Two years.

Why does it feel so fresh? So raw?

I sat on my couch, surrounded by a past I both missed and resented, hugging my knees to my chest. *What if I can't heal? What if this is who I am now? All I'll ever be?*

A loud knock on my door brought me to my feet, looking around in panic. If it was Tracy, I wasn't mentally prepared to defend myself or explain the scene around me. On the other hand, maybe it was time to admit to her that I wasn't okay.

Give up the pretense.

Resigned to facing whoever was there, I opened the door then froze and gasped. "What are you doing here?"

Dressed in jeans and a T-shirt, he walked past me as if I'd invited him inside. Piper greeted him enthusiastically. He bent, asked him to sit then petted his head. "It's good to see you." I wasn't sure if he meant me or Piper.

I said, "I didn't say you could come inside."

He straightened. "I know." He walked farther into my apartment, stopping to pick up a photo of Teddy and me from the floor. It was one of the last photos we'd taken together.

I closed the door and rushed toward Jared. "Don't touch that." He handed it back to me and I held it to my chest.

The tiniest part of me that had been ready to show this side of me to Tracy or my parents was in no way prepared for Jared to see it. It was humiliating. "You need to leave."

"Actually, you need to." He cleared a space on my couch and sat down. "How is Piper with flying?"

"You shouldn't be here." There was nothing about him that felt menacing but I tensed to the point that I began to shake. How was it that even while I stood there, clutching a photo of Teddy, I could be excited to see Jared again? I didn't want to be. "Piper's never flown and I thought I made myself clear that I didn't want to see you again."

"You did." Jared sat back and gave the place beside him a pat. Piper hopped up and laid his head on Jared's lap like they were old friends. "But there's something I need to show you."

With one powerful move he leaned forward, grabbed the sides of his shirt, lifted it over his head and dropped it beside him on the couch. I inhaled sharply as an unwelcome warmth spread through me. Every inch of him was chiseled muscle. This was a man in his prime, and although I had no idea what he wanted, my body argued with my brain that we should at least hear him out.

Before I had a chance to demand he put his shirt back on, he touched a round scar on the center of his strong chest. "This is from when my father put a cigarette out on me because I tried to stop him from hitting my mother." He touched a faint line on his jaw. "I earned this one from picking a fight with a complete stranger the day I heard my mother had died." He traced a jagged scar on his abdomen. "This is from a broken bottle a relative of one of my foster parents tried to stab me with. He was drunk and harassing one of the other kids in the home and I confronted him." He raised his hand to a mark on his eyebrow. "I made sure I received this one from a huge kid in the school I was transferred to. Why? Because the foster family I'd been staying with lied and said I'd attacked a friend of theirs for no reason other than that I had anger issues. So, I was moved, but the kid their friend was targeting remained behind no matter what I said."

Still shaking, but this time from an added confusing layer of sympathy, I stepped closer. "What happened to the child?"

"I have no idea," he said in a guttural tone then turned his head so I could see a mark on the side of his neck. "Which is probably why a year later, I taunted a known member of a gang and almost had my throat sliced because of it. If it wasn't for my friend Calvin, my temper would probably have me sitting in prison or dead."

I swallowed hard. Was his speech supposed to make me feel better about being alone? If so, it wasn't working.

"I carry a lot of baggage with me from my childhood. When I'm angry, I channel my rage to cage fighting and usually win. When I'm really angry, I do the same, but don't stop until I lose."

I brought a hand to my mouth as I realized that he had more scars scattered across his chest and arms. My heart broke for him. I felt broken, but this man . . . I'd never been through anything like he described. "Why are you telling me this?"

He leaned forward, picked up his shirt, and pulled it back on. I was both relieved and a little disappointed. Where had I thought this was headed?

"Sometimes the things we use to make ourselves feel better don't actually make anything better at all. All they do is keep us trapped in that place like a mouse running himself to death on a treadmill he doesn't know he can step off of." He picked up a Halloween photo of Teddy and me from high school. We were laughing because I was dressed as Christopher Robin and he was an enormous Winnie the Pooh. "You loved him."

"I did." It felt like a betrayal to put it in past tense so I added, "I do." I retrieved that photo from Jared as well, then sat on the arm of the couch looking at both images.

When Jared spoke again, he waved at the room in general. "I know what you're doing here—in Rhode Island as well as in the middle of all of this and I get it. This is your cage fight. And these photos are how you punish yourself."

I opened my mouth to say he was wrong, but he wasn't. In the beginning, looking at photos of Teddy had made me feel better, but over time that had changed. What had the last week been if not me torturing myself with memories because I'd wanted to meet Jared for tacos?

He continued, "The people we lose stay a part of us forever—in the best and worst of ways. No matter how it happens. And it would be easier to survive if the pain from it came all in one wave, but it doesn't. It can circle back and side swipe you just when you think you've beaten it."

"Yes," I said barely above a whisper. "And all you want to do is retreat from everyone until you have it under control."

"Or change your name because you need a fresh start and think that will erase your old life."

"You did that?"

He nodded slowly. "I was born Jared Smith, but Smith was my father's last name. I want nothing to do with him."

"He's still alive?"

"Not to me."

"I'm sorry."

"Don't be. It only bothers me when he tries to contact me."

I remembered something he'd said the day he'd given me a tour of the Wenham homes. "The text you said had you off-kilter the first time we met—was it from him?"

Jared nodded once.

The pain I'd seen in him that day now made sense. "What did he want?"

"What he always wants—to see me."

"And you don't—"

"He killed someone in a drunken fight. I felt bad for the

man who died, but not for my father. All I felt was relieved that he was sent to prison . . . somewhere away from my mother and me. I thought it would make our lives better, but it didn't."

There were no words to express how my heart ached for him. Compared to his life, my loss seemed inconsequential. He'd had no one. "How did you choose the name Seacrest?"

He shifted from one foot to another as if the question had made him uncomfortable. "It was the name of the first foster family I was placed in. They were very kind to me."

My chest tightened. "Are you still in touch with them?"

"No. I didn't leave them on good terms. Social services pulled me from their home to place me with my mother's sister. I knew she didn't actually want me. I thought the Seacrests should have fought for me."

"But you chose their name . . ." Emotion clogged my throat, making it difficult to get the words out.

"Like I said, they were kind to me when no one else was."

"I bet they'd love to hear from you."

"Maybe."

I shook my head. "Not maybe. Promise me you'll look them up."

There was no promise in his eyes or uttered from his lips. Still, I hoped he would. Instead of responding to my request, he glanced around my apartment, then said, "You can't stay here. Walk out of this place—today."

"And go where?" My heart began to race wildly. Whatever he suggested, my answer had to be no . . . didn't it?

"I have a jet waiting for us. You, me, and Piper are going on an adventure."

"I-I can't do that."

"Yes, you can."

"First—" I struggled to make a coherent argument when part of me wanted to throw caution to the wind and agree to go anywhere he wanted to take me. "I don't know you."

"That would change fast."

My breathing turned shallow. What did that mean? Was he expecting me to . . . an image of us rolling around naked on the floor of my apartment had my face flushing. "I might be lonely, but not enough to agree to be some rich man's plaything—" His laughter cut me off and my temper rose. "What are you laughing at?"

He shook his head and met my gaze. "That was a laugh of relief. I was beginning to question if I was doing this all wrong, but if you're imagining sex with me, I'm not totally bombing."

"I was not . . ." The lie caught in my throat and I let out a little growl. "I'm not going anywhere with you."

He glanced at his watch. "I'll give you fifteen minutes to gather up what you want to bring, then I'm prepared to carry you to the car if I have to."

"That's—that's . . ." Although I wouldn't have admitted it to him, imagining being tossed over his shoulder and hauled out of my apartment had me so turned on I was struggling to come up with a reason why that wasn't exactly what I needed. "Illegal," I finished weakly.

He smiled and shrugged. "I have it on good authority that it's not kidnapping if you want to come with me."

"We can't do this," I said breathlessly, suddenly unsure of which was scarier: leaving any part of Teddy behind or staying and not.

Jared stood and walked over to me, removing the photos of Teddy from my hands before leaning in so close his lips hovered above mine. "You needed this place in the beginning, Michawn. Just like I needed the cage fighting. It's time for us to break free. Come with me."

After what he'd shared about his life, I felt that he understood me in a way no one else had. I didn't want to lose that connection, but I was scared. "Where would we go?"

"Somewhere you'll love."

"You'll have to be a little more specific than that."

His breath was a warm tickle on my lips. "No." His kiss was gentle, but firm, and I swayed beneath it as my senses went into overload. He tasted as good as I'd imagined he would and his touch felt more right than it should. I'd been numb for so long I'd almost forgotten how good being attracted to someone could feel.

My heart was pounding. My body warmed and readied for more of his touch with an eagerness that made it difficult to remember what we'd been talking about. There was only him and how good that made me feel.

"Get your shit and let's get out of here," he growled against my lips.

Feeling like someone being asked to jump from a cliff without knowing what was below, I panicked. "I've only been with one man," I blurted. "I'm not the kind of person who . . ."

He touched my cheek gently. "You and I will have sex, but we don't have to rush. If that was all I was after, I'd have chosen someone a little less fucked up than you."

My mouth dropped open in surprise. *"Rude."*

"Honest." He bent so our eyes were level again. "But that's why I can be real with you. I need this as much as you do."

"This?"

"Adventure. Laughter. Whatever magic you were talking about the first time we met."

I clasped my hands in front of me. "I'm not that person anymore."

He took a moment to answer, then said, "I understand why you'd feel that way. I went from fighting to survive to fighting to prove myself. I couldn't imagine myself being anything beyond that. I'm beginning to think there's more to life. I intend to try things I've never done, fail at the ridiculous and excel at something that doesn't matter. I might make grapes into wine with my feet or pose nude for a sculpture I'll donate to a museum."

I chuckled at that last one. "I don't believe museums accept random nude sculptures."

"They do if they come with a big enough . . ." My eyes widened, then crinkled with laughter when he added, "*donation*. Get your mind out of the gutter."

For a moment we simply stared into each other's eyes and time slowed. There was nothing beyond us, no past, no future, just that undeniable pull toward each other. To counter the intensity of it, I joked, "Now all I can imagine is you naked and stomping grapes in one of those big wooden tubs."

"Sounds like the perfect memory for us to make together. They must have grape mashing tubs for two."

I blushed. "You're ridiculous."

"And you're beautiful when you smile."

I felt beautiful. And more alive than I had in a very long time. I took a fortifying breath and said, "If I said yes to going somewhere with you—"

He kissed me then, a gentle, brief caress that wiped whatever else I'd been about to say out of my head. "Five minutes." He nodded toward my room. "Grab your phone, your purse and whatever Piper needs."

"I'll need more time than that to pack."

"We can buy everything else wherever we end up."

This time when he held out his hand to me I took it and marveled at how right being with him felt. I looked around my apartment and all the mementos, and for once didn't feel chained to any of them. I would always love Teddy, but I didn't want to die with him. I was done carrying the guilt of not being there his final night.

I wanted—needed—to shake myself free.

I grabbed my purse, my phone, and a few of Piper's toys. Jared carried Piper's leash, food, and bowls to his car. It wasn't until I was in the passenger seat with Piper's head sticking out from the backseat between Jared and me that my decision began to feel real. I'd said yes to going away with Jared.

Away to where I didn't know.

With almost nothing beyond my phone, credit cards, and my dog.

Oh, and I was doing all that while dressed in my oldest pair of sweats and a T-shirt that used to be tight on me before my boobs shrank right along with my waist. I looked from myself to Jared and wondered if someone was paying him to be with me. I'd never struggled with self-esteem, but he was gorgeous, rich, and immaculately put together. I couldn't remember if I'd put deodorant on that morning.

How was this happening?

"Where are we going? How long will we be there?" I asked.

Jared pulled out onto the road. "Trust me."

"Just like that?"

He glanced my way then back at the road. "Just like that."

"What if I told you that I won't go anywhere with you unless you give me all the details right now?"

"I'd remind you that you're already in my car."

Good point, but still, I was a little irritated. "You're seriously not going to tell me?"

He turned slightly toward me, met my gaze briefly, and shot me a grin that was both infuriatingly confident as well as sexier than I wanted to admit. "Now where would be the magic in that?"

Teddy would have told me. He'd always caved whenever he sensed I was the slightest bit unhappy with him.

Not Jared.

He was nothing like Teddy, and I wasn't sure how I felt about that. "If it's for more than one day I should tell my landlord as well as the company I'm working with."

"Already done."

I whipped around in my seat to face him, nearly strangling myself with my seat belt as I did. After coughing, and adjusting the chest strap, I demanded, "I'm sorry—what's already done?"

"Your things will be moved into storage by tonight and you're free from the lease. You're also currently unemployed."

"You got me fired? Wait. Stop the car. You can't do that. And who gave you permission to touch any of my stuff?"

"Technically I had nothing to do with anyone wanting to sever ties with you . . . they mentioned quality of work and missing deadlines. The contents of your apartment will be safely stored in a pod by a moving company. It can be delivered wherever you'd like."

"No." I grabbed his forearm. "Stop the car. Now."

He slowed and pulled over to the side of the road. When his gaze raised from my hand on his arm to my eyes, I saw no apology—just determination . . . and desire. "You need to get out of that apartment."

"You don't know what I need."

He placed a hand over mine. "Maybe not, but you're not going back there."

"You're taking this too far," I said in a small voice. "You're starting to scare me."

His eyes darkened. "There's nothing back there for you, Michawn."

It was then that I realized I was gripping his arm tightly and relaxed my hand. His remained warm and firm on mine. I let out a shaky breath. "I don't like this."

"I know."

"Nothing that happened was your fault." I slid my hand out from beneath his and clasped it on my lap. "But it feels wrong to want to be with you."

Neither of us said anything for a few minutes.

When he spoke, it was with a sincerity that made me feel like he truly did understand what rock bottom felt like. "What happened to you wasn't right. It wasn't fair. If life is supposed to make sense, I don't know how. Sometimes it's a real fucking shitshow." It wasn't much of an inspirational speech, but it was the most real one I'd had in a long time.

"I've been there," he continued. "I'm confident I can survive whatever life throws at me—but I want more than to just get by. I want a reason to smile when I wake up in the morning. I want to go to bed grateful for something I can't buy."

My mouth went dry. Did he think that might be me? That I could be the reason he'd wake up smiling? There'd been a time when I thought I could be that for someone. He was putting a lot of effort into being with me. It had to be more than just his attraction. What was I missing? I glanced down at my clothing. "Be honest, are you here because someone sent you? I find it really hard to believe that I'm rocking your world right now when I can't remember the last time I shaved my legs."

He raised a hand and traced my jaw gently. "Is that where you think your value lies? In how smoothly shaven you are or the clothes you wear?"

"Of course not."

"I'm here because I met an amazing woman whose enthusiasm spoke to me about things I didn't realize I wanted."

I swallowed hard. "So, I'm paranoid to think someone sent you? You said you'd heard I wasn't doing well. Who told you that?"

"Hamilton Wenham. He hasn't renovated his place yet. He keeps hoping you'll come back to complete the project."

I chewed my bottom lip. "He sent you to convince me to?"

"No. He's okay if you don't. Gavin and Riley spend weekends in the house he bought them with Marina and

Hunter all the time."

I remembered Hamilton had mentioned his daughter-in-law was pregnant with twins. That felt like a lifetime ago. "The twins. They must be two by now?"

"Almost, their second birthday is in a few months. That should be quite the event since we already celebrate their births monthly."

"Wow. Monthly?"

"That's what I said in the beginning." He lowered his hand. "But it's an excuse for Hamilton to gather us on a regular basis. Life is busy and I'll admit it's nice to have a reason to get together."

"I never met Hamilton in person, but my parents said he was very kind when they spoke to him after . . ." I searched Jared's face.

"He understood." Jared cleared his throat. "I didn't get the memo right away, which is why I left you all those messages."

"I'd figured as much." After briefly pressing my lips together, I said, "I'm sorry I didn't respond."

"Don't be. You might have had a thing or two on your mind at the time."

I nodded. Odd how long ago that felt as well. Memories that had always been vivid were beginning to fade. To stop myself from digging them back up, I asked, "Have you known Hamilton long?"

"Yes. I met him at my college. He'd come to speak to the

graduating class. We talked and he hired me."

Jared's tone was casual, but I sensed there was more to that day than he was letting on. "And you've remained close. That's nice."

"He's been very good to me over the years." He tapped a hand on the steering wheel. "I don't have any real family I talk to, but I have the Wenhams and a few friends who've become family."

"That sounds real enough to me." I inhaled deeply. Despite our unconventional spot on the side of the road, there was an intimacy to our conversation that had me sharing more than I normally would. "I have a good family. Great parents. Two amazing brothers, a sister, and friends I've known my whole life. At least, I think they're still my friends. I wouldn't be surprised if they said they're done caring about me." Feeling suddenly self-conscious, I added, "I'm sorry. I don't know why I'm telling you this."

His gaze was intense and impossible to look away from. "Because you know I get it. You've been avoiding them because you can't deal with how they make you feel, but being without them leaves you feeling even shittier."

I tried to make light of the truth. "It's like you see my soul."

"Then believe me when I say that the only one who's disappointed in you is *you*."

"I wish that were true." Did I dare say it? Really, if I hadn't scared him off already, what would a little more honesty hurt? "My best friend from back home just got engaged and asked me to be her maid of honor. She's been waiting for a response from me and so far I've just left her hanging."

He waited without speaking.

I continued, "We've been friends since preschool. I love her. I'm so happy she found someone."

"But?"

"But I don't know him. And the idea of returning to my hometown . . ." I paused. "I can't handle when people ask me about Teddy. What if I fall apart at her wedding? I can't do that to her."

When he didn't say anything in response, I said, "I expected you to say I should put aside how I feel and do the right thing."

"I have no idea if you're capable of that. That's a you decision."

My temper rose a little. "You think I'm weak?"

"Are you?"

I folded my arms across my chest. "I fell apart when Teddy died, but I didn't stop being responsible. I found a job I could do and a place I could bear to be. I kept going, kept getting out of bed, even when it felt too hard. One foot in front of the other. One day at a time. I survived."

He took my hand in his. "Yes, you did."

"But maid of honor? The idea of standing up in front of everyone who would have been at my wedding . . ."

"That would be a challenge for anyone."

"A challenge," I chuckled without humor. "More like a recipe for disaster."

"So, don't go."

"I need to." I looked down at our linked hands and thought about my bond to Tracy and all the promises we'd made to each other. "And I will. I don't want to be the person who wouldn't go."

"What do you need to be able to be at that wedding?" His question rocked through me.

"I don't know."

His hand tightened on mine. "If you let me, I'll help you get there."

In a voice just above a whisper, I asked, "Why?"

"Like I said, I need this too."

I met his gaze and came to a decision. "What are we still doing on the side of the road? I thought you said you had a jet waiting for us?"

He brought my hand to his mouth for a quick kiss. "I do." He released my hand, shifted to face forward in his seat and we rejoined the traffic. "Still need to know where we're going?"

I weighed the question in that context as well as in a more general sense. Jobless and homeless—I was freefalling.

It should have been scary, but instead it made me feel alive.

"No, I trust you."

CHAPTER FOURTEEN

Jared

Y*ES!* Dominic had been right to call me out for how I'd approached her the first time. I'd doubted my ability to help her because I'd doubted myself. My success in business hadn't come easily, but I'd dug in with a determination that didn't allow for any other outcome. I knew what I wanted then put all of my energy into making it happen.

Michawn needed someone to take her by the hand and lead her out of the darkness, someone who believed in her enough to jump-start her believing in herself again. Calvin had done that for me. He'd guided me back from the brink of self-destruction to a place where I was confident enough to gain the attention of an employer like Hamilton.

I wasn't a different person because Calvin had come into my life, but I was a better version of myself because he'd believed in me. The same could be said for Hamilton. He'd smoothed out the worst of my rough edges and taught me how to navigate the world of the rich and powerful as if I belonged there.

In return, I taught his son humility. In the very beginning, Hamilton had pitted Gavin and me against each other in similar entry-level positions in his company. I understood the assignment. Gavin had been raised with money. He was soft and felt entitled. I hit the ground hungry and prepared, claiming promotion after promotion before him, winning over client after client while he floundered.

Things got a little ugly before they smoothed out. To say that Gavin didn't like me at first would have been an understatement, but that was another lesson Hamilton walked both of us through. He had zero tolerance back then for weakness, but he'd always encouraged collaboration and fair play.

Gavin learned how to earn rather than demand respect and I learned the power of a shared vision. As soon as Gavin and I started working together rather than against each other, the business soared.

Hamilton could have taken advantage of my dedication, but instead he encouraged me to start my own company with what I'd learned and invested in it. And when Gavin had decided to not take over the family company? Hamilton sold it to me because he wanted to keep it in the family.

Integrity. Loyalty. Commitment.

I hadn't grown up with much of any of those, but they were integral to the man I'd become. Michawn had no reason to trust me yet, but I'd been there once as well. It would take time and honesty to win her over.

I glanced at her and hated how uncertain she still appeared. It was understandable. I'd essentially swooped in and taken her out of her comfort zone. Although she said she trusted me, I knew we weren't quite there yet.

I'd cleared my schedule and was willing to give her the time she needed. Michawn was important to me. I'd stopped asking myself why or second-guessing it. I wanted to protect her, reassure her that the worst was over, fill her days with reasons to smile.

My gut told me that, despite how quickly I'd convinced her to leave her apartment, we needed to progress to the next level slowly. Not an easy feat when all it took from her was a look or the slightest touch to have my thoughts scrambling and my blood heading south.

What she'd said about not shaving her legs had me fighting back a smile. That was an issue I felt equipped to handle and one we could both enjoy.

I'd happily tackle any other areas she might have allowed to grow out.

Or appreciate a more natural landscape for once. I imagined exploring every inch of her, taking my time to taste and tease. There was nothing about her I didn't like, but a whole lot of her I couldn't wait to uncover.

My cock responded too enthusiastically to the imagery. I shifted and told it to calm the fuck down. It was too soon. When Michawn and I did have sex, I didn't want her to be battling with regret or uncertainty. I could wait until she was ready.

I pulled up to a large unmarked metal gate with a manned guardhouse, rolled down my window and was waved through before I said my name. As I parked the car on the tarmac near my jet, I watched Michawn's face with interest. She wasn't from money, nor did she appear overly impressed by mine. Her attention was instead on gathering Piper's leash and making sure nothing would be left behind when we exited the car.

I got out first and opened her door, offering to carry what she had in her arms. None of it stayed long in my hands since the jet's crew was immediately in attendance to unobtrusively assist. Frequent flights were a necessary component of running two businesses, but normally it was a useful, mobile office more than a luxury and the crew had been trained accordingly. They greeted Michawn in the same professional manner they would have a client and I appreciated that.

Not one of them so much as blinked when Michawn asked where she should take Piper to relieve himself before boarding the plane. When Michawn stepped away to a grassy patch beside the runway, my long-time pilot, John, came to stand beside me.

"A dog as a passenger," he said with light humor in his voice. "Will this be a regular thing?"

"I hope so." It was a fair question. I'd always insisted the interior of the jet be kept pristine. No one brought a pet onboard, not even potential clients. As a general rule, I'd kept my life free from clutter or chaos. Having grown up with both, I'd been determined to have neither when I had the choice.

That was why I'd originally dismissed Michawn's plans for Hamilton's homes. At the time, I'd valued the clean and crisp. I'd had two years, though, to change my mind. The more time I spent with Marina and Hunter, the more I wished they had the tree and fanciful library Michawn had imagined for them.

I'd also seen the two little ruffians spill juice on that pure white rug and been moved by Gavin's response. He consistently chose the happiness of his wife and children over any material possession. My father would have beaten me, my mother, or both of us for ruining anything of his.

Dominic's words came back to me then. *I would never raise a hand to my children or my voice to my wife. Every single day I hold to a promise I made to myself to be the man they deserve.*

Yes.

Dog hair could be cleaned up.

A spill stain could be removed.

There was so much that mattered more.

Michawn returned to my side after awkwardly handing a plastic bag of poop to John. "Sorry, I couldn't find a trash receptacle for it."

I coughed to cover my amusement and decided to give

John a raise simply for accepting it as if it was something he was accustomed to.

I couldn't hold back a chuckle, though, when Michawn dug hand sanitizer out of her purse, used some on herself then offered some to John when he returned from disposing of the baggie. He thanked her politely and accepted that as well. *That, sir, is how you guarantee job security.*

With Piper dancing excitedly at her side, Michawn looked from me to the jet and back. "That's quite a plane."

It was. I could have gone for a simple six-seater, but as my business had grown, having a bedroom and shower aboard allowed me to arrive rested and refreshed. "The Gulfstream is small enough to go most places, but big enough to get the job done."

Without skipping a beat, she said, "That's what he said."

And I barked out a laugh.

She smiled then blushed. "Sorry, I couldn't resist that one."

I took a moment to savor the glimpse of the woman who I hoped had returned. "No apology necessary, although now I feel that I shouldn't add that although many will try to say the bigger the better . . . some locations have size requirements, and you don't want to limit yourself."

Laughter shining in her eyes, she pressed her lips together, then said, "No, no one wants that."

I held out a hand to her. "Come on, we should board before this conversation takes a total dive into the gutter."

She hesitated then laced her fingers through mine. "I can't believe we're doing this."

I spun her so she was tucked to my side and murmured in her ear, "Me neither. You're my first kidnap."

She laughed nervously, paused to scan my face, then laughed again. "You probably shouldn't joke about that before I'm actually on the plane."

I bent and growled into her ear, "It's too late to escape now."

Her head snapped back but the look in her eyes was definitely not fear. She wanted our adventure to continue as much as I did.

Michawn laid a hand on my chest. "I'm not afraid."

"Good, because I have some amazing things planned for you," I said and bent to give her a brief kiss that I enjoyed almost too much to end. There was only one place I let myself lose control and that was during a cage fight.

When I raised my head I was breathing raggedly and struggling to remember why it was important to go slowly with her. She was molded to me, looking every bit as shaken.

Piper barked and licked one of my hands, calling me back from the brink. I gave his head a pat.

With a nod, which was as much as I could muster at that moment, I turned and placed a hand on Michawn's back to guide her to the jet. Piper bounded up the steps without hesitation, pulling his leash free from Michawn's hand and causing her to stumble.

I caught her, then kept an arm around her as we rushed to ensure Piper didn't burst out of the jet as energetically as he'd entered it. I shouldn't have been surprised to see him lying across a built-in leather couch with a pleased expression on his face.

Michawn called to him. "Oh, Piper, no. Get down."

Without moving, Piper looked to me. I shrugged. "He's fine, Michawn."

She tried again to call him to her but he rested his head on his paws and simply stared back at her. Shaking her head, she said, "I'm sorry, he usually listens."

I snapped my fingers. Piper's head lifted. "Come." He hopped off the couch and came to sit beside me.

Her forehead wrinkled delightfully. "Okay, now I'm offended. Piper, you do know I'm the one who feeds you, right?"

I smiled and decided to have some fun with the situation. "He's simply showing respect to the alpha in the room."

Her eyebrows shot up but there was amusement in her eyes.

I was enjoying giving her shit too much to keep a straight face. Still, I tried to sound suitably commanding when I said, "We'll only be in the air for a couple hours, but there are two bathrooms on board. One near the front and another with a shower inside the bedroom."

She had the most beautiful smile. "Of course your jet has

a bedroom."

"Would you like to see it?" I asked playfully, knowing full well she'd refuse.

She swallowed visibly. "Not just yet."

It was better than a no.

I waved a hand toward the club chairs that were opposite from the couch. "Choose your spot."

Tilting her head to one side, she asked saucily, "I don't have to defer to the alpha?"

I shot her a wink. "Not while we're in public."

Shaking her head, but smiling, she sat in one of the chairs and secured herself. I took the seat across from her. "Promises, promises."

That was all it took for heat to shoot up the back of my neck. Slow and patient was my plan, but that didn't seem likely if she kept talking like that. I spent so much damn time counting and calming myself down that by the time I realized I hadn't responded it was too late.

God, she had me upside down and turned around and I was loving every moment of it. A member of the crew announced we were ready for takeoff. Piper moved to lie at Michawn's feet, alert but unafraid. *Good boy.*

Michawn looked out the window before meeting my gaze. "I kind of like that I don't know where we're going."

"I know."

"I should tell someone in my family, though, just in case they try to surprise me by dropping by my apartment. I wouldn't want them to think—"

"They know where you are."

Her mouth rounded. "How?"

"I spoke to your family."

We left the ground with her gaping at me. "Whoa. What did you do?"

"I had dinner with them."

"No."

"Yes."

"I don't believe you. They would have told me."

I would have thought the same, but clearly they hadn't. "Feel free to call them if you'd like. The jet has a satellite phone."

She shook her head in disbelief.

I added, "Your father showed me his entire gun collection. Christopher threatened to skin me alive if I did anything to hurt you, and Megan grilled me for nearly an hour. They may now know more about me than my friends do."

A faint smile stretched her lips. "They did?"

"I hadn't planned to stay for dinner, but your mother wouldn't let me leave without eating, which I believe was a ploy to have more time to interrogate me."

"Sounds about right." Her expression turned more serious. "I still don't believe they would have been okay with this."

I debated how much to tell her and decided we had

enough issues without secrets looming. "Your friend Tracy can be quite persuasive."

"Tracy?" Her face flushed. "She was there as well?" She studied my face for a stretch before blinking quickly and looking away. "I don't understand. How is she involved in this?"

I leaned forward and laid a hand on one of her knees. "She cares about you, Michawn."

"I know that, but that doesn't answer my question."

"She reached out to Hamilton who reached out to me."

"About?"

I took a moment as I questioned if I'd chosen the right time to tell her about her friend's involvement. "It was after she'd asked you to be part of her wedding."

"Hang on, Tracy is the reason you came to see me at the dog park?"

"And Hamilton. He thought I might be able to help you."

"Why? Why you?"

Lies never led anywhere good so I didn't indulge in them. "Tracy thought you might be harboring guilt about the timing of when you and I met. She thought seeing me again might . . ."

Her eyes darkened. "No, she wouldn't do that to me."

I could understand how she might take Tracy's call as a betrayal, but I saw it for what it was. "Unless she was more concerned about your well-being than she was with upsetting you. Like your family, she was worried about you."

After taking several deep, audible breaths, Michawn shifted her leg so my hand fell off it and snapped, "What is this? An intervention? Thanks, but no thanks."

I sat back and rubbed my hands roughly down my thighs. Talking out anything related to feelings wasn't something that came easily to me. "Therapy didn't work for you. Time alone proved ineffective . . ."

Her mouth opened and closed several times before she folded her arms over her chest and looked away. "This was a mistake. I don't want to go anywhere with you."

"Too late, we just left the ground."

"Then tell the pilot to land because I'm getting off this plane—now."

"No, you're not. You're going to sit there and listen to me because it's time for you to wake the fuck up. There's a lot of people who care about you. They don't need to apologize for that. I'm here to help you, and that's what I intend to do."

"I didn't ask anyone to *help* me."

"Why did you say yes to coming with me at all?" Now that had my curiosity. "The sex? Has it been too long since you've been fucked?"

If looks could kill . . . "I should have said no. I did say no. You didn't care enough to respect that."

I sat back and counted in my head before saying, "This is me not respecting you? Not caring? Why the hell do you think I'm here?"

"To get me to go to a wedding?"

"I don't know your friend. Why would I care about her wedding?"

Huffing, she said, "I don't know, but I do know that I don't need your help. I don't need anyone."

The silence that followed her declaration hung heavy. I remembered lashing out at people who tried to help me and saying exactly those same words. Fear had driven my actions back then. I hadn't trusted anyone to stay so I pushed them away before they could leave me.

That was Bradley's theory on me, anyway. He wasn't wrong. Michawn probably wasn't angry with me or Tracy. She was embarrassed and uncertain. I'd punched people for less.

I thought about what I'd need to hear if I were in her place. "Tracy may have asked me to go see you, but she wasn't the reason I went. I've spent two years thinking about you."

This time her eyes shot upward and she searched my face.

"I'm not here to convince you to go to a wedding. I'm not even here for the sex, although that's still on the table if you're interested. I don't know where the hell this is going or if you'll be any better off because of your time with me, but I couldn't stay away." I leaned forward again until our eyes were level. "I'm not hiding anything from you. This is me, in all my fucked-up glory, doing the best I can to help you. Be angry with me, if you need to be, but I'm not going anywhere. I want to be your friend, your lover, and the reason you find your magic again."

Tears filled her eyes. She hugged her arms around herself and leaned forward looking like she might be sick. One of the crew motioned toward a bag. I signaled them to hold off. Piper stood, whined, and placed his head on her lap. She petted him absently, but his presence seemed to calm her. Her breathing slowly went from fast and panicked back to normal.

When she sat up, she wiped her hands across her cheeks. "Wow, I sure know how to make things awkward."

"Do I look bothered?"

Our eyes met again. "No."

"Good, because I'm not. You don't have to pretend with me. I don't need things to be perfect. Everything I've survived has toughened me." I softened my tone. "Any time you need them, these shoulders are strong enough for you to lean on."

For a moment I felt that I'd said what she needed to hear.

Then she burst into tears.

CHAPTER FIFTEEN

Michawn

T HE STORM I'D held back for so long surged and spilled out. When Teddy had first died I'd held everything in because I didn't want to upset people more than they already were. I was never truly honest in therapy because I wanted to be strong enough to handle things on my own. Each time I'd failed with a therapist, I'd held in my growing fear because I didn't want to worry people more. Then when I found myself feeling less and less alive every day, I didn't tell anyone because I'd already put everyone through enough.

What I craved was a safe place to break down, ugly cry and truly mourn. I didn't fight Jared when he released my seat belt and picked me up. He carried me to the couch, sat with me on his lap, and cradled me to him. I cried longer and harder than I'd ever allowed myself to. He rocked me gently, murmuring words into my hair.

Tissues were tucked into one of my hands. I blew my nose several times before closing my eyes and snuggling deeper against his strong chest. After sniffing one last time, I tried to make a joke. "You're the one who offered."

His chest rumbled beneath my ear as he asked, "Do you feel better?"

"I do, actually."

"So do I."

I raised my head and was shocked to see his cheeks were wet from his own tears. I raised a hand to touch the tangible proof of our connection. The childhood he'd endured had been full of so much more struggle than mine had. He could easily have told me that my loss was inconsequential in the face of his, but instead he chose to comfort me.

Until that moment, I'd thought nothing good could come from losing Teddy, but if allowing myself to release my pain into the universe helped Jared do the same . . . Teddy would have approved. Jared's journey would have touched his heart as deeply as it touched mine.

I thought back to a time in school when I'd caught a couple boys pushing Teddy around. I'd stepped in and punched the biggest one square in the face. Teddy and I had been fast friends after that.

I'd been craving the safe place Jared offered me, but I was beginning to see that I'd also missed being that for someone else. After Teddy, people had started treating me like I was fragile and I'd begun to see myself in that light. I wasn't fragile. At least, that wasn't who I'd ever been or who I wanted to be. Perhaps Jared and I really could help each other. I caressed his cheek and smiled. "Thank you."

"You're welcome, I guess. Just leave this part out of the

story when you tell people about the day I kidnapped you."

I chuckled. "You mean the day you tossed me over your shoulder, carried me onto your jet, and . . ." I stopped as my imagination took the image somewhere X-rated, and I wasn't ready for it to go there. Jared's must have as well, because evidence of his excitement came to life beneath one of my thighs. Something he said came back to me and I blurted, "I didn't mean to . . . I'm here for more than . . . more than . . . you know."

He smiled and kissed my forehead. "I know."

I glanced around. "Where did the crew go?"

"Probably the galley."

I rested my head against his shoulder. "Let me guess, they have instructions to leave you alone when you have company?" I regretted asking the question as soon as I'd voiced it. I didn't want to hear him confirm it.

His arms held me closer. "They understand when to make themselves scarce, but I don't use my jet to fly my dates around."

"Sorry, even if you did, it's none of my business."

"Not sure what you're sorry about. I like that you're curious enough to ask. Before you feel compelled to inquire: No, I'm not a virgin."

My elbow might have dug into his stomach a little in response. "That much I'm sure of." After a moment I must have decided to torture myself a little more because I asked, "Have you ever been in love?"

"Not even close. For a long time my life was rich with people who didn't believe in it."

Interesting. "And now?"

He let out a slow breath. "My closest friends have done complete turnarounds on the subject, found partners, and gotten married." Instead of asking another question, I waited, hoping he would say more and he did. "Calvin was the first to fall. I can't blame him, Bradley is an amazing cook and he's always hungry. Gavin and Riley make sense to me. She brings out a good side of him. Hamilton is the one that took me by surprise. I didn't think he'd ever get over his wife leaving him. My view of relationships might be jaded, but Hamilton had zero patience for women until recently."

"What changed?"

"Two of his friends died and going to their funerals woke him up to his mortality. Soon after that, he met Fara. She'd been abused by the father of her children but somehow remained the sweetest and most loving woman. She gave him the strength to try again. Now it's difficult to imagine him without her."

"So there's hope for all of us." My attempt at a joke fell flat.

"I'd like to think so."

I took a deep breath and tensed a little against Jared. Never had I imagined being so real with anyone, but he'd held back nothing from me. "I may one day be able to fall in love again, but that's not where I am today. I never want to feel the pain of losing someone like that again."

"That's fair."

"You?"

"I'm still a work in progress in that department. Until now I've adhered to the "do no harm, take no shit" philosophy when it comes to relationships. It's kept my social calendar drama free, but I'm ready for more than pleasurably passing time with women I don't care if I see again."

"That sounds healthy. I'll be happy if I can hold my shit together enough to get through Tracy's wedding."

"You will."

I glanced up at him. "You're not just saying that to make me feel better. You mean that."

He ran a strong hand from my hip to knee and back. "I'll accept nothing less."

My eyes widened. "Accept?"

He held my gaze. "To get what you want out of life you have to first know what that is."

"And what is it you want?"

He frowned. "I've been upfront about it, but I'll say it again if you need to hear it."

I went over our earlier conversation, then said, "You want to be my friend, my lover, and the reason I find my magic again."

"Yes."

Beautiful as that sentiment was, I couldn't see all of it happening. "I could use a good friend right about now. Even one who is as pushy as you are." I looked down before raising my eyes to his again. "There's definitely something between us, so I'm not saying the second part won't happen." I took a deep breath. "But the magic? I don't believe it can come back. I'm a different person now with a very different view of the world. And before you think that would change if I wanted it to—I've tried everything . . . even medication for a short time. Designing used to come naturally to me. It was impossible to not imagine spaces more playful, colorful, fanciful than they were. They were blank slates itching for the artwork that was already in my head. Now when I look at a fresh space I see nothing but what's there."

"Friendship is not a bad place to start." He hugged me closer. "And since I'm irresistible, you'll be waking up in my arms probably by the weekend."

"Oh, really?" I asked with a laugh.

He continued as if I hadn't heckled him. "Rediscovering the magic? I have a plan for that and I've always enjoyed a good challenge. I do need to warn you, however, that there is one part of the process that'll be difficult."

I tensed in his arms. "What part would that be?"

He rubbed his chin across the top of my head gently. "Where you find yourself saying, 'You're right' a lot. It'll be a struggle to say it the first time, but as my genius shines through, you'll find yourself compelled to say it more and more. Over time, it'll get easier."

I smiled behind one of my hands, then sobered as the

sincerity of his desire to see me create things again sunk in. He really was such a beautiful soul. "I'll do my best not to say it so often things get awkward."

"Feel free to express it sexually as often as you need to."

After shooting him a playful glance, I said, "I had no idea it could be expressed that way."

His grin warmed me to my toes. "Everything can be translated into sex. I missed you. I'm sorry. I hate you."

"Why would anyone have sex with someone they hate?"

"Because it's fucking amazing."

I couldn't see how that was possible. "Right."

"You don't want to want the person, but the heat of the moment makes it impossible to not."

I shook my head slowly.

"What did you and Teddy do when you argued? Sleep in separate rooms until it passed?"

"Teddy and I didn't argue."

He tilted his head to one side. "I don't believe that."

"It's true."

"No make-up sex."

"We never needed to."

He held me back from him so he could meet my gaze. "The two of you agreed about everything? Never got sick of each other? Neither of you ever got too angry and said something stupid that pissed the other off?"

I had to think about that one. "There were times when he annoyed me, but he was sensitive to criticism so I didn't say anything."

"Sensitive to criticism, okay."

"His father was critical and would belittle him. If Teddy felt he'd done something wrong he would shut down and . . ."

"Sulk?"

I didn't like the negative connotation of that word, so I corrected it with, "Withdraw." I felt the need to defend Teddy for that. "He was a good person. If everyone was as nice as he was, the world would be a much better place."

"I don't doubt it. Was he nicer than you?"

"Absolutely." I smiled at the memory of the time I'd defended Teddy against bullies and shared the story with Jared before adding, "I know his father didn't approve of me after hearing that I'd broken one of their noses, but his mother loved me for it." When Jared didn't say anything, I glanced up at him. "You would have hit the kid too."

"Absolutely."

He gave me a look I couldn't decipher. So I asked, "What?"

"Nothing."

"You look like you want to say something. Say it."

After a pause, he said, "Teddy and I are very different people. I could get in a heated argument with the wall."

A shiver went down my spine. "Is that a warning?"

He frowned. "I've never raised a hand to a woman and I never would if that's what you're asking."

I relaxed somewhat. "But?"

"I do have a temper. I don't pretend to like things to please others. I'm reasonably certain I could drive you to raise your voice and slam a door." He kissed my temple, moved his mouth lower, and whispered into my ear, "But then I'd spend the rest of the night finding the most delicious ways to get you to forgive me."

I shuddered and gasped as one of his hands slid up the inside of my thigh and stopped just before it reached my sex. I turned my face toward his, lightly brushing my lips across his chin as I did. There wasn't an inch of me that wasn't craving him.

His hand tightened on my inner thigh and I sucked in an audible breath. How had we gone from me ugly crying into his chest to me wanting to drag him off to that bedroom he'd asked if I wanted to see? Why the hell had I said no?

It could have been the emotional roller coaster of the day, but despite where my thoughts had gone, my body began to shake. I fought back a wave of disappointment when he tucked me back against his chest and murmured, "It's not a long flight, but there's time for you to take a shower or freshen up if you'd like."

I froze and my pride kicked in. "Are you suggesting I need to?"

He chuckled and kissed my forehead. "No intelligent man would ever do that, but there might be a surprise or two for you in the bedroom."

I tipped my head away to glance up at him. My gut told me that if he was trying to get me naked and in his bed he would be more direct. "What kind of surprise?"

His smile was irritatingly vague. "Guess you'll have to go take a look."

"Is keeping me in the dark supposed to make everything more exciting?"

"I prefer the lights on, actually."

My mouth rounded in a gasp just in time for him to claim it. His kiss was a hot demanding one that ended with him lifting me off his lap and onto my feet before him. "Go check out what I bought for you before I forget that my plan doesn't include me going in there with you."

Excited, confused, and a little angry without understanding why, I said, "I don't want you to buy me anything."

"Too bad, because I intend to spoil you."

"I'm self-sufficient. Anything I want, I can get for myself."

He rose to his feet. "What are you afraid of? Talk to me."

"I'm not afraid of a gift. I just would rather pay my own way."

He searched my face. "Did your mother work?"

I blinked a few times quickly. "No. She was a stay-at-home mother." I felt I needed to add, "And she loved it."

"But not all of it. What didn't she love about it?"

"I don't know, but it was really important to her that I could make my own way financially." I placed my hands on my hips. "She always says that raising the four of us brought her more joy than a job ever could have."

"But?"

I frowned. "Nothing. Just that."

He shook his head. "Why did you become an architect?"

"Because I've always loved creating things and . . ." I stopped and weighed the next words before uttering them aloud. My mother's voice echoed in my head, "Women need their own money. They should never have to choose between freedom and respect." My hands fisted. "My parents are very much in love. They argued, but over regular things. Nothing serious."

"Was she afraid to upset your father? Like you were with Teddy?"

I swayed back onto my heels as his words washed over me. That wasn't it. Maybe I'd tiptoed around Teddy's feelings, but my mother hadn't done that with my father. That didn't mean our marriage wouldn't have been as good. I shuddered. "My parents have been married over thirty years. My father respects my mother. They're solid. And happy."

He ran a hand lightly down one of my arms. "Were you planning to stop working when you had children with Teddy?"

"He didn't make enough to allow for that."

"If he had, what then? Would you have wanted to?"

"No," I said in a voice barely above a whisper.

"Why?"

I shrugged even as I dug for the answer within myself. "Having my own money was important to me too. I didn't want to ever put myself in the position of . . ."

"Of what?"

I remembered hearing Teddy's father talk to his mother as if she didn't matter and the memory angered me. I'd never wanted to give Teddy the chance to treat me the same way.

"Michawn."

I raised my gaze to meet his.

He pinned me with a look. "How did Teddy's father treat you?"

Not well, but I wasn't about to admit that. I didn't have to. Jared knew.

Jared leaned closer. "I would never allow anyone to talk to my woman with anything but respect." Fire flashed in his eyes.

I swallowed hard. "How Neanderthal of you."

"Is it? I've seen the opposite and I can't stomach it. If love doesn't include keeping someone safe, you and I must have different definitions of the word."

He was right, but I didn't like how our conversation was messing with my memories of Teddy. "Teddy would have said something if he thought it would have made the situation better."

Rather than disputing that, Jared simply held my gaze.

"He knew I could handle anything his father said." I

rubbed a hand over my face. What did it matter anyway? He was gone. "I don't want to talk about this anymore."

Jared nodded once then turned me and gave my ass a light pat. "Go see what I bought for you. Last door on the right."

I whipped partially back around and shot him a little glare. "Don't do that."

"What?" His attempt at looking innocent was so obvious I laughed.

"The ass slap. It's . . ." Too hot? Too intimate? I wanted to find it condescending but that wasn't at all how it felt.

It had me feeling . . . even if it was just for a moment . . . that I was his woman, someone he'd fiercely defend. And I wasn't prepared for how much I liked it.

"What if I promise to let you reciprocate?"

Warmth spread up my neck to my cheeks and I retreated before I gave in to the impulse to throw myself into his arms. I felt both eager and completely unprepared to take things further with Jared. Halfway across the room, I was about to call Piper to come with me when I glanced back and saw Jared already back on the couch with Piper lying at his feet.

I like him too, Piper.

I turned away again and made my way to the bedroom. Once inside, I closed the door, telling myself that the unsteadiness in my legs was due to turbulence. The room was lit both from the windows as well as lights that had come on as soon as I'd entered. It was definitely a man's bedroom—rich leather, plain in design with few accents.

My attention was drawn to the two dark pecan wardrobe trunks at the foot of the bed. They had an iconic 1920s vibe to them that made it feel as if I'd stepped into an old movie set. Matching pieces of varying sizes were on the bed.

Several of them were monogrammed with my first name. Jared had put thought into this gift. One of the bags even had Piper's name on it. That made me smile.

I opened one of the cases. It was full of intimate articles of clothing . . . bras, panties, socks . . . all in my size. Some were skimpy and made of silk. Some looked like comfortable cotton. My curiosity was piqued.

The next bag was full of hygiene basics. Deodorant, a toothbrush, makeup, and everything a woman might need if she unexpectedly started to menstruate. Embarrassing, but also so thoughtful I blinked back tears.

Tucked into the side pocket of the case were several velvet bags. I pulled them out. The first was full of individually wrapped condoms, extra-large. My eyebrows rose. *Okay, then.*

The next contained a box labeled *Gilded Luxury Collection.* I opened it and my mouth rounded. *Oh, that kind of collection.* I didn't know sex toys came in gold or what some of the ones in the box were for. I snapped it shut and replaced it.

The last velvet bag was full of something I was more relieved than insulted by—a variety of high-end shavers, nail files, and polish. If things were headed the way it felt like they were, I'd feel more confident with a little primping . . .

Curiosity in full tilt, I decided to open the trunk that bore my name as well. I needed to see what he thought I'd want. It was standing on one side and appeared to be meant to be opened that way. I undid the brass clasps and pushed the sides open.

On the right, wooden hangers held an assortment of shirts as well as a few dresses. Much like the intimate attire selection, there were more suggestive items as well as a pair of cotton slacks. The other side of the trunk had drawers. I shifted through them quickly and smiled. Shorts, jeans, a few long T-shirts, as well as a matching pair of sweatpants and a sweatshirt that looked a lot like what I was wearing—just new. Surprisingly enough, it was all in my size or close enough to fit. A bag beside the trunk revealed shoes of all different styles.

I thought about the conversation we'd had on how my clothing could be taken as a message. I looked down at what I was wearing then again at the choice before me.

I wasn't ready for the little black dress.

But I also didn't want to change into the newer version of what I was wearing.

Shorts and a nice shirt it is.

I gathered what I'd need to make that a complete, as well as a less furry option and headed toward the bathroom. The image that met me in the mirror wasn't a promising one. My nose was red, my eyes swollen, and my hair as wild as if I hadn't brushed it that morning.

He'd been upfront about what he wanted from me.

Friendship wouldn't require that I looked perfect.

Sex . . . a man might overlook a few things for that.

But helping me rediscover my gift? What did I have that was inspiring that level of investment in me? Since the first day at the dog park I hadn't done much more than tell him to go away, that I didn't need him, and then bawl all over him.

What did he see that I didn't?

I stood there for a good long time simply staring at myself in the mirror before I stripped and turned on the shower. Beneath the warm spray, I imagined what he'd say if I returned to him in the same condition I'd walked away.

He might give me shit, but in a way that would make me smile. His opinion didn't rely on the superficial. I was a hot mess, but so far that hadn't stopped him from wanting me.

I can do this.

And it's time.

If someone had told me putting on a little makeup and wearing clothing that was more modest than most of what I'd worn before losing Teddy would have left me feeling exposed, I would have thought they were crazy. It did, though.

For the past two years I'd done the opposite of trying to attract a man. Jared would know he was the reason I'd spent the last hour fussing over my hair and painting my nails.

I felt a little ridiculous. Painfully obvious.

When I stopped to give myself one last once-over in the mirror before heading back to Jared, however, I also felt triumphant. I recognized the woman who looked back at me this time. She was someone I hadn't seen in a long, long time.

CHAPTER SIXTEEN

Jared

I STOOD WHEN Michawn reentered the main cabin. Piper did as well, but I'm sure not for the same reason. Yes, she was thinner than the woman I'd met at Hamilton's house, but a glow was returning to her and it took my breath away.

There was a spark of confidence in her eyes as she approached. Tempted as I was to cross the room to her, I was beginning to see that part of her journey was to choose to come to me.

She stopped within touching distance. The smile she flashed me was a little shaky, but her voice wasn't when she said, "Thank you for the gifts. You're incredibly considerate."

I held her gaze. "Not many would describe me that way."

She looked away then back. "The ones who know you best would."

I inhaled sharply. I don't know if words had ever been uttered that'd affected me more. In her eyes I saw the man I wanted to be. I wasn't too broken . . . I could be the man she deserved.

A weight I hadn't realized I'd chosen to carry was lifted.

Dominic's words came back to me. *"Being with her felt a whole lot better than being without her. Jared, when it's right, you won't need to punish yourself to quiet the chaos in your head. She'll bring you that kind of peace."*

I'd wanted to believe that was possible, but years of punishing myself made me doubt I was capable of another way. Abby had freed Dominic from a prison he'd created for himself. Could Michawn do that for me?

No one else had brought me close to believing I could have something normal . . . and good. I didn't yet have the words to articulate that but I knew one day I would, so I cupped her face with my hands and gave her a gentle kiss and did my best to show her. When I raised my head, she was all eyes.

Taking her hands in mine, I said, "I may have gone overboard shopping, but I wanted you to have everything you need."

"I can't think of anything you missed."

"What did you think of the toys? Did I choose well?"

Her face flushed. "They . . . they . . . I'm sure they'll be fine."

"Good, because I never had a dog and I don't know Piper well enough to know what he likes besides a ball."

"Piper?" she choked out her dog's name. "You bought toys for him?"

Her embarrassment suddenly made sense to me. "You

didn't look in his luggage, did you?"

If it were possible her face flushed redder. "No."

A grin spread across my face. "Well, then, we're not talking about the same toys." She was so damn adorable I gathered her against me. "But while we're on the topic, did you have any thoughts you'd like to share about the ones I bought for *you*?"

She gave my chest a light swat. "No."

"But I chose well?"

With her eyes averted, she said, "I'm sure they're wonderful."

"Are you not into them?"

She cleared her throat. "What did you buy Piper?"

I laughed. "Oh, is that how it is?"

Without looking up, she said, "I'm not ready for this conversation."

I put a finger beneath her chin and raised her face until she met my gaze. "Hey, there's no rush, but promise me something."

She blinked quickly then seemed to hold her breath.

I continued, "Don't hold back with me. Tell me what you don't like." I leaned down and kissed her between my next words. "And. What. You. Do."

Beautifully flushed and smiling, she said, "I bought a small vibrator once. You know the kind you could take in the shower? I tried it a few times and it was nice, but I lost the charger, and I was too embarrassed to ask Teddy to help me look for it. He didn't know I had it. I didn't want him to think he wasn't . . . enough?" She closed her eyes briefly. "That wasn't what you wanted to hear, was it? I'm sorry. I don't know why I keep bringing him up."

I did. I didn't like that she hadn't felt comfortable enough to be herself with the man she'd planned to start a family with, but I understood that Teddy was the only man she'd ever been with and part of letting him go involved talking about him. "Did you ever find the charger?"

Her eyes flew open and she wrinkled her nose. "My sister did when she helped me move. It was with some shoes under the bed. Thankfully, I'd already tossed the toy."

She still looked in need of reassurance, so I raised my right hand. "For over a decade this hand and I have had what could only be described as an intimate relationship. During my teen years, some might say we were inseparable."

She smiled shyly.

I continued, "No matter how good you and I are together there may be a time when you walk in on me and this hand having a moment. Don't take it personally. Sometimes you've got to do what you've got to do. Now if you want to join in, help out, or have a little fun on your own at my side . . . it's all good, and all welcome."

She wrinkled her nose. "Fun on my own at your side?"

What kind of vanilla sex had she and Teddy had? "Michawn, you can't say things like that when I'm doing my best to take things slow with you."

She seemed about to apologize, then tilted her head to one side and desire lit her eyes. "You keep telling me not to hold back. Pick a lane."

Damned if she wasn't right. I hauled her tighter to me and kissed her deeply. Her hands made their way up my neck to dig into my hair. Mine went lower to grip her ass and grind her against the raging hard-on she'd given me. It was hot and primal and likely would have ended with our clothing on the floor had a voice not come over the intercom and announced that we would be landing.

I broke off the kiss and we stood there, still in each other's arms, breathing raggedly for several long moments. I'd never get enough of her. I tucked a loose tendril behind one of her ears. "We should get in our seats for the landing. It might be rough."

The heated look she gave me was nearly my undoing. "Who knows, I might like that too."

I shuddered from pent-up desire and gulped down a breath. *Well, okay then.*

CHAPTER SEVENTEEN

Michawn

WITH SOME PHYSICAL distance between us, I had too much time to think again. I looked out the window as the jet came to a smooth landing and tried to focus on the wonder of the trip. Jared's face when I'd joked that I might like it rough had been priceless.

My mortification when I'd realized his initial question about toys had been about what he'd bought for Piper had quickly been replaced by a giddiness that had my heart racing.

Although I'd anticipated feeling pressured by Jared's gifts, I didn't. Not even from the sex toys. I liked that he wanted to know my feelings on them even though I might have overshared with my response.

I wondered what he would have said had I told him I had no interest in them. Something told me it wouldn't have fazed him at all to throw them out and ask me what I did want. Speaking openly about sex was something Teddy hadn't felt comfortable with. If I suggested something, he took it as meaning what he was doing wasn't right. I'd accepted it as how things would be, but I couldn't deny that at times it had been frustrating.

Sometimes, just to appease Teddy, I'd pretended to orgasm. I saw it as easier and an act of kindness. His pride was a fragile thing I'd felt protective of. Had there been anything he'd wanted but never found the nerve to ask for? I was beginning to think meeting Teddy when we were both so young had stunted the maturity of our relationship.

No wonder we hadn't fought . . . we'd both held back, both played so nice with each other that I wondered who we would have become over time. Would one of us have grown tired of not being free to be ourselves? Begun to resent each other or worked it out and grown closer?

I'd never know.

And I didn't want to go down that rabbit hole. I didn't like that I was beginning to pick apart my relationship with Teddy. Was it an unconscious way of freeing myself from him?

That wasn't how I wanted to do it.

In my mind, I spoke to Teddy. *It's time. This isn't healthy and I don't want to end up hating you.*

I'll never stop missing you. You were my best friend.

But I need to start laughing instead of crying, living instead of mourning. I don't know if Jared and I will last a day, a weekend, or a lifetime, but right now he's a beacon leading me out of the darkness.

If you're still here with me, it's time to let me go.

We'll meet again on the other side and I promise if I find out anyone is picking on you there, I'll kick their ass no matter how many angels try to stop me.

I've never been one to put much stock in ghosts or the paranormal, but I felt a tingle on one of my cheeks as if he'd bent and kissed it as he often did before he'd headed off to work.

Then he was gone.

And I felt lighter.

Forgiven.

I glanced down at Piper who was wagging his tail. Had he seen Teddy? If so, it seemed to have left him feeling better as well.

The jet came to a stop. Jared released his seat belt, stood, and offered a hand to me. I freed myself and joined him, placing my hand in his.

"All good?" he asked.

"Getting there." The smile we shared warmed me to my toes. "Ready to tell me where we are?"

"No, but I'm ready to show you." He snapped his finger and Piper went to his side as if he'd been trained to. Jared bent, put on Piper's leash, and said, "This is as much for you as it is for her so be on your best behavior."

"Now I'm intrigued."

"Well then, let's get going."

The giddiness of before returned and, as we walked toward the exit of the jet, I joked, "I suppose I should be grateful I didn't also receive a lecture on behavior."

His grin was sinfully sexy. "You're allowed to be as naughty as you want to be."

I laughed. "I'll keep that in mind."

The runway looked like not much more than a very long driveway in the middle of a field. As naturally as if they'd done it a hundred times, Jared walked Piper over to the grass to relieve himself.

A black SUV pulled up and a driver opened the rear door. "Mr. Seacrest," the man said in greeting then nodded toward me.

Jared said, "Miss Michawn Courter and her friend Piper."

The man nodded toward me again, but smiled at Piper. "Welcome." Once again, addressing Jared, the man said, "Another car will come for your things. Do you have everything you require for now?"

"Yes," Jared answered but turned toward me to confirm. "Michawn?"

Considering I had no idea where we were going or what I could possibly need there, I shrugged. "I think so."

The man motioned for us to get into the car. I did first and was quickly joined by an excited Piper. Jared didn't seem to mind that Piper was seated between us. I could have asked a hundred questions, but I couldn't remember the last time I'd been truly surprised and I'd forgotten how fun it could be.

We drove down a dirt road until the jet disappeared from view behind us. We pulled up to an enormous metal gate with a guardhouse. It was flanked on either side by two-story, stone, fortress-like walls. We were waved through.

My mouth dropped open as I took in the scene before me. On both sides of a grass road there were rows of cottages with dog bone-shaped mailboxes. There were several loose dogs lounging on the small porches or on the lawns. It was all immaculately manicured. "I'm so curious. Why is the street covered with grass?"

The driver answered, "The dogs prefer grass over pavement—easier on their paws in the summer."

"Of course," I murmured. "What is this place?"

Jared smiled and leaned over to speak softly in my ear. "The parents of a friend of mine are a little eccentric. This is their version of a dog rescue." He lowered his voice even more. "And possibly a manifestation of a little psychosis."

The driver either didn't hear Jared's answer or decided to ignore it. He said, "Six years ago the Livingston family saw a need for stray dogs both in the United States and around the world. They decided to create a place capable of giving every dog a voice. Dogs are brought here, evaluated, medically treated, then trained by top animal behavior specialists. Many are adopted out. Some choose to stay and live out their lives here."

"That's so beautiful," I said, taking note of the dogs that were lounging on the porches of the houses as well as playing in the yards. They were all loose and looked relaxed. "How many dogs are here?"

"The average is a hundred, but we have thousands of dogs placed with foster families all over the world." The SUV made its way slowly down the center street. "Would you like to see where you're staying or have an overview tour first?"

I spontaneously answered, "A tour please." Then turned to Jared for confirmation. "Unless you've already seen the place."

"Only heard about it. A tour sounds perfect."

When Piper barked at a dog on the side of the street, I took hold of his leash. "No, Piper."

The driver said, "He's allowed to bark here. He'll stop once we introduce him to other options."

I wasn't sure I liked that. "What other options?"

The driver slowed the vehicle and pointed to one of the cottages. "Every dog who comes here is taught how to use a communication board. You can see an example of an external one on the wall beside each front door. Yes. No. More. Hungry. Pet me. It's important for us that the dogs are able to articulate their needs."

I grabbed Jared's arm. "I've seen videos about that. There are big buttons that say something when the dog presses it. I've always wanted to try that with Piper."

"Then it's a good thing I arranged for Piper to learn how to do that while we're here."

My smile could not have widened more. "You did? Oh

my God, you have no idea how excited I am to see him say something."

Piper barked to add his approval.

Jared placed his hand over mine. "A smile looks good on you."

There was a warmth in that moment that had me looking away shyly before meeting his gaze again. "It feels good."

I reluctantly pulled my attention from Jared to our surroundings. Once out of the neighborhood section, we drove between what appeared to be huge industrial storage buildings. The driver explained they were essentially indoor soccer fields, places where dogs could be trained regardless of the weather.

"What's inside them?" I asked.

"Depends on the building. That one is full of obstacle courses. The one on the right has a track they use for exercise."

"With a pool?" I couldn't imagine a place like this not having one.

"Not at this time," the driver answered as he made another turn.

A large expanse of open grass came into view. "The dogs must love running there."

With a shake of his head, the driver said, "That area hasn't been developed yet so it's currently off-limits."

"Oh," I said, leaning so I could see out my window better. "Do you know what they have planned?"

"Nothing is on the schedule yet."

Jared's hand squeezed mine briefly. "What would you put out there? What does Piper love?"

I glanced down at Piper and asked myself what he'd want. The area began to transform in vibrant color in my head. "I'd create a pond with stationary floats the dogs could sunbathe on. A beach with buried bones and toys they could dig up that would be put back each night. And see that hill? That would be the perfect place for a tennis ball launcher. It would all be connected with paths and tunnels. It would need to be inviting for people as well so I'd add benches and shade, but nothing so obtrusive that it would take away from the feeling of being in the wild. I'm picturing a campground theme."

"I can see it," Jared said.

My mouth dropped open as his words echoed in me and I gave his hand a shake. "Me too. I see it, Jared. Oh my God, I didn't think I could do this anymore, but it's all there, and it's . . ."

"Magical?" he asked in a voice thick with emotion.

Still reeling from the tsunami of gratitude that was rising within me, I said, "Yes. Well, to me, anyway." I felt as if I'd spent two years banging on a locked door in frustration and had just been handed the key to it. Looking at the area through Piper's eyes had shaken the wheels of my imagination free. I wanted to laugh, cry, grab a sketch book, throw myself into Jared's arms and thank him with every inch of my body.

"Would it make Piper's inner pup smile?"

"It would." A huge smile spread across my face. "It would. Thank you. How did you know?"

He dipped his head in a rare act of humility. "You love your dog. It made sense that you'd know what would make him happy. I guessed that it might jump-start your creative side."

"It worked." I brought a hand up to caress one side of Jared's face, skimming a finger lightly over one of his scars. He was a complicated mix of gentle and jaded, caring and stubborn. Stretching upward, I kissed him, moving my lips over his in a heartfelt expression of my gratitude.

When I sat back, his face was flushed, but we shared a smile full of promises for later. He cleared his throat. "You should share your ideas with the Livingstons. They've been looking for a way to improve the place and a contract with them would be quite lucrative."

"A contract." I echoed the part that gave me pause. Was I ready to take on a project like that?

Jared's gaze turned steady and reassuring. "When you're ready you can go back to using your spare income to fund public playgrounds, but imagine how many animal shelters you could help improve with that money."

Jared didn't say, "If you're ever ready . . ." To him, this was a process, one he was confident in.

I took a moment to soak in how monumental that was.

Jared had survived things no child should ever endure and somehow hadn't stopped believing in himself . . . and others. If he could summon that kind of resiliency, so could I. "There are many shelters with cement runs and fencing because they don't have funding for more, but it doesn't have to be that way."

"Use your gift to change that . . . one shelter at a time."

I looked across the open field again. My vision of the area was still strong and clear. "You're right. I would love that."

"What did you say?"

"I should share my vision for this area with the Livingstons."

"No, before that. What did you say before that?"

"About the dog runs?"

"After that."

As my attention reverted fully back to him, I played our conversation over in my head. What part did he want me to repeat? *Oh.* Smiling, I shook my head and gave my chest a pat. "You're right again."

"I do love hearing it, but I liked how you said it earlier."

I cocked my head to the side. "Did I say it earlier?"

He leaned over and kissed my parted lips lightly then murmured, "You did—like this."

"Oh, yes. I did." A panel between the front seat and rear went up and I laughed into the kiss. "Is that a hint that we should stop?"

Digging a hand into my hair, Jared growled, "No, it's a sign that we have a savvy driver."

Piper chose that moment to serve up a wet kiss that started on my cheek and ended on Jared's. We broke apart, laughing, and wiped at our faces. I asked, "And that?"

"A sign Piper needs a friend of his own." Jared was smiling as he ruffled the fur on Piper's head. Piper whined but lay back down between us. "And that he shouldn't be in the bedroom."

I caught my breath. That was where this was heading. Was I ready?

The heat in his eyes said he was, but there was also more patience and understanding than I would have expected from a man who had known very little of either in his life. "Now I regret telling the Livingstons we'd have dinner with them tonight."

"What time is dinner?" I asked in a husky voice.

His eyebrows rose. "Not for several hours, but I could tell them tomorrow would be better."

Taking a deep breath, I came to a decision. "I wouldn't mind continuing this tour later."

He knocked lightly on the panel the driver had raised. When it lowered, Jared told the driver we were ready to see where we were staying. The driver didn't appear at all surprised.

As we made our way back toward the neighborhood section of the compound, Jared took my hand in his and gave me a look every woman understands. I bit my bottom lip, held his gaze, and flushed from head to toe.

In a heartbeat we stopped in front of a little house tucked away at the end of one of the streets. A woman in khaki shorts and an oxford shirt met us as we exited the car. She was young, perky, and tan. "Hi. My name is Olivia. I've been assigned to your family for your time here." Rather than shaking our hands her attention immediately went to Piper. Her voice rose with excitement. "Is this Piper?" Piper's tail wagged at her enthusiasm. "Well aren't you beautiful?"

"He says thank you," I said.

Jared asked, "When you say you've been assigned to us, what exactly does that mean?"

With her attention still on Piper, she said, "I help introduce dogs to the facility as well as to each other. I'll be the one giving Piper lessons on how to use the communication boards. In general I'm here to support you with anything Piper might need. In fact, since today was a travel day for you, I'd love to take Piper for a walk. That is, if he feels comfortable separating from you in a new place."

Unused to Piper going anywhere without me, I glanced around and was surprised by how anxious I suddenly felt. Piper wasn't a valuable breed. He was a medium-sized mix of so many it was hard to say what was in him. They certainly wouldn't want to steal him.

It was odd that I was more nervous at the thought of letting someone take him for a walk without me than I'd been agreeing to fly off with Jared. I took a breath and faced the source of my fear—I couldn't bear to lose him too.

Jared put a hand on my back. "You can say no."

I took another breath and relaxed my grip on Piper's leash. "I'll let him decide. Piper, would you like to go for a walk with Olivia?" Piper bounded around, tongue hanging out, looking so damn happy at the opportunity I didn't have the heart to not hand his leash to the other woman. "Looks like he would."

"I'll take good care of him," she promised.

"We'll probably use that time to rest," Jared said smoothly. "How long do you think you'll have him? Two maybe three hours?"

That sounded like a long walk to me, but Olivia didn't so much as blink. "I can do that. I'll show Piper around and text you when we're on our way back."

"You have my number?" Jared asked.

"Sure do." She smiled at me. "All of my information is on a card on the kitchen table. If you decide you'd like Piper back sooner or simply want to check in with what we're doing, I have a phone on me at all times. Feel free to call me."

Piper began dragging Olivia toward the lawn. Olivia laughed. "Someone is eager to explore. Along with my card, there's your butler's contact information. I'll tell him to hold off on coming to meet you. Your luggage is already inside, but if you need anything, anything at all, please contact him.

He has been assigned to your family for the entirety of your stay as well."

"Thank you," Jared said. "I'm sure we have everything we need for now. We're going to head in and get some rest."

Olivia waved and walked away with a very happy Piper bouncing ahead of her.

"A butler. I've never seen one of those at a dog rescue," I said.

We both watched Olivia and Piper disappear down the street.

"The Livingstons are old money. I doubt they know that's not the norm. They're a little odd though. Their son Rick sent me to check on them, but he's just as odd. If you want to have an interesting conversation with someone regarding the real shape of the earth, if the moon landing was fake, or prehistoric giants, Rick will offer to fly you to archeological digs in China to hunt for sixteen-foot human skeletons."

"Have you been?"

"No."

"That's a shame. Imagine the stories you'd have to tell."

He cocked his head to one side. "Wait, you'd want to go? Tell me you don't believe there were really giants."

"Going anywhere sounds tempting." I shrugged. But it was more than that. "Even though I've always considered myself an open-minded person, I didn't realize how set in stone some of my beliefs were. There was only one path for me and I was certain about a lot of things. The past two years were humbling, but maybe that wasn't such a bad thing. I'm now well aware there are many things I don't understand . . . even about myself . . . and for the first time in my life I might be okay with that."

With a wink, he said, "I'll check back with you on how open-minded you are after you spend an hour talking to Rick."

"You do that." Was the next step after this crazy dog rescue adventure to meet his friends? My heart started thudding wildly in my chest. Jared didn't see this trip as being the extent of our time together. I was beginning to believe it could be the start of something important as well. The moment was too intense to not ease with a joke, so I pursed my lips and said, "All that talk about needing to rest. You must be exhausted."

"I intend to be," he said cheekily and lifted me into his arms like I was a bride he intended to carry over the threshold. "I'll tell the Livingstons we'll see them tomorrow."

I was about to protest and tell him to put me down, but instead wrapped my arms around his neck and let myself enjoy the romance of it. With him, I felt youthful and alive—and I didn't want the feeling to end. He strode up the path to the house, shifted me in his arms so he could open the door, carried me inside, then kicked the door shut behind him.

Strong.

Confident.

And all mine for the next two to three hours.

CHAPTER EIGHTEEN

Jared

I'D HAD A good share of women. Some had been pretty sexually adventurous, but easy enough to walk away from. What we'd done together didn't matter in the bigger scheme of things. That wasn't at all how this felt. I'd had two years to imagine being with Michawn and I wanted our time together to mean something.

Be the beginning of something.

I wanted to explore every inch of her. Learn her secrets, her fantasies, perfect how to drive her wild then do it over and over again until her voice was hoarse from crying out my name.

I lowered her slowly down my body. She arched impatiently against me, bringing the softness of her flush against my hardening cock. Her breasts, although smaller than they'd once been, fit perfectly into my hands. I ran my hands over her curves while holding her gaze and trying to remember to breathe.

Her hands began an exploration of their own, starting at my shoulders, sliding down my stomach before teasing their way down the front of my thighs. I opened my mouth to tell her we could take it slowly but those words fell away unuttered when one of her hands settled possessively over my dick.

I brought my hands up to cup her face while I claimed her mouth. She opened for me without hesitation, and I savored that hot, wet offering. I took my time, circling and withdrawing, delivering the most intimate of promises of what was to come.

Her hand moved up and down on my cock, exciting me to a near painful level. I needed more of her, so I lifted her shirt over her head and tossed her bra across the room.

When she pulled my shirt loose from my jeans I finished the job for her, tossing it aside as well. We stood there, both bare chested, breathing raggedly as the air throbbed with our anticipation.

"You're so fucking beautiful," I growled.

"I was about to say the same," she answered huskily.

I stepped out of my shoes, unzipped my jeans, and slowly stripped the rest of my clothing away. She did the same, kicking her shorts and underwear off in the direction of the shoes she'd also shed.

After sheathing myself in a condom, I closed the short distance between us. With one hand, I cupped one of her bare breasts and grazed her hardened nipple with my thumb. I ran my other hand down her stomach to her shaven sex. "I like it," I murmured, dipping my middle finger gently between her folds. "But just so you know, I would have also enjoyed shaving you myself. Before you, I would have said I wasn't a possessive man, but you're mine." I bent and took her other breast in my mouth, circling her nub with my tongue. "All mine."

Her wetness allowed me to easily slip a second finger inside her. I worked them back and forth while seeking out and settling my thumb on her clit. In and out, back and forth. I loved the way she spread her legs farther apart for me and arched against my mouth.

She gripped one of my shoulders to steady herself, while her free hand sought my cock again, this time encircling it and pumping. Her talented fingers cupped my testicles. I groaned and kissed my way up her neck.

We both became less gentle. I crooked my middle finger within her, experimenting with positioning until she gasped and bucked against my hand. Oh, yes. Her head rolled back as she gave herself over to the pleasure of it, her hips moving back and forth as if I were already inside her. I took my time learning her. The sounds as her pleasure rose had me rock-hard and eager, but there was no need to rush. This was just the beginning.

When I felt her getting close, we kissed deeply, roughly, as I continued my intimate assault. She cried out into my mouth, shuddered from head to toe and clenched around my fingers. I withdrew my hand, hauled her up the front of me and lowered her onto my cock.

She wound her arms and legs around me, hot and wanton for more. I slammed her into the nearest wall and began to pound into her. We knocked into a table and there was a sound of something crashing to the floor, but neither of us broke tempo. Nothing mattered beyond how fucking good it felt to be enveloped in the taste, smell, and wet sex of her.

She rode me as hard as I rode her. Her hands dug into the muscles of my back as her hips met mine thrust for thrust. Deeper and deeper, with less and less control, I drove into her. She was moaning and writhing against me. I grabbed a handful of her hair and dragged her mouth up to mine so I could fuck her mouth with my tongue while I came.

Raw, intense sounds were followed by her breaking off the kiss and issuing guttural instructions. "Don't stop. I'm coming again; don't you dare stop." I continued to pump roughly until she shuddered and slumped against me. We took a moment, neither of us moving, simply soaking in the aftermath of release.

Still wrapped around my cock, she looked up at me, face glowing and said, "Holy shit, that was good."

I ground my hips against hers. "It sure was." I chuckled. "I know I should put you down, but I could get used to this."

She flexed her vaginal muscles around my cock in the most intimate of caresses. An amused light entered her eyes. "It would eventually get awkward."

My dick twitched, already coming back to attention within her. "And there are drawbacks." In her ear, I growled, "I can't reach your pussy with my tongue from here."

Her legs tightened around my waist. "So what do you suggest?"

I lowered her briefly to the floor, disposed of my condom, then took her by the hips and raised her until her sex was level with my face. "Put your legs over my shoulders," I ordered.

Laughing nervously, she did. I moved us closer to the wall so she could brace herself against it. With two fingers, I parted her folds and began to learn and love her all over again.

She dug one hand into my hair, holding me to her. And the sounds she made could easily have been the soundtrack of a porn. Oh, my sweet little Michawn was deliciously vocal. The scent of her, taste of her, enveloped my senses and had me as close to being in heaven as a man could reach while alive. I circled her nub, teased it, stroked it, put the good-sized tongue I'd been born with to work bringing her pleasure.

My free hand massaged and gripped her ass, grinding her against my mouth. Not able to get enough of her, I kissed my way up and down her mound, back and forth along her thighs, and back to her clit. Each time I returned, her reaction was stronger and her moans louder. When she started writhing and gripping my head tightly, I ramped up my speed and pressure until she called out my name and came with a full body shudder.

She slumped against the wall, laid her head back, and closed her eyes. "Oh, my God."

Shifting my body so I could lower her legs, I slid her down me, her wet sex grazing its way down my chest to settle on me just above my quickly hardening cock. She brought her hands to my shoulders again and looked me in the eye as my shaft bounced intimately against her. "Rumor has it there's an indoor Jacuzzi somewhere in this house." I cupped her ass to hold her as I moved away from the wall and began to walk. Her breasts jiggled delightfully against my chest.

Breathlessly, she asked, "You're just going to carry me around while we look for it?"

I paused, put her down for a moment, and ignored her disappointed look. It took me only a second or two to locate a second condom and roll it on. "Come here," I said.

She stepped closer.

This time when I lifted her, I thrust myself in as she wrapped her legs around my waist and I gave my hips a roll. "You're right, this is better."

She adjusted her position so I could slide in deeper and I took a step forward. "Don't drop me," she said as her whole body tightened around mine.

"I won't." Although, I'll admit it was incredibly difficult to remember where I wanted to carry her off to when I could feel her vaginal muscles flexing on my cock. We only made it halfway through the first room before I needed more.

When she began to kiss my neck, I stopped at the bottom of the stairs and began to fuck her against the wall there. I put a foot on the first step to gain even more leverage. As inspiration hit, I withdrew and turned her, so she faced the stairs. I spread her legs wide and eased her forward until her arms were braced against a carpeted stair.

Running my hand up her back, then around her stomach, I pulled her ass up and drove myself into her from behind. She cried out my name, begging me to keep going, as if there was an option of stopping.

I pounded into her, leaving all gentleness behind in my need to claim her. Deeper and deeper. Harder and harder. She pushed her ass higher, meeting me thrust for thrust. I wove a hand through her hair and pulled her head back so she arched for me. "You're mine now, Michawn. Say it."

"I'm yours. And you'd better be mine."

I paused, chuckled, and growled, "Oh, I am. Sure you can handle me?"

"Shut up and fuck me," she whispered.

So I did—on the stairs, once again in the hot tub, and then toweled her dry after I intimately washed her in the shower. Cuddling her naked in my arms beneath the sheets of the bed we'd found our luggage next to, I kissed her on the cheek and said, "I could get used to this."

"Me too," she murmured against my chest before closing her eyes.

CHAPTER NINETEEN

Michawn

DESPITE CLOSING MY eyes, I was far from falling asleep. I didn't want to compare being with Teddy to being with Jared, because there was no comparison. My entire impression of what sex was had just been blown out of the water.

It wasn't a sweet, pleasant expression of love between two people that you hoped ended in an orgasm. No, it thundered in like a tornado you couldn't escape. Spun you around until you were completely out of control, sent you higher than you'd ever gone, then sent you crashing through an orgasm in a way that left you feeling a little shattered but also craving that high again.

I'd never been vocal during sex.

I'd certainly never sworn at Teddy.

Opening one eye, I checked to see if Jared was sleeping yet, but found him watching me. His smile sent little flutters through me. Was sex always like that for him?

"What are you thinking?" he asked.

I blinked quickly, giving up the pretense of sleep. "Nothing I should say." I groaned. That hadn't come out the way I'd meant it to.

He tucked some of my hair behind my ear. "I'm ridiculously hard to offend. Say it."

I shook my head. "It's not bad."

He made a face. "I hope not. I don't know about you, but I enjoyed everything we did. Very much."

"Me too."

"But?"

I ran a hand over my face. "I don't know how to do this . . ."

"This?"

"Talk to someone I don't really know after sex."

He spoke slowly. "Because you've only ever been with someone you loved."

I closed my eyes and waited for guilt to rise within me, but it didn't. I took a deep breath. "Yes. So, I don't know what the rules are. Does it change anything? Does anything we say during sex matter or do you always tell women they're . . ." I couldn't say it.

"Mine?"

"Yes."

He took a moment before saying, "That was intense for our first time, wasn't it?"

I nodded and waited.

He rolled onto his back, continuing to hug me to his side as he did. "I don't want to be with anyone but you, and I don't want you to be with anyone but me."

"For . . . how long?" God, I hated that I needed clarification, but my emotions were all over the place. Half of me was dying for him to declare he loved me. Half of me was certain I'd sprint right out of there if he did. How long did most lovers last?

He ran a hand down my back. "How do you want me to answer that?"

I tensed against him. "I don't know."

He tipped his head back so he could look me in the eye again. "I like who I am when I'm with you. If you like who you are when you're with me, let's not ask questions neither of us knows the answers to yet."

I let out a shaky breath. "Okay."

He caressed one of my cheeks. "Just so you know, sex with someone you don't know well often doesn't change anything at all. In the heat of the moment, to get what they want, a lot of people will say all kinds of shit they don't mean. That's never been me. So, what I said about you being mine? Yeah, when it comes to you, I'm feeling territorial." His hand moved down beneath the blanket to cup my sex. "Is that a problem?"

I spread my legs for him even though I was still a little sore from the intensity of our last session. "I don't think it is."

He plunged a finger into my sex and rolled it deep within me. "Hold on, you can still think? Then I definitely haven't fucked you enough today."

I gasped as his finger went deeper, sending waves of warmth through me. He couldn't be ready for another round, could he?

He rolled away, opened one of the bags he'd bought for me, and returned with the box of toys. "Ready to come again and again until you're begging me to stop?"

How was it possible that my body was already revving up again? I'd never understood people who said they had all day romps, but suddenly a few hours didn't feel like enough. "Oh," I said breathlessly, as he placed the tip of the vibrator on my clit and turned it on. "God, yes."

CHAPTER TWENTY

Jared

MICHAWN WAS STILL napping when Olivia texted to say she was on the way back with Piper. In a T-shirt and lounge pants, I met her at the door. Piper looked as happy to return as he had been to go.

"He was wonderful," she said as she handed me the leash.

Piper almost jumped on me, reconsidered, then sat at my side. "Good dog." I praised him with a pat on the head.

Her smile was bright and she politely didn't mention that I was looking a little disheveled. "I'll be back at nine in the morning to work with Piper unless you have other plans for him. If so, just text me."

"I will. Thanks." After a pause, I asked, "Hey, how did he do? Michawn will want to know."

She bent and smiled at Piper. "He's a peach and very easygoing when it comes to meeting new people as well as other dogs. Just a big bundle of love." She straightened. "The communication board will take practice. He's not sold on it, but it takes time with some."

I thanked her again and told her I'd text her if anything

changed for the next day. When I released Piper, he just sat there, tongue hanging out one side of his mouth. "Did you have a good day?"

He stood and wiggled from head to toe.

I laughed. "You hungry? Me too." He bounded a few steps ahead of me then back, which I took as a yes. I located the butler's information and requested a meal for two delivered discreetly, then went in search of Piper's food. It had been set beside his bowls in the kitchen. I took a guess and gave him a cup of it, figuring Michawn could give him more when she woke if that wasn't enough.

While he ate, I made myself a coffee and leaned against the counter. "In case you're wondering, she's fine. Just sleeping." Piper kept eating without looking up. I continued, "Priorities, I get it. I just thought you'd be a little more protective."

"He was with Teddy," Michawn said from the doorway. "Not so much with me, although he adores me."

I took a moment to soak in the beauty of her still flushed from sleep, wearing nothing but one of my shirts. I'd never seen anything more beautiful. "He knows a strong woman when he sees one."

She hugged her arms around her waist, an act that raised my shirt a few inches higher, revealing the curve of a part of her I'd never get enough of. "Strong? I'm not so sure sometimes."

I could have gone to her and taken her into my arms but

the view was too fucking good. "Do you know what I learned from fighting? Even the biggest, baddest of opponents can be brought down by an unexpectedly vicious strike. And they don't always get back up. When the body receives a blow it can't deal with, you don't have any choice but to let it heal."

She nodded. "Everyone kept telling me to move on, but I couldn't."

"And now?"

She chewed her bottom lip before answering. "It could be because I just came more in one day than I think I have in my life, but I'm feeling pretty good."

I knew she was joking, but I was proud of myself for how many times I'd brought her to climax. With others it had been enough to know that they'd enjoyed themselves as much as I had, but I'd found a new addiction. I absolutely loved watching her come, especially when she didn't think she could again.

She yawned. "Thank you for feeding Piper." At the mention of his name, or maybe because it was timed with him finishing his food, Piper bounded over to her and jumped up on her, almost knocking her over. "Easy Piper," she said with a laugh and gave his nose a kiss even as she told him to sit. He happily ignored her.

"Down," I said firmly.

Piper sat.

Michawn wagged a finger at Piper. "You're making me

look bad, dude."

I placed my coffee on the counter beside me and walked over to her. "That isn't possible." I ran my hand up the back of her legs to cup her bare ass beneath the edge of the shirt and bent to graze my lips over hers. "Dinner will be here soon."

She wound her arms around my neck and arched against me. "Are you suggesting I put bottoms on?"

"Never," I growled against her ear. "But maybe don't answer the door like that. I'll have the meal set up for us then call you out."

She searched my face. "Thank you for all of this." She yawned again. "Sorry. Although it's your fault I'm so tired. I'll go to the bedroom, but I can't guarantee I won't fall back asleep."

"If you do, I'll find some delicious way to wake you up."

"That's not really a threat." She blushed, buried her face in my chest and made a funny sound. "I mean, who could blame a woman for feigning slumber after hearing that?"

I hugged her to me, then turned her and gave her ass a light swat. "Get back to the bedroom before the butler walks in to the sight of you on your knees giving me dessert."

The heated look she gave me had me texting the butler and telling him to leave the food in containers in the hallway rather than coming in and setting up. Sure, my stomach was rumbling, but I was craving something sweeter first.

CHAPTER TWENTY-ONE

Michawn

I WOKE THE next morning feeling both tired and refreshed at the same time. When I took Piper out into the backyard I thought I'd never seen the sky look as blue, the grass as green, or a more peaceful morning.

So, that's what a sex marathon does for you. *I get it now.* I was so relaxed I melted onto one of the patio chairs and absently threw the ball for Piper each time he brought it back for me.

My phone buzzed with a call from my mother. I answered quickly. Afraid I might wake someone in one of the other houses, I kept my voice hushed. "Morning, Mom."

"Morning. Your father and I just wanted to make sure you're okay."

For once I was. "I am."

"How's the dog rescue? Is it as fancy as Jared described?"

My mouth dropped open in shock that she knew where I was, then I remembered that Jared had gone to see my parents. "It's unlike anything I've ever seen." I described the rows of small homes, the staff that came with the house, and the warehouse-sized buildings they used for training areas.

"It sounds amazing."

"It is." Unable to contain my excitement, I said, "And guess what, Mom?"

"What?"

"Jared took me to this huge open area yesterday that the owner is considering renovating as a recreational space for the dogs and you're not going to believe what happened—"

"You saw a vision of what you'd build there."

"I did!" My eyes misted up. "I can still see it in my head, just like I used to be able to see what I wanted to build. Mom, it's back."

My mother's voice became thick with emotion. "That's so wonderful, baby. I knew it was only a matter of time."

I sniffed and blinked a few times quickly. "I'd stop believing it could."

"Your father and I didn't doubt it for a second."

I really did have amazing parents. "Mom, why didn't you tell me Jared went to see you?"

She didn't answer at first, but then said, "Your father and I went back and forth about if we should. He didn't like the idea of you going away with someone we'd only met once, but we called Hamilton Wenham and he spoke highly of Jared. He considers him one of his sons."

"I'm just surprised you didn't say anything. Weren't you worried how I'd react to having my apartment emptied?"

"Baby, I've been worried about you for two years. Worrying that I'm failing you is all I've been doing. When Tracy told me it had been her idea to send him to you because you'd felt something for him when you'd met him—"

I brought a hand up to my face. "It wasn't like that, Mom."

"I know. She told me. Just a spark you didn't act on. Completely natural."

I groaned. There was no denying that I was in a better headspace than I'd been the day before, but I still didn't like how many people knew something I'd told Tracy in confidence.

As if my mother heard my thoughts, she added, "Don't be upset with her. These past two years have been hard on everyone."

"I'm the one who lost a fiancé." I cringed as my words echoed in my ears. When had my loss reduced to a shield to deflect things I didn't want to hear? I didn't like it and resolved then to stop doing it.

My mother's voice was gentle. "And Tracy lost her best friend. She loves you and has stuck by you even when you didn't appreciate it. It wasn't her fault you told her something you wanted to pretend never happened."

"That wasn't why—" I stopped because despite how well I knew myself, my mother knew me better. "Oh, my God, that's it. I was angry with her because I'd told her. It made it real and I felt so guilty."

"She understood that, Michawn. Maybe not at first, but we've done a lot of talking while you've been away. She misses you as much as the rest of us do. It's killing her that you might not be part of her wedding."

I cleared my throat. "About that . . . I'm okay with it now."

"Really? Have you told her yet?"

"No, but I will."

"This makes me so happy to hear. And you sound so much . . . lighter."

Lighter. Yes, that did describe my headspace. "The change in location has been good for me."

"Have you slept with Jared yet?"

I blushed to my toes. "Mom!"

She laughed. "Come on, we're both women now. I couldn't talk to you about Teddy because you were so young and for a while I needed to pretend you weren't doing what we all knew you were. But I'm happy for you this time. You needed—"

"I love that you're happy for me. But this is still awkward."

"If you tell Tracy, I'll hear about it anyway."

"No you won't," I stressed. "Tracy is going to remember how to keep her big mouth shut."

"Well, aren't you suddenly feisty? I like it. Jared is bringing out a good side of you."

That hit me as a strange thing to say. "Mom, did you not

like Teddy?"

"You loved him and that was all that mattered to me."

"That wasn't what I asked."

She sighed. "I didn't like his father. He wasn't nice to Teddy's mother and that wasn't easy to watch. He thought he did it in ways no one noticed, but I was glad when they divorced. She's finally free to be herself."

"They divorced? I didn't know."

"He didn't leave her much of a choice. He blamed her for Teddy's death. He stopped hiding the way he treated her." She took an audible breath. "I hated that Teddy never stood up for his mother. It meant he wouldn't protect you either . . ."

I almost repeated what I'd said a hundred times to myself over the years, that I didn't need his protection, but that wasn't the truth. I didn't allow myself to be disappointed in Teddy because I loved him, but looking back I wished I'd been more honest with him. "Teddy was afraid of his father too."

"I know you loved Teddy and he was a good boy, but you need a man who is as strong as you are. You always jumped in to defend Teddy. He should have done the same for you."

"I don't want to rehash everything I had with him, Mom. He's gone."

"I understand, but I don't want you to settle for that again. You deserve someone who will go to battle for you the same way you've always done for others. Why do you think Tracy is so loyal to you? You always had her back."

I closed my eyes briefly. "Except when I hurt her by pulling away, but I'll make it up to her."

"She'll just be glad to have you back, baby. We all will be." In a lighter tone, she asked, "So, tell me, how is the sex, anyway?"

"Amazing. I can barely walk today." My hand flew to my mouth. I couldn't believe I'd just said that to my mother, but she laughed.

And I laughed along until I heard Jared chuckle behind me. I spun in my seat. "Mom, Jared is a little stinker. He was standing right behind me listening and now he looks all proud of himself."

Jared's grin made it difficult to actually be upset with him. "Good morning, Mrs. Courter."

"Tell him to call me Janice," she said. "And put me on speakerphone."

I did both.

She said, "Jared, you be good to my daughter, you hear?"

"Yes, ma'am." He pulled up a chair and sat next to me.

My mother's voice softened. "When you guys get back, I want to see the two of you over here for a family meal. No excuses."

Jared looked to me for confirmation. When I nodded, he said, "I look forward to it."

"How long will you be gone?" she asked.

"That depends," he answered, holding my gaze, "on Michawn and what she wants."

Smiling, I linked my hand with his. "We're supposed to meet the Livingstons today; they're the people who created this dog rescue. One of their trainers is working with Piper. There's so much to see here. I'm not in a rush to leave, but I'm sure Jared has to get back."

"I cleared my immediate schedule. We can stay as long as you'd like," Jared said, and I nearly swooned.

"Call me every day," my mother instructed.

"I will," I promised.

"If she doesn't, Jared, I'll send my sons there to check on her and they're tougher to win over than I am."

Humor flashing in his eyes, Jared gave my hand a squeeze. "Oh, I remember. Hear that, Michawn, call your mother daily."

"And Michawn," my mother said, "your father's worried about you and he might take a little longer to warm up to Jared as well, but we're happy if you're happy."

I sniffed. "I know, Mom. I love you."

"Love you too."

After the call ended, I asked Jared, "What are we doing today?"

He raised my hand to his lips and gave it a kiss. "The Livingstons are looking forward to meeting you. Olivia will be here in a few minutes to pick up Piper if you're still okay with her working with him."

"I am. He seemed to like it."

Jared leaned over and nuzzled my neck. "And it gave us some time alone."

"It sure did."

"So," he murmured against my cheek. "It was amazing, huh?"

I met his gaze. "You can't pretend you didn't hear that?"

"Are you kidding? I might have it made into a T-shirt. *I can barely walk today. Thank you, Mr. Amazing.*"

"Really?" I asked with sarcasm and a smile.

He snapped his fingers. "Or just *Amazing. When you know you know.*"

I laughed while shaking my head. "What if I wear, 'Is that your ego growing or are you just happy to see me'?"

He chuckled. "That's not bad, actually. I'll have one made up for you. As long as you don't wear it around your brothers, because apparently, they would come for me."

I wrinkled my nose. "They have become kind of protective. I guess I had everyone worried, but I feel past the worst of it now."

There was tenderness in his eyes when he said, "I'm glad I could be part of that." Then he winked. "The amazing part."

"Oh, boy." I stood up and dropped his hand, but I was laughing. "I'm going to shower and get dressed. Piper is already fed."

Jared rose to his feet. "Should I carry you upstairs? You

know, since you can barely walk?"

I was still laughing as I walked away. A quick glance back confirmed that Jared was grinning. I wiggled my ass at him and loved the way his cheeks flushed. "If Olivia takes Piper soon, you're welcome to join me."

He was on his phone and texting before I got the last word out.

CHAPTER TWENTY-TWO

Jared

L ATER THAT DAY, I couldn't stop smiling while watching Michawn interact with Darcy and Graham Livingston. We were seated at a table in a beautiful garden at their home in the rescue. The staff seamlessly filled our waters and put salads before us.

Any worry I'd had that Michawn might feel awkward around them quickly dissolved. She had a relaxed confidence that made it easy to understand how she'd attracted so many wealthy clients. She was polite enough to compliment their home, but casual enough to put them at ease.

I'd seen the home Michawn had grown up in. Comfortable. Modest. It was the classic older home of a blue-collar working family. It had likely been paid off then mortgaged and remortgaged to fund the education of Michawn and her siblings. And yet she didn't look at all out of place in the Livingston's lavish home.

Graham took a sip of water then said, "I hope you find the accommodations comfortable. I would say you're our first official guests, but Jared is family."

Michawn shot me a side glance I wasn't quite sure how to interpret. "I like that."

I smiled then took a bite of my salad rather than answering. Is that how they saw me? We'd spent a good amount of time together during my college years but I hadn't thought they felt much toward me one way or the other.

Darcy added, "He and our Rick were inseparable through college."

"We've stayed in touch," I reassured them.

"Then why don't we see you?" Graham asked, cutting the lettuce on his plate into smaller and smaller pieces.

Darcy shook her head. "Rick is the same way now—always too busy."

I opened my mouth to explain that running two successful companies was time consuming but stopped when I realized what they were actually saying was that they'd missed me. "I'll come by more often."

Darcy smiled then turned to Michawn. "After Jared told us about you, the first thing we did was look up your work." Her hand went to her chest. "I loved what you did for your clients, but the playgrounds you designed for public parks—so imaginative."

"Thank you," Michawn said with a humble lowering of her head.

"You can't learn talent like that," Graham said. "You obviously have a gift. And from what we've heard, you helped fund those public projects. That's admirable."

"I haven't in a while." Michawn looked away then back. "But I hope to be in a position to do so again in the future."

I reached out and covered one of her hands with mine. "You will." I turned back to the Livingstons and said, "The world is a blank canvas to Michawn. All she has to do is look at a space and she can visualize how she'd transform it. Yesterday we went to the empty field on the west of your property."

"Ah, yes," Graham said after finishing a bite of salad. "Our driver said something about that. I'd love to hear your suggestions."

I gave Michawn's hand a supportive squeeze.

She met and held my gaze for a moment, then started to describe how she'd use a campground theme to keep the area as natural as possible while transforming it into a recreation area for the dogs. They loved her idea of creating a pond with filtered water the dogs could swim in. Darcy clapped her hands in excitement when Michawn suggested they base each area around it on something dogs naturally love to do: dig, chase, swim, nap. Obstacle courses would be blended into the nature setting. When Michawn took out a pen and began to sketch her vision on a scrap of paper she'd pulled from her purse, both Graham and Darcy were enthralled.

"I love it," Darcy exclaimed. "Michawn, tell me you could fit us into your schedule. You and Graham can work out the details, but I need to know our dogs will be able to experience what you just described. Anything less would be a disappointment."

Michawn shot me a quick look then flashed a smile. "I'm sure I could squeeze you in."

"That's settled then. Send me a proposal and we'll come to an agreement." Graham nodded toward me. "We also ask that the details of the project aren't shared with anyone. This is a private rescue and all of our employees have signed NDAs."

"Of course," Michawn said.

The Livingstons avoided the public eye. They avoided people in general as well. As eccentric as their son, they used their money to buffer their family from the world.

Rick had grown up extremely sheltered, tutors and limited exposure to other children. He credited me for being why he now had friends. He'd hit college painfully shy. Fresh from changing my name and leaving my life in foster care behind, I'm sure I'd come across as equally awkward. Rick had taught me how to temper what I said to fit in. I taught him to walk with his shoulders back and look people in the eye. His parents had met me once, seen the transformation in their son, and given me a place at their table.

Our salads were taken away and a soup was served. As Graham and Darcy spoke to Michawn about the area she'd grown up in, I thought about how sad it was that she'd moved away from her family.

I understood, though. Family could be complicated. I certainly didn't want to see any of mine.

Rick had started avoiding his when they'd become ob-sessed with stray dogs. My decision to bring Michawn to their rescue had stemmed from a well-timed call from him. He'd asked me to check in on his parents.

I smiled.

Now I get to tell him I not only approve of their rescue, but that Michawn and I will help expand it.

Where was the harm in any of it? Rick's parents sounded like they really enjoyed helping the dogs. I'd never seen them with a pet previously, but it was a good cause.

Michawn asked the Livingstons about their own child-hood homes and seemed to genuinely enjoy the long and winding stories that question elicited from them. Her kindness toward them touched my heart. A lot of people sidled up to the wealthy with the intention of getting something out of the connection. That wasn't Michawn.

As I watched them with her, she reminded me more and more of the woman I'd met at Hamilton's. Warm. Open. Full of life. Hamilton and Fara would adore her. I could imagine her getting along well with Gavin and Riley as well as their children. Calvin would tell me I was an idiot if I didn't marry her and Bradley would make it his mission to put some pounds on her.

I could imagine a future with her and that was a first for me. A scary first, but not one I rejected. We had a long way to go before we were in that place, but *that's my woman.*

The one that comes once in a lifetime.

The one no one else would ever compare to.

Our plates were cleared away and Darcy's smile was warm as she looked from Michawn to me and back. "This has been the most enjoyable visit we've had in a long time."

Graham took her hand in his. "I agree. Jared, she's a keeper."

I met Michawn's gaze. "I know."

Her face went a delightful pink and her eyes reflected the emotions running through me. The connection was too intense to maintain in front of an audience. She looked away first.

Darcy said, "Seriously, Michawn, I understand why your dog looks so happy. You have a nurturing soul."

"People used to tell me I did." Michawn turned her hand and wove her fingers through mine. "I'm coming out of a tough spot. Thankfully Jared didn't listen when I kept telling him to go away."

I leaned over and gave her cheek a kiss. "I always knew being a poor listener would one day be an asset."

Darcy brought her hands to her chest. "Graham, would you look at them? Remember those days, when we couldn't get enough of each other?"

Graham moved his chair closer to hers. "I do, and I hope they cultivate it the way we have." He put an arm around the back of her chair. "Every year with you, no matter what life throws at us, is better than the year before . . . because we're together."

She cupped one of his cheeks with her hand and gave him a brief kiss. "Yes. Thank you, Graham, for not thinking I was crazy to want to start this rescue."

"Oh, you're certifiable, but my life always has been and always will be better with your crazy self in it." Graham's tone was so warm and sincere it filled me with a yearning to be accepted so completely.

Michawn and I shared another long look. Was she thinking the same?

Darcy's voice brought my attention back to her. "I wish Rick understood. Jared, perhaps you could talk to him for us. I've tried to explain why this rescue is so important to me, but he doesn't take it seriously."

That was certainly true. "Not sure my opinion on the matter would carry much weight, but what you're doing here is helping a lot of dogs—and that's beautiful."

Darcy's expression turned sad. "He refuses to even try to understand. I know we made mistakes in the beginning, but neither Graham nor I ever had pets. My parents always said they brought filth into the house."

"My father was allergic," Graham interjected.

"But we've hired full-time trainers. It's not just Graham and me in a house full of dogs we can't control anymore." Darcy shrugged. "Rick won't come out to see the changes we've made. He thinks we've lost our minds."

"We may have," Graham added with dry humor, "but if he wants to stay in our will he needs to get over it."

With an impatient wave of her hands, Darcy said, "I've never judged him for believing aliens walk among us or that some of our ancestors now live in middle earth or whatever the nonsense of the month is that he has chosen to believe in."

Graham gave his wife's back a pat of support. "As long as what a person chooses to believe in involves making the world a better place, does it really matter?"

"It shouldn't," Michawn said gently.

"My parents always said I could have a pet after they were gone." Darcy sighed. "My father passed away from a heart attack and my mother died soon afterward."

"I'm so sorry to hear that." Michawn's grip on my hand tightened.

"Thank you." Darcy paused then said, "After my mother's passing, I began to have the dreams."

Michawn exchanged a look with me. Yeah, I didn't know where the conversation was headed either.

"Dreams?" Michawn asked.

"Yes. Dogs everywhere. So many of them. Barking at me as if they were trying to tell me something."

"All strays," Graham added. "That's when Darcy realized her parents were trying to send her a message."

"A message," I echoed. "To adopt a stray?" Odd, but I'd heard stranger from Rick.

Darcy lowered her voice as if to prevent others from hearing. "To find them. My parents believed in reincarnation. They're back but not in human form."

"Oh," I said, not doing a great job of disguising how unlikely that sounded.

Michawn leaned forward, a smile of delight on her face. "That's why you're teaching the dogs to communicate . . . in case one of them is your parent."

Darcy clapped her hands together. "Yes. I don't care if anyone believes me, all that matters is that my parents are out there, waiting to be found."

Nodding, Graham added, "And along the way we've discovered we really enjoy rehabilitating and finding homes for dogs that would otherwise be considered nuisances. Some of our rescues go on to be medical or emotional support dogs, others have been snapped up by search teams. We've had a couple end up with acting gigs. It's all done very discreetly with no mention of our facility. We want neither compensation for the dogs nor recognition for helping them. It's enough to know they end up in loving homes."

It was bizarre . . . but kind of sweet in an old-people-are-weird kind of way. "Do you actually have conversations with the dogs?"

"With the intelligent ones," Darcy said enthusiastically.

"It depends on what you consider a conversation," Graham clarified. "They're trained to press a button with a pre-recorded message. Some seem to understand what they're doing and others just want the reward which is usually a treat. The yes and no buttons are the hardest for them to learn because they are less contextualized."

Michawn wrinkled her nose. "That makes sense . . ."

Graham raised a hand. "Take the treat button for example. Every time the dog hits the treat button he's given a treat. It's not difficult for them to understand or even that amazing. So, whenever they want a treat, all they have to do is touch the button to receive one. It's nothing more to them than that."

"Piper does love treats. He must be in heaven," Michawn joked.

"They don't just ask for food," Darcy said. "We had a German shepherd mix that learned about . . . Graham, was it two hundred words?"

Graham sat back in his seat. "She was so impressive. She almost had me believing she knew what she was doing."

Pursing her lips, Darcy shook her head. "But she didn't believe in reincarnation."

"Or couldn't figure out what the word meant," Graham added. "This is where it gets complicated. How do you translate that concept into a button? I completely believed her when she would say, "Tara want scratches." Or "Tara done. Tara hungry." But do I think she understood when we asked her if she believed people can come back from the other side? That's a stretch."

My skepticism must have shown on my face, because Darcy said, "I know how ludicrous this all sounds, but one day I'll find dogs who do understand that question."

Michawn looked at me. "I lost someone who was very dear to me and there are things I believe that others might not, but I wouldn't want anyone to challenge those beliefs. They're what makes it possible for me to accept what I lost and go on."

Dabbing at the corners of her eyes, Darcy said, "Yes. You do understand. This place brings me peace. I was so sad after I lost my parents. Rick moved away and I needed something." She gave Graham's face a pat. "Luckily, I have the most incredible husband. How much does he love me? I brought home a pack of strays who destroyed our house in the Berkshires. Instead of getting angry, he hired more staff and had this place built."

Graham hugged his wife. "Like I said, certifiable, but my kind of crazy. Life with you has never been boring, Darcy, and I hope that never changes."

Looking like she was fighting back tears, Michawn asked, "Do you still have that German shepherd?"

Darcy shook her head. "She was adopted by a speech therapist who adores her. We get updates about her via the foster family she was placed with just before she was adopted. We hear she works with nonverbal children and teaches them to label things."

Graham shrugged. "See. Associating a word with an object. Now that I believe you can teach a dog to do. Are they capable of a deeper understanding? I'm not sold on that being possible."

Darcy tipped her head to the side. "I had several good conversations with Tara. Maybe you're the one, Graham, who isn't capable of deeper understanding."

"Burn," I said with humor.

Graham didn't look at all bothered. He shrugged. "Maybe. I just can't become too invested in a conversation that pauses so one of us can lick our genitals."

Michawn and I exchanged a look and a laugh. She said, "That would be distracting. What do you think, Jared?"

Coughing on another laugh, I attempted a serious tone. "I'm with Graham on this one." Then to see if I could make her blush said, "Although in certain situations it might make things interesting." Her face went pink and she swatted my abs.

Later that evening, Michawn and I chose to walk back to our place. I was still half smiling from the number of times the Livingstons had said goodbye but continued talking, essentially keeping us there until we attempted to leave again. I was glad I'd agreed to come check on them. It was easy to get wrapped up in work and lose track of people.

Michawn pulled me to a stop and smiled up at me. "I laughed more tonight than I have in a long, long time. Thank you."

In that moment I understood why Graham was living at a rescue, entertaining the idea that his wife was having meaningful conversations with canines. Nothing felt better than knowing I'd played a role in the happiness I saw in

Michawn's eyes.

Well, not much felt better. I bent and growled, "Want to argue about something tonight and have angry sex?"

Her eyes lit with interest. "I'm intrigued. A little scared. But okay."

For effect, I lifted her and tossed her over one of my shoulders and started walking again. Laughing, she asked, "Am I supposed to be angry about this? Because it's kind of hot."

"No talking."

"Oh, right, because I'm angry with you."

I gave her rump a strong smack, not enough to hurt, but enough to get her attention. "Do I need to get duct tape?"

"You wouldn't dare."

"Keep talking and find out."

She didn't say anything after that and it was difficult to not laugh and tell her I was joking. I let her stew on whether or not I was serious for the rest of the walk back to our place. With her still slung over my shoulder, I kicked the door of our house closed behind us. I put her roughly down on her feet and decided to clarify that there was always an out. "Do you know what a safe word is?"

"I think so," she said slowly.

"No matter how excited I get or what we playfully say to each other, all you have to say is: Jared, stop. And we stop."

She seemed to ponder this deeply, then tipped her head to one side. "If my mouth is full, would a nipple twist work too?"

I choked on a laugh. My sweet Michawn had a wicked side to her and I loved it. "We could come up with a less painful cue."

She shrugged and whipped her shirt over her head. "And here I was thinking angry sex was rough. How disappointing." She kicked out of her shoes as she dropped her bra to the floor.

I don't think I've ever scrambled out of my clothing faster.

CHAPTER TWENTY-THREE

Michawn

THE NEXT MORNING, fresh from taking Piper out in the backyard of our house at the rescue, I sat on an overstuffed chair near a window and took out my phone. Jared had closed himself off in another room to make some work calls, but I knew it was really to give me time to talk to Tracy.

I chose her number then held my breath while waiting for her to answer. There was so much I wanted to say I didn't know quite where to start.

"Hi, Michawn. Hang on. I'm just getting into my car and my phone will switch over to Bluetooth. Hopefully I don't lose you."

"No problem. If that happens, I'll call back." God, that felt good to say. I didn't want to lose her either. A friendship like we'd had didn't just happen. It had to be strong enough to have survived me stepping away from it when I needed to.

A moment later, she asked, "Can you hear me?"

"Yes. I'm here." I took a deep breath. "Right out of the gate, I want to say I'd be honored to be your maid of honor.

And, I don't want to miss a moment of it. If you haven't chosen your dress yet, I'd love to go with you. I want to make a ridiculously large scrapbook of the whole process and cover it with ribbons from your bridal shower. Whatever you want . . . that's what I want you to have. You deserve it."

"Are you sure? I don't want you to take on more than you can handle. The most important part for me is that you're there. I can't imagine getting married without you. I love you, Michawn. You're my sister from another mister."

I blinked quickly and sniffed. "I love you too. So much more than you know. I'm sorry about . . . about everything. I felt guilty after Teddy died. I wanted to pretend I hadn't met Jared that night. And I couldn't because I'd told you. I didn't understand until recently how I held that against you." I cleared my throat. "It wasn't right and wasn't fair. If it's any consolation, I wasn't any kinder to myself than I was to you."

"Oh, Mich, you were never bad to me. I understood. We all loved Teddy and not a day goes by when I don't miss him. You need to know, I never judged you for what you said that night. The timing of it was the only thing that gave it importance."

I let out a shaky breath. "It was bad timing."

"The worst, but life is like that sometimes. Like me meeting the man of my dreams right after my best friend loses hers. It killed me to be so happy when I knew you weren't."

"What's his name?" I groaned, hating that I didn't know. "I should have asked my mother. Don't hate me for not knowing."

"I could never hate you. And how could you know about someone I didn't work the courage up to tell you much about? His name's Corey Gagnon. He's from South Kingston. Do you remember that clam shack near Narragansett Beach?"

"Of course. You and I were there all the time the summer we were lifeguards."

"Corey's parents owned it. Apparently Corey spent that summer working up the nerve to come out from behind the register to ask me out, but by the time he was ready we'd stopped going."

"Oh, my God, he isn't the one with green eyes you mooned over that year, is he? The one you bought that red bikini for . . . hoping he'd notice you?"

"He sure is. Funny, how things work out, isn't it? I had no idea he liked me and he had no way of finding me when we stopped going back. When you moved away, I was sad and headed down to the beach to think. He was working the register that day because someone had called off and he owns the place now. The way he tells the story, he announced to everyone in line that they'd have to come back because his future wife just walked by and he wasn't going to let me get away again."

"That's so beautiful!" It really was . . . and as romantic as

Tracy had always wanted a man to be. "So he just chased you down?"

"Essentially. I was a little freaked out at first. The way he ran up to me I thought something was wrong, but then I recognized him. He asked me out, I said yes, and we've been inseparable since."

"Tracy Gagnon. It has a nice ring to it."

I could hear the smile in her voice when she said, "It sure does. I can't wait for you to meet him. I know you're going to like him."

"I will love him because you do."

"And because he makes the best clam cakes and chowder in New England. It's a family recipe that even I can't know until I marry him. When I want to spice things up, I joke that I hope it doesn't come out of a can. He says it doesn't bother him but his neck gets a little red and then I tease him that he looks guilty. You should see his face. Bottom line, he's probably a better human than I am. But at least he knows what he's getting."

"He sounds incredible." I laughed. "You always did bring the trouble, but I've missed having that in my life."

"And I missed your laugh. It's good to hear you sounding happy again."

"I'm getting there. At first I felt like I needed to be alone to heal and then I felt trapped in that decision."

"Everyone understood, but it was hard to watch. We were afraid we'd lose you too."

I inhaled sharply. I could have denied that I'd gotten close to that dark place but that would have been a lie. "For a while there I was afraid of losing myself as well. I didn't see a way back."

"But you do now?"

"I do. I don't know where this is going, but Jared was a good choice to send for me. He didn't give up."

"I had a feeling he wouldn't. Hamilton said it was obvious that Jared felt something for you. Do you realize that you single-handedly ruined his social life? Hamilton told your mother Jared pretty much stopped dating anyone after he met you."

"No." I warmed from head to toe at the idea that he might have been as affected by me as I'd been by him.

"It's true. Jared told your father that with or without his blessing he was getting you out of that apartment. I thought fists were going to fly when Christopher stood up and asked Jared where he intended to take you. When Jared told us about the dog rescue, your mother melted and I knew I'd made the right choice. Jared is your Corey."

It felt disloyal to give him that title. "You don't think Teddy was that?"

She sighed. "You were the best thing that ever happened to Teddy . . ."

"But?"

"I'm not sure you wouldn't have outgrown him. Everything was on his terms and you went along with it because you wanted him to be happy, but I wanted to see him stand up for you . . . just once. Even though he loved you, he didn't go out of his way to do anything special for you."

"I've always been independent and he let me do what I wanted."

"*Let you.* That's what I never liked. You never needed his permission to be an architect, but somehow he convinced you that you did."

"Stop, Tracy. Teddy wasn't like that."

"No? Why did you buy a house before getting married? He wanted that. Why did you move in without completely renovating it into one of your magical, wonderful spaces? He wanted a traditional home. And that would have been perfect if that was what you wanted too. But you'd always dreamed of living somewhere with hidden rooms and staircases, weird furniture that transformed with a press of a button, and I wanted you to have that."

I sat heavily down on the arm of a couch. It was all true. How hadn't I seen it? "I loved him."

"I know you did, but I think it's okay to allow yourself a chance at the life you always talked about wanting. You are one of the most creative people I know. Don't let Jared or anyone else make you feel like you need to confine that side of yourself to work. Be you—all the time—no apologies."

Tears filled my eyes. "I will."

"So, all that aside, how's the sex? Your mother said it's awesome."

I laughed. "We need to talk about how comfortable the two of you have become with oversharing."

"So I shouldn't ask if you're able to walk today?"

Smiling, I shook my head. "You are both lucky I love you."

"You did say you missed having the kind of trouble I bring in your life. I'm baaaaack! And worse than ever because I've missed you."

"Oh, Lord."

Her tone turned more serious. "What are your plans? For after the dog rescue?"

I tensed but answered honestly. "I have no idea. We talked about staying here for a week, but things are still pretty new with Jared. I don't know if there'll be an 'after the dog rescue.'"

"There will be."

"I'm not ready to think about that yet. I'm still trying to wrap my head around the fact that I'm here."

"It's good, though, right?"

"It is."

"Corey and I are only a phone call away, and he already offered to kick Jared's ass if he hurts you."

With all I knew about Jared's MMA experience as well as his current Gladiator fitness level, I couldn't see that happening easily, but it was nice to know Corey cared. "Jared has been nothing but wonderful to me so you can tell Corey to stand down, but that I love him for the offer."

Our call ended with both of us promising to talk the next day. I was still smiling when I went in search of Jared. A night of deliciously rough and wild sex should have left me eager for a break, but instead I was hungry for more.

Starving.

Impatient to have him on me, in me. His kiss was a healing addiction I couldn't get enough of.

He was on the phone in the bedroom and raised a finger in the air to ask me to wait while he finished what he was saying. I nodded in agreement then slid out of my shoes.

Holding his gaze, I unbuttoned my shirt and let it slide to the floor, undid my bra and dropped it to the floor as well. Jared's face flushed and he absently answered the person on the phone then asked them to repeat themselves.

I shed my shorts and panties then sashayed my way over to the drawer on my side of the bed. Raising one finger to my lips in a request that he say nothing. He'd told me a little fantasy he had of how I'd use one of the toys he'd bought for me. Hearing that I'd affected his ability to date gave me the level of confidence required to make that fantasy come true for him. I turned on the vibrator and boldly placed one of my legs up on the bed and spread myself wide so he had a good view of my sex.

I moved the vibrating tip over my clit, over my wet center, then back to my clit again. Jared's nostrils flared and his voice sounded a little strangled as he answered questions. My eyelids lowered as my pleasure mounted.

I shifted the tip of the vibrator back and slid it deep within me, aligning part of it so it could still touch my clit. In and out, deeper and deeper, I imagined it was Jared filling me. He ended his call but stayed where he was.

I brought my free hand up to one of my breasts to play with my excited nub and discovered turning him on was incredibly exciting. I licked my finger and traced a circle around my nipple, imagining the path his tongue would take. He groaned audibly.

In a husky tone, I said, "Sorry, I hope I'm not distracting you."

"Not at all," he said in his velvet 'I love what you do to me' voice.

Sliding the toy in and out to a delicious rhythm, it was a struggle to continue my little game, but I was having too much fun to end it. "You didn't need to end your call."

"Oh, but I did." He undid the top of his trousers and released the evidence that he was enjoying this as much as I was. "When I come in your mouth I want to fully enjoy it."

I lowered the speed on the vibrator. "Then you'd better get over here because I'm close and my favorite way to come is together."

I didn't need to say that twice.

He was naked from the waist down and standing before me in a heartbeat. The kiss we exchanged was so hot it seared my very soul. I lowered my leg to the floor, adjusting my position so the toy continued to sit just right as I went down onto my knees before him.

He filled my mouth deeply. His hands grasped my hair and tightened just enough to cause the kind of pain that only heightened my excitement. My sex spasmed around the vibrator as I began to love Jared's cock with my tongue and lips.

Never had I thought I could find so much pleasure in giving head, but the scent of him was intoxicating. His balls filled the palm of my hand perfectly and I began the slow caress he'd taught me to drive him wild. Without the toy, this time might have been for him, but I spread my knees so my free hand could begin to move the vibrator again.

I gasped and moaned as I began to come. He shot his load down my throat while I was riding a glorious orgasm. Sheer perfection.

He hauled me to my feet, tossed me backward onto the bed, and began to kiss his way from my ankles up my legs. Mostly forgotten, the toy began to slide out but he took over control of it as he settled himself between my legs. Still sensitive from my climax, the high setting he changed the toy to was almost too much—but a few heartbeats later and it was just enough.

He kissed my thighs, nipping lightly as he moved his way up to my sex. The magic he worked with his tongue, fingers, and that toy had me screaming out his name and begging him to not stop. The first climax had been amazing, but the one he was boldly driving me toward was mind-altering.

Relentless.

Demanding.

Skilled.

He brought me close several times until I dug my nails into his shoulders and growled X-rated demands. I didn't want the toy in me, I wanted him.

He told me to be patient, but I couldn't. I wiggled down until my greedy hands found him and I brought him the rest of the way to how I needed him. Then I tossed my still vibrating toy aside, straddled him, and rode him with a wild abandon that left us both sated and shaken.

Side by side, neither of us moved. The only sound in the room was our ragged breathing as we came back to earth. Eventually he scooped me up and cuddled me to his chest. I wanted to stay in that moment forever.

After a time, he said, "How did your conversation with Tracy go?"

I breathed in the scent of him. Friend, lover, reason I could see designs in my head again. He really was good at reaching goals. "Better than expected."

Without speaking, Jared lightly traced a line up and down my back. The steady beat of his heart had a calming effect on my own. Never had I felt so safe and at peace with someone. Wanting to share more with him, I said, "It was like no time had passed at all. Isn't that crazy? We talked about her fiancé, you . . ."

"Teddy."

"Him too."

"And?"

I sat up and hugged my knees to my chest. "It's unsettling to hear that the people closest to me didn't think Teddy and I would work out."

He shifted so his back was against the headboard. "What other people think doesn't matter."

"I know that. And, I'm not saying we're serious, but if we ever are serious, and decide to live somewhere together, I need you to know that I will renovate the shit out of the place. It'll be expensive, way over the top, there'll be secret passages and . . ."

"As long as I could find you in that house I'm sure I'd love it."

I searched his face. "You're serious?"

"It'd need to have a gym."

"That could have a dungeon theme?"

"As long as it's functional, sure."

"A staircase that turns into a slide with a press of a button?"

"Sounds fun."

"Theoretically, as long as I could afford it, I could modify that house any way I want to?"

He gave me an odd look. "What is this really about?"

I swallowed hard and dug deep for the answer. "I don't want to be wrong again."

"Come here," he said.

I slid forward and into his arms, resting my head on his chest. He kissed the top of my forehead. Jared's warm hand caressed my bare back. "Were you kind to him? Was he kind to you?"

"Yes, absolutely. It bothers me, though, that Tracy thought—"

His hand stilled. "What did she think?"

"That I changed for him. That I was better for him than he was for me." I told him what she'd said about the house we'd bought together.

"And that upset you."

"It's not how I want to remember him."

"Then let yourself remember him the way you want to. The woman I met was very much in love with the man she planned to marry."

I hugged him tightly. "Thank you. I needed to hear that."

A smile pulled at the corner of his mouth. "You are stronger than you know, Michawn Courter. And smarter than you give yourself credit for. People can think what they want, but I met you when you were with Teddy. Maybe you'd made some concessions, but you looked happy to me."

"I was."

"That's all that matters."

I smiled. "You're right."

His face lit up. "Am I? Again?"

I rolled my eyes. "Yes."

"Would you mind saying it again? Lower? With your lips wrapped around my dick?"

A laugh burst out of me. "You're shameless, you know that?"

He laughed along, then wiggled his eyebrows. "So . . ."

I kissed his lips, his neck, then worked my way down his stomach . . . and lower.

CHAPTER TWENTY-FOUR

Michawn

A WEEK LATER, I stood next to Jared on the fake indoor turf of one of the training buildings. His tie was slightly crooked so I adjusted it. "I like you in a suit," I murmured just before kissing him.

He wrapped his arms around my waist. "I like you in whatever you wear, but you do look stunning in this dress." In my ear, he growled, "Keep it on later. I love the idea of you on top of me wearing only that."

Heat seared through me. A week of exploring what I liked and discovering what he did should have lessened the intensity of being with him, but all it took was a look or a touch to have me craving him again. "I suppose you've earned it by getting all dressed up for Piper's big moment."

"It's not every day I attend a canine graduation."

I smacked his chest lightly. "It's not a graduation. He's taking his level one test. This will be his first certification. My dog is a genius."

"Why am I wearing a suit for this?"

I fluttered my lashes at him and purred, "Because I like

you in them."

His grin was one I'd seen many times over the last week. It appeared just after I did something that had him so turned on our clothing wouldn't stay on long.

A week of laughter and lovemaking. I loved that we'd stepped outside of our lives to enjoy each other and the rescue. Piper had attended training every day, but Jared and I had taken a more leisurely schedule for ourselves. We took some classes on problem solving common canine behavioral issues, but mostly we took advantage of uninterrupted time with each other.

Each night I fell asleep in his arms. Each morning I woke in a tangle of sheets and his limbs. Never had I imagined I could feel so at peace again. I tried to not think about what would happen when our time at the rescue ended, but we couldn't stay there forever.

I didn't have a place to live.

Or a job until I started the work for the Livingstons.

Were Jared and I a couple or was this a fling?

How did we feel about each other?

Where did I want things to go with him?

What did he want?

"Hey," Jared said. "What are you thinking?"

I let out a breath. "Our time here is almost over, isn't it?"

He searched my face. "Unless you'd like to stay longer."

"I do and I don't." Staying would only postpone the conversation we needed to have. "What happens after this?

When we leave?"

"What do you want to happen?"

I could have shaken him then. "Answering my question with a question isn't helpful."

"It's not?" When my lips pressed together in frustration, he raised his hands with a chuckle. "Sorry, I couldn't resist." My response was to hold his gaze and wait. He sighed. "This week was intense."

"Yes," I said breathlessly.

"It would be difficult to go from this to casually dating."

"It would."

"You shouldn't go back to Rhode Island."

"I agree. I left because in my hometown I couldn't face all the memories, but I need to go back at least for a little while. If I decide to not live there anymore I want it to be because I don't want to, not because I can't handle it. Does that make sense?"

"It does. Looks like I'll be working remotely for a while."

I held my breath. "Are you saying you'd come back with me?"

"Unless you don't want me to."

"So we'd . . . get a place . . . together?"

"We could live separately, but . . ." He kissed me, then parted my lips, claimed my very soul, and I gave it to him willingly. The heat of our passion didn't allow for holding back or second-guessing. It burned hot, overwhelmed completely, and silenced my doubts. "Do you really want to wake up without me?"

Smiling against his lips, I joked, "Wow, you're so . . . humble."

"Should I have led with how I don't want to wake up without you?"

I chuckled. "Maybe." As I let his suggestion sink in, I sobered a little. "Getting a place together is a big step."

"I know what I want. Do you?"

I was tempted to throw my arms around his neck and declare that I did and it was him, but it was all happening so fast. "Would we be—Would that mean that—"

"What happened to not answering questions with questions?"

I grabbed the lapels of his suit jacket. "I am completely freaking out on the inside about this. It's amazing and scary and I want to do it and I don't want to do it. I didn't think I could ever be happy again and you're making me think I can be, and it's scaring me."

He took both of my hands in his. "What do you need for this to be less scary? Time? I don't have to go back to your hometown with you. We can take this slowly."

Did I want to slow things down? See less of him?

Panic began to nip at me and my breathing turned shallow.

"Talk to me," he commanded softly.

I couldn't. My brain was shutting down and I was fighting a strong urge to turn and run. I hated not feeling in control.

He pulled me closer, wrapping his arms around me. "Breathe."

I forced myself to take a deep breath and then another. "Sorry."

"Don't be."

Wrapped in a cocoon of his strength, I began to calm. "I don't want to care about you so much that if I lose you I'll . . . I can't do that again."

He tucked my head under his chin and simply held me for a moment. "I understand. I spent a portion of my life convinced I couldn't trust anyone to stay. I vowed to care about no one but myself because I was the only person I could depend on. Calvin proved me wrong by sticking by me. Then Hamilton . . . and Gavin. I'm not going anywhere, Michawn, but I get that it'll take time for you to trust that."

I hugged him tightly. "If you come home with me, my family will assume it means something."

"It does mean something. It means I want to be in your life and I want you in mine."

It wasn't a declaration of love, but it was enough. "Okay. Let's do it. Let's get a place together. You can meet all my crazy friends—"

"And you can meet mine."

A recorded voice interrupted our moment. "Treat. Treat. Treat."

I stepped out of Jared's embrace and turned to see Piper

standing next to Olivia. She was holding a board against her side that he seemed determined to press the buttons on even though it appeared that she didn't yet want him to. Finally, she held the board above her head. "Are we ready for his test?" she asked as she walked toward us with Piper at her side.

I linked hands with Jared and smiled. "I'm ready."

"Go for it," Jared said.

Olivia instructed Piper to sit, which he did obediently. However as soon as she put the board down on the ground in front of him, he slapped his paw down on one of the buttons. "Treat."

"Not yet," Olivia said.

Slowly, deliberately, Piper sat, reached, and pressed the button again, this time twice. "Treat. Treat."

"Wait," she said firmly.

He raised his paw.

She gave him a look.

He lowered his paw.

"Look how smart he is," I exclaimed, dragging Jared closer.

Olivia explained the method she'd used to train Piper. "Some dogs learn the process quickly. Some require more practice. They all learn at their own pace and are all wonderful regardless of what mastery level they achieve."

Under my breath, I whispered to Jared, "What is she trying to say?"

He made a face. "He may not be a genius."

I elbowed him.

Olivia continued, "There are differences between breeds. Some use their communication boards to shape their environment. Others are more passive and do it more to please their handlers. We've trained search dogs to clarify what they've found. Level one normally tests for comprehension of four buttons, but Piper has learned three of them: treat, walk, and play."

Piper stealthily moved his paw forward and pressed one of the buttons. "Treat."

Olivia gave him a treat. "Piper *has* shown that he understands those three buttons, but he tends to fixate on one in particular."

I bit my bottom lip and said, "I wonder which one?" then shot Jared a playful glance.

"It's a real mystery," Jared murmured.

"He does know the other two." Olivia held up a lead leash and looked down at Piper.

Piper pressed the walk button.

"Good," she said. She took a ball out of her pocket.

He pressed the button for play. She threw the ball. He chased it, brought it back to her and sat perfectly at her side. I was impressed.

"What do you want?" she asked him.

Piper hit a button with his paw repeatedly. "Treat. Treat. Treat."

Olivia gave him a treat.

"The idea is to consistently reward with what he requests and slowly add more buttons, but considering how food driven he is, I'd suggest you limit his time with that particular choice."

"Oh, Piper," I said with a laugh. "No certificate today?"

"I'm sorry. Will you be staying another week?" Olivia asked. "If so, we can certainly work on that goal."

I exchanged a look with Jared. "No, we'll be leaving soon."

"Treat. Treat. Treat." Olivia handed Piper another treat.

"We'll be sorry to see you go, but it was a pleasure to work with Piper." Olivia bent down, retrieved the board from in front of Piper and handed it to me. "This board is yours to keep. You have my number, contact me with any questions. I can also provide you with some instructional videos so you can continue working with him at home."

Piper came to my side and pressed one of the buttons with his nose. "Treat."

"I don't have one with me, Piper," I said and was subjected to the saddest expression from him.

"Are we sure we want him to share more of what he's thinking?" Jared asked.

"With some dogs it's an incredible experience." Olivia looked down at her watch. "I have another training session after this. Do you have any questions?"

Ouch. I shook my head. "No, but thank you so much for

everything."

Jared thanked her as well.

Piper wagged his tail happily then used his nose to press his favorite button on the board again. "Treat. Treat. Treat. Treat."

Olivia handed him one last cookie then waved and made a hasty retreat. I turned the board so the buttons were facing away from Piper and looked down at him. "Piper, what does it say about your behavior that Olivia looked relieved to be returning to work with stray dogs? You, sir, are spoiled. You can't have everything you want." In response, Piper barked at me then whined at the board. "I told you I don't have any."

He whined again. "He wants something," I said to Jared. "Clearly."

"No, I mean, something else. I know him. He likes cookies, but not as much as he seems to right now." I turned the board around again. This time he pressed the button for out.

"Now that is a request we should honor," Jared said and I agreed.

Unleashed, we led Piper to the door of the building. As soon as he was on the other side he bolted out of sight and I swore. Jared and I took off running after him. With so many loose dogs, I was afraid that our time at the rescue might end on a bad note. So much for celebrating how well trained he was.

We followed the sound of him barking. As we rounded the building, we saw Olivia leading an Australian shepherd toward one of the other buildings. Piper was a good distance ahead of us and didn't respond to my call to come. Olivia turned. The dog beside her sat. Piper sat next to the shepherd, his tail wagging wildly.

Jared and I were both a little out of breath when we reached them. "I'm so sorry," I said as I clipped a leash on Piper's collar.

Olivia said, "No, I understand. These two have played together a lot this week. I should have taken Sadie over to say goodbye to Piper. He didn't get to see her today."

Sadie was wagging her tail and whining to go to Piper. Olivia said, "Okay, go."

I released Piper from his leash.

The two ran circles around each other happily then both came to sit in front of Jared and me. Piper nudged at the board in my hand until I turned it for him. He pressed the button for treat, then touched his nose to Sadie before repeating the motion.

Jared laughed. "At the risk of sounding sexist, I think he named her Treat." He put an arm around me.

Piper bounded in a circle, then pressed his nose to the board again. "Treat. Treat. Treat." Before pressing his nose to Sadie's again.

A huge smile stretched my lips. "Oh, my God, that's adorable."

Olivia took out a treat and showed it to Piper but he wasn't interested. He only had eyes for his lady friend.

"Fascinating. I haven't seen a dog make up his own meaning for a button yet, but I do believe you're right. If you were staying I'd change the treat button to her name, but since she's not going with you, perhaps just change the button's label to cookie."

Piper looked me right in the eye, touched Sadie with his nose, then whined. "Oh, Piper, we can't take her with us."

Olivia's shoulders raised. "She *is* available for adoption. She's also highly intelligent. She has perfect recall, mastered over thirty buttons, is agility trained as well as therapy dog certified. What she hasn't found yet is a family with a dog she gets along with, which is necessary because she has anxiety when left alone."

I met Jared's gaze as a desire to say I'd take Sadie welled within me. He nodded as if he could read my mind, then said, "Sadie, I've never had a dog. You'd have to be a better listener than Piper." It could have been something in his voice, but she sat up straight like she was ready to report to work. "Come, Sadie."

She went to his side and sat. Piper sat beside Sadie, both on Jared's side and I laughed. "I'm not sure I have a dog anymore. Jared, you might have two."

Olivia interjected, "Sadie's made her decision, but if you're still on the fence, let me show you how smart she is. Tell them both to go play."

I did.

The dogs bounded off, chasing each other in a large

circle around us. Olivia called out, "Sadie, bring Piper."

Sadie took Piper by the collar and brought him over to Oliva. I was clapping my hands in amusement. "No, way. Sadie, bring Piper to me." She led Piper to me. I glanced at Jared. "I need her."

As soon as Sadie released Piper's collar, he pressed a button again. "Treat."

I bent and looked into Sadie's beautiful blue eyes then into Piper's. "Yes."

Piper barked and wagged his tail.

Jared put his arm around me again. "Looks like we have two dogs."

We. My heart started thudding crazily in my chest. I had never imagined I could feel so much for anyone again, yet there it was . . . the butterflies, the anticipation of sharing more with someone. Unexpected. Terrifying. Wonderful. I said all I was ready to: "Looks like we do." The words felt inadequate.

He nodded in response.

Everything beyond him fell away the longer I looked into Jared's eyes. Olivia said there was somewhere she needed to go. Where? Neither of us cared enough to ask.

"Jared?"

"Yes."

"You just said we. *We* have two dogs."

"I did."

There was no uncertainty in his eyes. He'd said he wasn't

going anywhere and he'd meant it. I rose onto my tiptoes so my breasts brushed over his muscular chest. "You're a big softy beneath all your growl, you know that?"

He gave me a mock scowl then kissed me again. "Don't tell anyone. I've built an empire around being a scary son of a bitch."

"It'll be our little secret."

We shared a laugh. *God, I could get used to this man and this feeling.* Lost in the emotion of the moment, I forgot I was holding the communication board until I heard it hit the ground and jumped. As I bent to pick it up, I said, "I hope I didn't break it."

Jared glanced from me to Piper who was standing happily next to Sadie looking like he'd just won the lottery. "Not sure he needs it anymore. Looks like he already has everything he wants."

I knew the feeling.

CHAPTER TWENTY-FIVE

Jared

NOT TOO MUCH made my stomach twist with nerves, but pulling up to the Courter home for the second time in a matter of weeks did. I'd stepped into rings to engage in illegal MMA bloody fights with more confidence.

Michawn's family was wholesome and loving, but they also had no qualms about putting a person on the spot. There was a lot Michawn and I were still figuring out. From the backseat of my car, Piper barked in excitement. I glanced back. Sadie was sitting quietly.

After flying the dogs back on my jet and settling them into my apartment in the city, Michawn and I looked for a place in her hometown. All of the changes were confusing for Sadie. I understood that. Neither of us liked change. We'd both survived being abandoned by people we'd loved so we approached new situations and relationships with caution. We were overachievers—something that likely stemmed from never again wanting to be whatever it was that had made us so easy to discard the first time.

Michawn was smiling again. I'd caught her on the phone

several times reconnecting with friends, telling them she was moving back, and sounding so damn happy about it. I was beginning to wonder if she'd soon look at me and realize I didn't fit into her picture-perfect hometown.

Did she even need me? She didn't care about being wealthy. Now that her creative vision was back, she could easily build back up her business. The sex was phenomenal, but was that enough to keep two people together?

Michawn laid a hand on my arm.

"Jared. What's wrong?"

"Nothing."

"Look at me," she said.

I did and forced a smile that failed to impress her.

She continued, "You already had dinner with my family. Without me. This has to be easier."

"It's not that." I took a moment to appreciate the pink in her cheeks and sparkle in her eyes. Every side of her was beautiful to me, but more and more she was resembling the Michawn I remembered from Hamilton's—like a flower blossoming after a long winter. If things didn't work out between us, I'd never regret being part of her journey back? "You're glowing."

She blushed. "That might be your fault."

I caressed her cheek. "Might be, but I also know you're excited to be back."

She searched my face. "I am."

"And that's a good thing."

"You're a horrible liar or I just know you too well now."

"Michawn, I'm fine." I looked toward the house. "And your father is standing on the porch watching us."

She glanced toward the house then back at me. "I'd say let him wait, but I don't want him to worry."

I opened my door, slid out, then went around to open hers. "It's all good, Michawn."

She took me by the hand and gave my fingers a squeeze. "We can talk later, but I'm glad you're here. And my family is too. Some of them might be awkward at first, but only because they care about me and they're still trying to figure you out. Once they see how happy I am, they'll relax."

She called Piper and Sadie out of the car. "I almost forgot the board." She released my hand to dig into the backseat of the car for the board of speech buttons we'd modified so Sadie and Piper could share one. "I can't wait to show them what Piper learned."

Sadie came to my side and sat without having to be instructed to. When she leaned against my leg, I felt the tension in her and understood. She didn't know what we were doing there either. I pet the top of her head and said, "You're a good girl, Sadie. This is just a visit. We don't live here."

I have no idea if she understood some or none of what I'd said, but she relaxed a little. She stayed at my side while Piper bounded up the steps and jumped up on Michawn's father, nearly knocking him over. "Easy, Piper," he said with a laugh.

Michawn took a step toward the house as well, then turned and nodded to me. "Come on."

Under my breath, I said, "You heard her, Sadie, we're going in."

Sadie emitted a low whine but didn't move.

"I get it," I thought. "I don't know if I belong in there either, but what's the worst that could happen? They don't like us? We've gotten this far in life without them." No, there was a worse possibility. "Nothing is forever. If Michawn and Piper decide they don't need us anymore, we'll survive. That's what we do."

Sadie licked my hand, which didn't make her a telepath, but likely meant she could sense my apprehension. I hated that I couldn't walk in there with the same confidence I strode into meetings with the rich and powerful. The difference was I didn't care what those people thought of me.

Michawn was laughing as she pulled Piper off her father. They said something to each other that she seemed to agree with after giving me a long look. Holding on to Piper's collar, she led him into the house and her father started down the steps to me. *This should be interesting.*

"Mr. Courter," I said in greeting.

"Charles." He stopped and bent to a crouch. "Well, hello, Sadie."

Sadie stayed glued to my side. "She was a stray until a few months ago. She's cautious around new people."

Charles straightened. "That's understandable." Neither of us said anything for long enough that I was half-convinced he was going to tell me I wasn't welcome in his home. "I didn't agree with you taking Michawn anywhere."

"I know."

"She's been in a vulnerable state since losing Teddy."

"Yes." What else could I say? He'd said as much the first time we'd met and I'd seen Michawn teetering firsthand.

"Taking her to the dog rescue was genius."

My eyes were drawn to his. "Thank you."

Nothing in his expression was warm or welcoming. "I hear you had a good time there."

I was not about to touch that one.

He continued, "And that you helped her land a contract to design a park for the rescue owners."

"All I did was introduce her to them. Her ideas won them over."

He made a sound deep in his chest. "I heard the two of you are renting a house in town."

"We are."

"And that she's excited to be in Tracy's wedding now."

I nodded.

"That's a fast turnaround."

I couldn't deny that.

He hooked his thumbs in the front pockets of his jeans. "Where do you see things going between the two of you?"

"I'm not sure what you want me to say."

"Michawn has been through hell and back. I want you to tell me this isn't some casual thing for you. Don't build up whatever you're doing into something she may not survive if you change your mind. Don't do that to my daughter."

"I'm not going anywhere."

"Really? An important man like you with not just one but two companies waiting for you back in Boston. And you want me to believe you're willing to settle down in a small town?"

"I don't care what you believe."

He stepped closer. "Careful, son. You may have won over Michawn and my wife, but dads are a whole different animal. You don't scare me. And I'm not yet impressed. All that matters to me is my family's safety and if you want to play house with my daughter you'd better damn well convince me you're doing more than playing."

I pinched the bridge of my nose to stop myself from responding with sarcasm. "I'm not playing at anything."

He gave me a long look. "Do you love Michawn?"

I took a breath and asked myself the same thing. "I don't know how to love anyone, but I care about your daughter enough to try to learn to." It probably wasn't what he was hoping to hear, but it was the truth.

The air was thick with tension as neither of us spoke or moved. "How long do you intend to stay with her?"

"Forever if she'll let me."

His expression revealed how much my answer surprised

him. "Here or in Boston?"

"I have no idea. We're figuring this out one piece at a time."

"You have family?"

"By choice, not by blood."

"I'll want to meet them."

"They'll want to meet you."

"Christopher approves of you. He never approved of Teddy."

"That's a shame because from what Michawn says Teddy was good to her."

Charles nodded slowly. "How do you feel about children?"

"In theory?"

He frowned. "Michawn will want them."

I swallowed hard. She would. "I'm not opposed to a family if that's what she wants."

"Doesn't sound like you want them."

With a shrug, I said, "Just not sure I'd be good at parenting."

He let out an audible breath. "Anyone who tells you they know what they're doing when it comes to raising kids is either an idiot or a liar. Look at me, my kids are grown and I'm out here grilling you like you're a criminal. I can't help it though, I love Michawn so much. I don't want to see her hurt."

"I don't want to see her hurt either."

He put a hand on my shoulder and looked me in the eye. "I like you, Jared. You came here today even though this has to be uncomfortable for you. Michawn said you agreed to come back for as long as she needed to be here. There's no denying you make her happy. I'm going to let you have dinner with us for a second time."

My eyebrows rose. "Thank you."

His hand dropped from my shoulder. "Don't fuck this up."

"I'll do my best . . . Charles."

He nodded again. "Hopefully the day will come when you call me Dad." His eyes narrowed. "Not today. You earn that shit."

I made a face. "Yes, sir."

He flexed his shoulders. "Come on, let's go in. I'm getting too old to keep this up. I need dinner so I can work up the energy to threaten you a time or two more before you leave today." He winked. "Being a father is exhausting. I'm ready to be a grandfather. From what I hear that's a lot more fun."

Michawn appeared at the door again. She sent Piper down to get Sadie then called out, "Dad, stop grilling Jared and come eat. Megan has a conference call in an hour. Plus, you promised you'd be nice to Jared so if you said anything rude to him please apologize before you come in."

I met his gaze and tried not to let my amusement show. *Not such a toughie now, are you, Charles?* I thought it, but didn't say it.

Piper ran circles around Sadie until she took off in a run up the steps and into the house with him. A kinder man would have taken pity on Charles, but he needed to know who he was dealing with. "No apologies needed," I said as we made our way up the steps together. "Your father was just asking me to call him Dad. I was touched."

Michawn smiled, but looked skeptical, "Really?"

"Oh, you will be touched, if you push me," Charles said as he raised a mock fist in my direction.

I mouthed, "Dad" to him with a smirk.

Charles rolled his eyes. "I'd like to say you're too much of an asshole to come inside." His tone wasn't as cutting as his words.

"Dad!" Michawn exclaimed.

Charles raised both hands in surrender. "I said I'd like to. However, all he did was prove he'll fit in fine. I should warn you, Jared, everyone in that house would have done what you just did—with no remorse, just as gleefully. Welcome to the family."

CHAPTER TWENTY-SIX

Michawn

AN HOUR LATER, after everyone helped clear the table and moved to sit out in the backyard around a firepit, I slipped inside with my mother. She was tidying her already clean kitchen.

"I was hoping we'd have a moment alone," she said with a smile when she saw me at the doorway. "Tonight went well."

"It did." I gave her a hug from behind that made her smile then stood beside her at the sink. We shared a window view of the group. Jared was having what seemed like a comfortable conversation with Tracy's fiancé. "Corey is great. I'm glad Tracy brought him to meet us."

"We adore him."

"He and Tracy fit. I'm so happy she found someone."

The moment of silence that followed told me my mother was deciding how to say something. If it was about Jared, I wasn't sure I wanted to know. I said, "I was worried when Dad wanted to talk to Jared alone, but they seem to have worked things out. Jared doesn't look eager to leave, so I'm taking that as a good sign."

My mother took a moment to respond. When she spoke it was slowly and in a gentle tone. "We all love seeing you smiling again . . ."

"But?"

"It does scare us a little that it's happening so fast."

I gripped the edge of the counter. "I'm never on the right schedule, am I? I mourn too long then I heal too fast."

"Oh, baby, I'm not saying that." She pressed her lips together briefly then added, "This is only our second time meeting him. And now you're living with him. It's a lot to take in."

"You were happy enough at the idea of us sleeping to-gether. What changed?"

"That was—" She stopped, then restarted. "No one wants to see you get hurt again. What are you and Jared doing? Where is this going?"

I sighed. I couldn't blame her for asking the same ques-tions I'd asked myself a week ago. "I don't know, Mom. We might not be able to make this work, but I like who I am when I'm with Jared. He's a good man. Not a perfect one, but that means I don't have to be perfect either. And he cares about me."

"Do you love him?"

I let her question soak in. "I'm heading that way. I'm not a child anymore, Mom. I loved Teddy, but I might have been more in love with the idea of us than him. We were always living for what was next. I put up with a lot because I was so happy about the dream I'd created in my head of our future together. I'd charted it all out and letting that go was as hard as letting Teddy go. With Jared it's different. I don't know what tomorrow will bring, but I know how happy he makes me today."

There was no judgment in her eyes, only concern. "That's enough for me. But promise me that no matter how much changes, the important things will stay the same. I've missed you so much."

Tears filled both of our eyes. I took one of her hands in mine. "I needed to pull away to understand how much I had here. I might stay in the area or if things work out with Jared, we might end up closer to the city, but you won't lose me again because I'm no longer lost."

She hugged me and gave my forehead a kiss. "How did my little girl get so wise?"

I held on tight. "I was raised by amazing parents."

She chuckled and released me. "Flattery will get you everywhere." She stepped back, then in a more serious tone, she said, "Christopher and Thomas are now team Jared. Megan will come around. Of all of us, she took you moving away the hardest. You were her role model. When you crumbled, it shook her up. She wouldn't talk about it, but spend a little extra time with her when you can. She needs to see this side of you."

"I will, Mom."

"And if you need any help organizing things for Tracy's wedding—"

"I will consult you every step of the way."

Her pleased expression confirmed how much she wanted me to. "Only if you find it helpful."

"Who else would I trust to pick out the strippers?" I asked with a straight face.

A laugh burst out of her at that. "People don't actually do that, do they? Is that a big city thing?"

"I have no idea, but it seems like a topic you should look into for me."

Smiling ear to ear, she said, "Your father would die."

"I wonder if there are pamphlets you could leave round the house."

She laughed into her hand. "He collects the mail. I could sign up for coupons or a calendar."

"Oh, my God, if we found someone who could knock on the door with a résumé . . ."

We were laughing uncontrollably at the idea when my father and Jared appeared in the kitchen door. "That, Jared, is the sound of trouble," my father said with a shake of his head.

I met Jared's gaze and as I wiped tears of laughter from my eyes. "Don't believe him. We're innocent."

Still fighting back a laugh, my mother said, "Honey, all we're doing is throwing around ideas for Tracy's wedding."

Laughter gurgled in my throat. "And discussing the research necessary for my role as maid of honor."

"It's a difficult, time-honored role requiring the meticulous attention of a mother. Close, close attention in some cases," she joked and I nearly peed myself from laughing so hard.

I hadn't realized Tracy had also joined us until she spoke. "Oh, Lord. I do not want strippers if that is what either of you are planning."

That brought a roar of guilty laughter from my mother and me. Fighting to catch my breath, I said, "Would we do that to you?"

My mother wiped at her cheeks. "Michawn, tell him what you said about the résumé."

"Only if you tell him your idea about coupons and calendars."

"They're plotting to kill me," my father said to Jared.

Tracy was chuckling. "Coupons? I didn't know they had those. Corey, if they find a good deal, we might have to have strippers at our wedding. You know how I am about sales."

Without missing a beat, Corey put his arm around Tracy and said, "I thought strippers were for the bachelor and bachelorette party, but if you need some walking down the aisle with you—I'm in. I mean, only if we get a good deal."

Jared looked around and smiled.

My father frowned at him. "Don't encourage them, Jared. And never let them see your fear. They feed on that."

I crossed to where Jared was standing and slid beneath

his arm. "Dad, are you still upset about the clown dinner?"

Another roar of laughter erupted.

Tracy said, "Even I was in on that one. It was glorious."

"What's a clown dinner?" Jared asked, looking amused.

"That one was my fault," my mother said as she wrapped her arms around my father's waist. "The kids just ran with it."

Christopher entered the kitchen. "What's the ruckus for?"

From beside him, Thomas jokingly accused, "They were going to leave us out of the joke. Michawn, how could you?"

"I would have looped you in," I assured him with a huge smile. "But we should probably chill a little because Dad is still scarred from the clown stuff."

"I told them they were taking it too far," Christopher said.

I wagged a finger at him. "Liar. You rented the costumes."

His mock outrage was hilarious. "Only because you were determined to make it happen."

Laying a hand on Jared's chest, I smiled up at him. "I'm not sure how exactly it started but we were all in our teens and—"

My father cut in, "Your mother and I took all of us to a circus and she asked me why we'd never gone before. I admitted I've always been creeped out by the clowns."

Laughter bubbled out of me again. "Unfortunately we

heard him say it."

Jared's eyes lit with amusement. "And?"

I said, "Mom joked that it would be funny if he walked in one day and she was cooking dinner dressed as a clown."

Tracy added, "Then Michawn and I said we'd get matching costumes. Megan didn't want to be left out, so she said she would too."

Thomas interjected, "There was no way I wasn't going to be a part of something like that."

"I couldn't let them half-ass it," Christopher said.

Shaking his head, but smiling, my father said, "I came home from work one day and the whole damn family was dressed in clown outfits . . . full made-up faces . . . acting like they weren't the biggest assholes on the planet."

Jared's laugh was deep and blended with ours. "That's . . ."

"Diabolical?" my father asked.

Gazing down at me with a grin, Jared said, "Insightful."

I smiled at him and shrugged. "I have layers."

"And I like all of them," he said.

My cheeks warmed.

Still laughing, Thomas said, "The best part, Dad, was that you pretended you didn't notice so we just went about what we were doing. I finished my homework dressed that way. We made it through most of dinner pretending nothing was off."

Without looking away from Jared, I joined in, "It was

hilarious. And then Dad cracked and mumbled that he was trading all of us in for a nicer family."

"I should have," he grumbled. I glanced over in time to catch him give the side of my mother's head a kiss. "It was effective, though. Guess what? Clowns don't bother me anymore. My family? They scare the shit out of me."

In the quiet that followed, Jared joked, "So, will there be strippers or clowns at Tracy and Corey's wedding?"

"Or both?" Corey asked with humor. "Most memorable wedding ever."

Tracy raised a hand. "All joking aside. I've missed this."

The mood sobered. Christopher nodded toward me. "We all have. It's good to have you back, Michawn."

"It's good to be back," I answered. Tucked against Jared's side, I wondered if he had any idea how impossible this had felt before him? I doubted a lifetime would be enough to thank him.

Just then Piper ran into the kitchen with Sadie at his heels. They both lay down in the middle of the room, seeming perfectly comfortable to be in the mix.

I glanced up at Jared. The worry that had been in his eyes when we'd arrived was gone. I went onto my tiptoes and whispered in his ear, "I'm glad you're here."

He hugged me closer and seemed to breathe me in before answering, "Me too."

CHAPTER TWENTY-SEVEN

Jared

TWO WEEKS LATER, we parked in the driveway of Hamilton's house, something that had seemed like a good idea until Michawn visibly tensed as she looked around. "What is it?" I asked.

She shook her head without speaking.

Things had been going well, really well. We'd moved into a small house a few blocks from her parents', but had decided to split our time between there and my place in Boston. It was a compromise that was allowing her to reconnect with people in her hometown and me to schedule meetings that had to be done in person.

Sure it required a little shuffling around, but the payoff was falling into bed with Michawn every night, waking up with her in my arms, and discovering what it was like to be half of a couple. So much of it involved things I'd never considered . . . taking turns doing the dishes, organizing and doing the laundry, planning the meals we'd share. None of that had been part of my childhood and as an adult I hired people to handle the household chores. We didn't have staff in our home in Massachusetts and I had to admit I liked it.

With Christopher's tutelage, I mowed a lawn for the first time in my life. It could have been the beer that Christopher said was essential to yard work, but I enjoyed the process and felt surprisingly proud of how the lawn looked when I finished. Michawn's father showed me how to change the oil in my car. I didn't have the heart to tell him I'd never cared what was under the hood of a vehicle and, after seeing it up close, didn't need to ever see it again. I had a garage in the city full of collector cars that were maintained by a full-time mechanic. I couldn't remember the last time I'd put gas in one of my own cars.

I'd agreed to learn to change a car's oil because it had seemed important to Michawn's father. According to Michawn, it meant he liked me and was looking for a way to bond with me. How could I say no after that?

Michawn had grown up in a world I was still learning how to navigate, but I no longer felt like an outsider in it. Her friends were nice enough. The town was small, but not suffocatingly so. I could imagine living there—at least part-time.

It was time to introduce Michawn to my family. I hadn't expected her to look so nervous. I reached for her hand but it was secure in the vise grip of her other hand on her lap. "You said you wanted to come."

"I did. I just didn't think it would bother me. This was where . . ."

I'm an asshole. How did I not consider that the last time she'd been there had been the night her life had fallen apart? "We don't have to do this. I'll tell Hamilton something came up."

Her breathing was shallow and quick, but she shook her head. "No, I'll be fine. I just need a minute."

I released my seat belt and turned toward her. "I want you to meet Hamilton and his family, but we don't have to see him at his house. I understand. There are things that are too much for me no matter how much time has passed."

She nodded slowly. "Your father."

"Yes."

"The idea of seeing him makes me physically sick. I could never look at him without thinking about what he did to my mother, what he did to me, and I don't want to be the person seeing him again would bring out in me. If being here is too much for you, don't feel like you have to push through it for me. I get it."

Her shaking hand sought mine. "You're amazing, do you know that, Jared?"

I winked. "That's what she said."

She rolled her eyes and let out a reluctant chuckle. "Really? Is that what's on your mind?"

I grinned, hoping a little humor would help her shake off what was haunting her eyes. "Guilty."

It almost worked. She looked from me to Hamilton's house then back and sighed. "Is it crazy to think Teddy sent me here? He had a huge heart and beyond everything else he and I were friends. Was it a coincidence that you and I met just before he died? I'm not sure. I feel like we were meant to meet."

Meant to meet. I'd never believed in fate, but there was no denying how right it felt to be with her. "I've heard crazier ideas."

She swatted at the air between us. "I'm serious. I can feel Teddy here and he approves of you. He wants me to be happy."

Teddy would always be with us on some level because she'd known him for most of her life. Another man might have been jealous of his memory, but I couldn't be. He and I were certainly different, but he'd been good to her and for that I was grateful.

Was he there with us? No idea.

Can people reincarnate into stray dogs? Who am I to say what's possible?

Life was full of questions I was becoming okay with not knowing the answers to. If believing Teddy approved of us was part of Michawn's healing process, I wouldn't deny her that. "Teddy, if you can hear me, thank you for bringing Michawn to me. I'll take good care of her and you're welcome to hang around as long as you stay out of the bedroom."

Michawn made a comical face. "And the living room."

"And the shower," I added as heated memories came

back from how we'd enjoyed one together that morning.

She shared a smile with me. "It's probably a good idea for him to stay out of our apartment."

"And the car," I said without missing a beat.

Laughing, she said, "I'm sure he gets the idea." Her hand tightened on mine. "Thank you for not hating when I mention him. I'd want to be remembered."

There she was, the woman I wanted to spend the rest of my life with. She was stronger than she knew and so damn beautiful inside and out. I took a moment to savor looking down into her eyes, then said, "Ready to go in?"

She leaned forward and gave me the sweetest kiss, the kind that brings even the strongest man to his knees. "Absolutely, but let's not stay too late."

I chuckled. "Oh, is that what's on your mind?"

Her smile was shameless. "Guilty."

I wanted to stay in the warmth of that moment forever, but another car had pulled up behind ours and a quick glance confirmed it was Dominic and his wife. *Oh, boy, here we go.*

"Michawn, Hamilton was excited about our visit. Looks like he invited more than us to dinner."

"Oh." She looked around. "Who else is here?"

"Dominic Corisi and his wife."

"No." Her eyes rounded. "I know you said you know him, but I still can't believe it. *The* Dominic Corisi? Tracy and I had the biggest crush on him when we were six or maybe seven? I forget. God, he was all over the news because he'd kidnapped a schoolteacher then married her. We thought that was the most romantic thing we'd ever heard. That was over twenty years ago. How *old* is he now?"

I coughed back a laugh. "I need you to tell him that story and end it by asking him his age *just like that.*"

"That's awful." Her mouth rounded in surprise like she didn't know I had an evil side too.

So, I let it shine. "If we can find a cane for you to hold out to him as you ask him, it would be perfect."

She laughed. "I could never do that."

She could totally do that, but it was probably too much to ask for their first meeting. We could always work the joke in later when she knew him better.

"That's probably for the best. I owe him. He's the one who convinced me to get you out of Rhode Island, even if you didn't want my help at the time."

Her hands clasped over her heart. "Did he? I want to say that was so wrong, but I was drowning and needed to be dragged out of the water. So, I owe him as well."

"Well, you'll get a chance to meet him because it looks like he's spotted us and is heading this way with his wife." I opened my car door. "Ready or not, here we go."

CHAPTER TWENTY-EIGHT

Michawn

I SCRAMBLED OUT of the car and was adjusting my dress before Jared made it around to my door. Jared had won over my friends and family. I wanted to do the same. Of course, none of my friends were American icons.

I squared my shoulders. It wasn't their wealth that made the Corisis intimidating. I'd worked with many affluent clients, although none at their level. No, the Corisis were a fascinating mixture of dangerous and philanthropic. People joked that Dominic must have been a magician in his last life because anyone who spoke out against him disappeared.

The chiseled man who walked toward us in an Armani suit with his hand on the back of a beautiful woman in a long flowing dress had an edge to him . . . but dangerous? No, not with the easy smile he gave the young man who trotted up beside him as well as the young woman who increased her pace to catch up.

At my side, Jared said, "Dominic's wife's name is Abby. His son's name is Leonardo. He's brilliant, but shy. His daughter's name is Judy. She'll test you, but she means well.

When I first met her she challenged me to a game of chess. I'd never played chess. My counteroffer was to teach her not only how to deliver Baji's heart-stopping elbow strike, but also how to effectively block the move if someone else tried it. We've been buds ever since. She's lived an extremely sheltered life and it shows in her social skills. As she matures she'll work that out. Think of her like Sadie. If she becomes too much, just calmly, kindly correct her."

"She sounds sweet," I said weakly.

"My point is—don't let her intimidate you. She loves to solve puzzles. You love to create things. Although you have differences, you're both passionate about what you do. If you meet on that common ground she'll respect you."

"I'll keep that in mind. No tips on how to handle Dominic?"

Jared put an arm around me and bent down to speak softly as they approached. "There likely isn't much he doesn't know about you and he approves. Now me? We're still figuring each other out."

Abby Corisi was the first to speak when they joined us. "Don't mind us as we chase you across the driveway. I'm Abby. This is Dominic." Her introduction was warm and down to earth. I found myself relaxing. "Our son, Leonardo, and daughter, Judy."

I shook her hand vehemently. "Michawn Courter. It's such a pleasure to meet all of you."

Dominic gave me a long look then nodded at Jared before holding out a hand toward me in greeting. "You look happy."

"I am." I linked hands with Jared after he shook Dominic's hand. "Very."

Dominic continued, "Good thing Jared took my advice."

"Dad!" His daughter rolled her eyes skyward. "Don't embarrass Jared."

"What did you advise him to do?" Leonardo asked.

Abby shook her head at her husband. "Please don't."

Everything I needed to know about Dominic was revealed right there in the look that passed between him and his wife. He respected her opinion. He leaned toward his son and said, "I told him that when a man finds a woman as special as Michawn is to Jared, as special as your mother is to me, he doesn't give up until he finds a way to make her smile."

Leonardo looked from his father to Jared. "That's what he said?"

Without skipping a beat, Jared said, "He sure did. And he was correct." He raised our linked hands. "The proof is right here."

Judy folded her arms over her chest. "I'm sure that's not how he said it."

"Judy Marie Corisi, be nice," Abby said gently. "We talked about this."

There was a brief, tense pause, before Judy smiled at me and said, "I'm excited to meet you. After comparing your early designs to your later ones, I have questions.”

Keeping what Jared had told me about her in mind, I said, “I’d love to answer them. And then I’d love to hear about what you’re interested in. I’ve always been passionate about creating spaces that take a person out of their normal reality and into a magical place where anything and everything is possible—”

Judy frowned. “I have an uncle who makes bunkers and they’re amazing. He has made some that make you feel like you’re outside, but magical is a bit of a stretch, don’t you think?”

“Not to me. A person’s imagination *is* a magical place.”

“Sorry, I prefer to keep my feet planted in reality.”

“Then you’re missing out,” I responded. “To create anything new and innovative you must first be able to imagine it. The places I design encourage people to cultivate their creative side, which if followed by action, changes their reality.”

“That’s an interesting perspective,” Judy conceded. “I like it.”

Leonardo chimed in, “Schopenhauer said, ‘Talent hits a target no one else can hit; genius hits a target no one else can see.’” He looked me straight in the eye and said, “If my parents agree, will you build me a space so magical it changes my reality? I may one day be taking over for my father and when I do I’ll need a lot of really good ideas. He’s brilliant.”

Dominic ruffled his son’s hair. “I’m not going anywhere

anytime soon, Leonardo, but I like the way you think. One day, you and Judy will take over and that'll be a big responsibility. It's never too early to start preparing." He nodded toward me. "When you have time, we'll talk more about this. We'll choose a property or two for you to do your magic thing."

"I'd love that." Did that really just happen? Did the Corisi family just hire me for a project? Okay, so it had a lot to do with the man holding my hand, but the idea of creating something for someone with their likely budget made me giddy as ideas for it started flooding in.

Jared motioned toward the door of the house. "Fara is waving for us to move this party indoors."

Judy fell into step beside me. "Have you ever considered integrating technology into your designs? Or pairing it with security? My aunt Alethea made a career out of breaching top security systems and I do it for recreation, but they're predictably straightforward and stale in design. Someone like you could incorporate enough distractions and decoys that even an AI would be confused. I'd love to talk to you too."

I smiled. "I know very little about security systems, but sure. I'm fascinated by something you said, though. How do you breach security systems for recreation? And is it as fun as it sounds?"

Judy's expression transformed with delight and as we walked, she gushed about the latest one she'd beaten and how addictive that feeling was. Jared's hand settled on my lower back. I glanced at him, and the approving smile on his face brought a flush to mine.

An older gentleman with kind eyes welcomed us at the door. "In a minute I was going to send out a rescue team for you."

The petite woman at his side greeted us with a warm smile. She took both of my hands in hers. "Well, don't you look lovely? No wonder Jared carried a torch for you for so long."

I smiled awkwardly.

"Michawn," Jared cut in. "This is Hamilton Wenham and his wife, Fara."

"It's nice to meet you both in person," I said.

"Please call me Hamilton."

"And Fara," his wife added, releasing my hands. "We've heard so much about you."

"All good, I hope." When that was neither confirmed nor denied, I added, "Thank you for being so understanding when . . ."

"Of course," Hamilton said before taking a step back and motioning for us to enter. "We've held off on renovations, holding out hope that you'd come back and finish your redesign."

"No pressure," Fara said quickly, "but if being here again sparks an interest in completing that project, we loved your ideas."

"I . . ." It was a little overwhelming.

Jared put an arm around my waist and murmured into my ear. "Breathe. You've got this."

I smiled at Fara. "Thank you."

When Hamilton and Fara greeted Dominic and his family, I turned to Jared. "You don't have to have everyone you know hire me. I can get clients on my own."

His eyebrows furrowed. "Hamilton was already your client when we met. You won the Livingstons over on your own. And believe me, the Corisis are not easy to impress. If they want to talk to you about designing something for them, that has nothing to do with me and everything to do with their opinion of your previous work."

I wanted to believe that. He was right about Hamilton. The Livingstons? Maybe. But I wouldn't have met them without him. And the Corisis? That was the hardest one to wrap my head around. It wouldn't have always been that way. Two years ago I wouldn't have questioned my ability to woo new clients. Apparently, regaining my confidence would be a process, just like mourning was.

"Everyone's in the family room," Fara said. "Calvin will be glad you're here. Marina and Hunter are crawling all over him. He's looking a little frazzled."

"He said he's ready for kids," Jared said lightly. "They're a good test."

Hamilton winked at me. "Jared said that like he doesn't adore my grandchildren. Wait until you see them together."

I didn't doubt that kids would love Jared. Piper and

Sadie worshipped him. Children and animals could sense the good in people. "Is Bradley here as well? I'm looking forward to meeting him."

"He's in the kitchen with our chef," Fara said. "We've told him a hundred times he doesn't have to help out, but he likes to tweak the menu."

Jared leaned in. "It drives the chef crazy, but there's no denying it's always an improvement. I told him he should write a cookbook."

From behind us, Dominic said, "He'd be better off opening his own cooking school. I'll talk to him."

Arm around me, Jared turned to Dominic. "As long as you hear him if he says he's not interested."

Dominic frowned, but his irritation seemed to pass quickly. "Is that any way to speak to your best man?"

Jared coughed.

Fara clapped her hands together. "Jared, does that mean what I think it means? I knew the two of you got a place together, but I didn't hear you'd proposed."

Wait. What? I froze and I'm sure my eyes doubled in size.

"I didn't . . . yet," Jared said while looking pointedly at Dominic.

Abby hugged her husband. "Dom, don't tease Jared in front of Michawn. We're still trying to make a good impression."

Leonardo came to stand beside me and spoke in a confidential tone. "You can't be sensitive and survive in this family."

I smiled. "I have two brothers and one sister. We grew up tormenting not only each other but also our parents. Bring it on."

Leonardo's face lit with an answering smile. Judy nodded in approval.

"She can handle us," Dominic said with confidence. "If you doubt it, ask her sometime about their clown dinner."

My eyes flew to Jared's. His narrowed and in a low voice meant for only me to hear, he said, "I didn't tell him. I won't ask how he heard the story because I don't want to know."

Jared had said Dominic made sure he knew everything about everyone, but that had the hair on the back of my neck standing up. "Understood."

As if the conversation hadn't just taken a dark turn, Fara said cheerfully, "Don't delay too long on that proposal. Calvin and Bradley retained an adoption lawyer and are actively looking now. Jared, if you and Michawn have children soon you could raise them all together." She laid her head on Hamilton's arm. "These houses would be overflowing with children."

He smiled and hugged her closer. "That's the dream."

We began walking toward the family room while I tried to catch my breath. Marriage. Children. Was it all back on the table? I was still struggling to label what I felt for Jared. Distracted, I stumbled. Jared caught me and gave me a concerned look.

"We can take things at our own speed," Jared said in that deep reassuring voice that always calmed me.

I sent him a thankful look.

I didn't deserve him, but that didn't make me less grateful to have met him.

We were both smiling as we entered a chaotic family room. As soon as they spotted Jared, two toddlers sprinted over to us. One of them came running up to Jared and held her arms out to him in clear request to be picked up. "Uncle Jarry," she squealed as he swung her up and spun around with her.

"This is Marina," Jared said to me.

I greeted her. "Hello, Marina. My name is Michawn."

"Shawn," she repeated.

Close enough.

Her brother demanded to be scooped up as well. Jared turned to me with a child on either hip. I couldn't imagine anything more beautiful than a mountain of a man with more than a few battle scars hugging two toddlers like it was the most natural thing in the world. "And you must be Hunter," I said to the little boy. "I'm Michawn."

"Dawn."

I could work with that one as well.

"Dom Dom," Marina squealed, wiggling down to run to another powerful man who melted at her enthusiastic greeting. It was difficult to remain apprehensive of Dominic as it became obvious how much he cared for the Wenhams as well as Jared.

A couple who looked about our age walked over. She had jet-black hair and striking gray eyes. Dominic's little sister, Riley. I recognized her from photos. The man beside her fit Jared's description of Gavin—athletic, polished, confident.

Riley gave me an extra-long hug and said softly, "You've got yourself a good man there. And he adores you."

I glanced back and caught Jared watching me with a warm expression in his eyes. "I know."

Her husband shook my hand warmly. "I've never seen Jared look so happy. I'm glad you took a chance on his sorry ass."

"Thank you," I murmured.

Calvin was the next to hug me. "If he ever gives you the tiniest amount of shit, you call me and I'll straighten him out."

I chuckled. "I'll keep that in mind."

Bradley returned from the kitchen and came over to greet me with a hug as well. "You are every bit as lovely as Jared described."

Their warmth took me by surprise. I expected them to be nice, but this felt like the kind of welcome a person received when returning home after a long trip. I joked, "Do you say that to all the women Jared dates?"

Bradley waved a hand through the hair. "Girl, we never even learned their names. Now you—we all knew you were important from the first time he met you."

My breath caught in my throat. "Two years ago?"

Bradley nodded. "Meeting you shook him up, but in the best way. Everything happens for a reason and seeing the two of you together confirms that for me."

I couldn't say I liked the idea of Teddy's death being part of a greater plan, but I did want to believe meeting Jared was. That didn't make sense, but I decided it didn't have to.

Fara brought me a glass of wine, which helped to settle my nerves. She told me about how she'd met Hamilton and the wonder of how much her life had changed since. Love had healed parts of her she'd thought would always be broken.

I snuck a look at Jared who had Hunter on his shoulders and Marina holding one of his hands, while he spoke with Bradley and Dominic about something that had them all laughing. I liked these people, who Jared was when he was with them, and how much they seemed to care about him.

Love was something I thought I couldn't feel for anyone again. It had felt like too big of a risk, but as I stood there watching Jared bend to hear something Marina said, I handed my heart to him.

That's the man I want to laugh, cry, and heal with.

Wake up to every day.

Raise a family with.

I brought a hand to my mouth as warmth spread through me.

I love him.

CHAPTER TWENTY-NINE

Jared

WEEKS LATER, I walked to the window of my Boston office, took a small velvet box out of my suit pocket, and flipped it open. The simple one carat flawless diamond was the one Tracy had assured me Michawn would prefer. It was sized according to Michawn's mother's recommendation. Christopher had met me in the city the day I'd picked it up. It'd be a miracle if my intentions were still a secret to Michawn.

How had I not yet said the three words a man should before he asks a woman to spend the rest of her life with him? Nothing mattered more to me than her happiness. With her, I felt centered . . . at peace for the first time in my life. The days when I stayed at work until midnight were gone. I finally had a reason to go home.

Home was no longer Boston.

It wasn't a small house near her family.

Both were nice enough, but location was irrelevant. Home had become wherever Michawn was. I flipped the lid of the velvet box shut.

So, why was I holding back? I loved her more than I thought I could ever love anyone. How were the words still hard to say?

I took out my phone and faced something that had been weighing on my mind. My father had sent me another text message—this time sounding openly impatient. I wasn't one who enjoyed delving into how I felt about anything in my past, but if his messages had the ability to prevent me from telling Michawn I loved her . . . that wasn't good.

I considered responding to him, but I had nothing I wanted to say to him. There was nothing he could say that I wanted to hear—nothing. I couldn't forgive him and all that his attempts to contact me did was fill me with a burst of uneasy adrenaline I no longer had an outlet for.

The buzz of my phone was a welcome distraction. "Hey, Tracy."

"Is Michawn with you?" she asked.

"No. I thought she was with you. Aren't you dress shopping today?"

"We're supposed to be. Everyone else is here, but not her. Do you think she decided it was too much for her? She's not answering her phone."

"When I spoke to her this morning she was excited. I'll call her." As soon as I hung up, I tried Michawn's number. Nothing. I texted her. Nothing.

There'd been a time, in the beginning, when I would have considered the possibility that she'd retreated again—

but that wasn't where her head was at anymore. No. She wouldn't blow off such a big day for Tracy.

So, where was she?

She could be stuck in traffic and have accidentally left her phone at our apartment. I'd never thought it was necessary for couples to track each other's location, but I had a bad feeling, and no way to find her if she'd run her car into a ditch . . . or if she'd fallen at home and hit her head.

I texted her again.

Still nothing.

My fingers rapidly typed a message to someone I knew could locate her. **Need your help. Michawn is missing. Are you able to track her phone?**

Dominic answered almost immediately. **Yes. Danger level 1-10?**

My gut says 15, but this could be nothing. I paced my office. It had been a long time since I'd felt helpless. There was nothing concrete to base my reaction on, but when a person's very survival has depended on their instincts, they tend to trust them. Yes, it was possible that I was overreacting, but I would have bet my life Michawn was in danger.

A few minutes later, a text came in from Dominic. **Her phone is in the garage of your apartment building. I have someone trying to access the camera system there. It'll take a minute.**

I burst out of my office and sprinted past my secretary without stopping when she called out to me, answering Dominic only when I was in the elevator heading down to the garage. Our apartment building was only a few blocks away. Michawn might be struggling with old memories, but I felt I needed to get to her. **I'm heading to my car now.**

Dominic's next message confirmed my fears. **We have access to the security cameras in the garage. She's in a car. Her car. There's a man in the vehicle with her.**

With any other woman my thoughts might have gone to infidelity, but Michawn wasn't like that. **Are they talking? Does she look scared?** I made it from the elevator to my car in record time.

Impossible to say. The man has a tattoo on his right elbow—a cobweb.

I nearly threw up in my mouth as I peeled out of the garage and sped toward our apartment building. I knew someone with that tattoo. He'd gotten it during his first year in prison when his sentence had loomed before him. **Can you track a phone from a number?**

My people can do anything.

I read off a number to him as I drove and fought to keep the rage welling within me in check.

A moment later I instructed my phone to read Dominic's next message aloud. **The phone linked to that number is in the vehicle with Michawn.**

If my father hurts her, I'll kill him.

CHAPTER THIRTY

Michawn

*N*EVER LET THEM *take you to a secondary location. Never get into a car with them.*

I'd heard the advice and remembered wondering why people didn't drop to the ground screaming and kicking when someone tried to abduct them—now I knew.

There's a paralyzing period of disbelief that a perpetrator can take advantage of. I'd been happily distracted as I'd made my way to my car in our apartment's parking garage. Between digging through my purse for my sunglasses and going over a mental checklist of everything I'd promised to bring that day, I'd completely missed that I wasn't alone until a large man had stepped out of the shadows.

He'd asked me my name and I'd knee-jerk-reaction answered him, wondering if he was new to the security team or the building. The hair on the back of my neck had gone up when he asked me if I was alone.

I'd immediately started backing away.

He told me to not be afraid, which only put my senses on higher alert. I was preparing to bolt when he grabbed my arm. We struggled. I kicked at him. His hold on my arm tightened so painfully I gasped. With my free hand I grabbed my key fob. My intention was to hit the panic button, but he grabbed it from me and used it to unlock my car.

I screamed but we were alone.

I begged him to let me go. He told me all he wanted to do was talk, but not in the garage. There was something he needed to show me.

I did fight, but he tossed me in the car with such force I hit my head and was temporarily stunned. By the time I reached for the door handle to let myself out, he was already in the passenger seat holding me in place by my shoulder. "You have no reason to be afraid."

Mace would have been helpful, but I'd never believed it necessary.

A good self-defense move might have worked as well, but I didn't know any. Sure, I'd thrown some punches in middle school, but nothing I could muster would take down a man of his size.

"Drive," he ordered.

I shook my head.

His hand fisted on my shoulder and I braced myself for a hit. "I don't want to hurt you," he said in a tight voice.

"Then let me go," I answered in the calmest voice I could muster.

"Did you hit your head?"

I raised a hand to my forehead. It was wet with . . . yep,

blood. He'd clipped my head against the top of the door when he'd tossed me inside, but I wasn't about to argue with him.

He ran his hand through his hair. "It wasn't supposed to go this way. If you hadn't started screaming . . ."

I should have watched the masterclass on hostage negotiation. I remember wanting to, but thought: when will I ever need that skill?

"You don't have to do this. If you let me go now, I have no idea who you are and no one needs to ever know this happened."

"Why did you have to make this so fucking difficult? All I wanted to do was talk to you. Now your forehead is messed up and that'll ruin everything."

I kept my breathing as even as I could and tried to assess the situation for a method of escape. There was a pen in my cupholder. Could I stab him in the eye? Did that kind of thing only work in the movies? I was an artist, not a ninja.

If I turned and put my back against the door, could I kick him? I shifted in preparation of doing just that.

"I'm not a murderer," he said. "I was drunk. I was angry. He was an asshole who deserved the beating I gave him. If he'd lived, it would have been like any other bar fight. No one would have cared."

Oh, boy. I shifted a little more in my seat wishing I'd practiced kickboxing instead of yoga back in college. All that slow stretching hadn't prepared me for how to get my leg up with striking speed.

His eyes narrowed. "If you kick me I will punch you in the face. Even if I don't want to. I don't respond well to being hit."

I inhaled a shaky breath and lowered my leg. "I would never try something like that."

"Good, because I already feel bad about your head." He rubbed a hand over his chin. "All I want to do is talk to my son."

"Your son?" Did I want to know?

"Jared Smith . . . that's who he is, no matter what he told you. Changing his name didn't change who he is."

Every story Jared had told me about his father swirled through my head, raising my panic level. This was the man who'd beaten Jared as well as his mother. He'd had a violent temper and prison didn't appear to have changed that. "Is that why you're here? To talk to Jared?"

"He won't take my calls. He ignores my texts. I had no choice."

Could I use that to my advantage? "I could ask him to contact you . . . and I will . . . if you let me go."

He shook his head. "No. If he thinks I hurt you he won't listen to anything I say."

Thinks? I cleared my throat. "What do you want to say to him?"

His hand fisted and he punched his thigh. "I was not the father he wanted, but his mother's death had nothing to do with me. She was a junkie when I met her. I tried to help her, but he never saw anything good I did."

"I'm sure he did." I moved a hand behind me, slowly. If I could get the door to open I might be able to drop out and scramble away faster than he could move around the car to get me.

"No. All he sees are my mistakes. He never visited me in prison because he blamed me for everything. I wasn't perfect. I admit it. But I've had a lot of time to think about what I could have done better. I never told him I loved him. I should have. He's my son."

"I'm sure he knows." I moved my hand fully behind me and felt for the handle. When I located it, I tried not to reveal anything in my expression.

"I paid my dues for what I did. He can't pretend I don't exist."

The sound of a car squealing into the garage grabbed Jared's father's attention. When he looked away, I pulled the handle of the door hard and threw myself out, ignoring the pain of the landing as I scrambled to my feet.

I reached the rear of the car only to discover he was already there, blocking my escape. I screamed and spun in time to see Jared jump out of his car and run toward me.

At Jared's appearance, his father froze. I didn't waste a second, I met Jared halfway, threw myself into his arms, but found no comfort there. He was coiled with fury, his eyes flashing with a look I'd never seen in them.

He held me back from him, inspected my face and my bruised upper arm then pushed me behind him. "Get in my car," he growled.

I wanted nothing more than to run and hide, but not without him. Unlike his father, he didn't scare me . . . not even when he looked about to commit an act of violence.

Although I'd never faced the kind of abuse Jared had, I understood how seeing his father with me, especially with me looking banged up, would bring back the horror of his childhood. In that frame of mind, with that kind of rage resurfacing, a man might cross lines he never normally would.

Jared shook off the hand I placed on his arm and closed the distance between his father and him, not stopping until he was within striking distance. "Were you disappointed prison didn't put you on death row? Is that why you hurt the woman I love? A death wish? I can help you with that."

Woman he loves? I shook my head. We could talk about that later.

His father puffed with his own anger, and although they were similar in height, I had no doubt that Jared would win if they fought. Unless his father had a weapon. *Please don't let him be armed.* "This is your fault," his father snapped. "You couldn't answer one of my texts? Not one? Do you know what that does to a father?"

Jared shook his head. "You think I care about you or how you feel? I don't. I was happy when they put you in prison. I prayed you'd die in there. Why? Because all you do is hurt people. I am not the boy you used as an ashtray and you seriously fucked up when you came here."

I went to Jared's side. "Jared, don't."

"Don't what?" he growled. "Let him leave here alive? Don't worry, I won't. Not even if it means I'll rot in prison. He's never going to hurt anyone I love again."

His father took a step back and I didn't blame him a bit for it. Jared meant it. I touched his arm again. His was pulsing with rage and although I understood why, I couldn't lose him to it. "The man I love is not a killer, Jared. Don't do this. You're not him. Don't let him take everything from you."

"Take what?" his father snarled. "I've never asked for anything. I have a job and a place to stay. I don't need your fucking money. I just wanted to tell you"—he stopped and his voice lowered—"that you're still my son. You always will be. And I love you."

Jared shuddered then surged against my hand. I could taste the rage he was holding back. I directed my next comment to his father. I raised my hand to the cut on my forehead. "You both need to stop and listen to each other."

His father growled, "I'll stop when he stops thinking he's better than me."

I implored Jared with my eyes, but he shook his head. "Go, Michawn. You can't be here. We'll never be safe if I don't handle this. We won't be. Our kids won't be. The next one he takes could be one of them. Could you live with that?"

I couldn't, but there had to be another way. I met his father's angry gaze. "You say you love Jared, but this isn't love. Love isn't angry or violent. This—what you're doing right now—is whatever unhealthy thing someone did to you. You can't make someone love you and you can't punish them when they don't." I held up my blood covered hand between us. "Look—really look at what you're doing and tell me—is that going to make Jared love you?"

Jared's father seemed to falter. He looked from me to Jared and back. "I never had a father. I had whoever my mother brought home and they were never kind. All I ever wanted was to do better for my son . . . to be there for him."

"You failed at that," Jared said in a tight tone.

"He knows that, Jared. He does." I gave his arm a squeeze. I held his father's gaze. Jared had stood between me and the darkness once and saved me from it. I would do no less for him. "You need to let Jared go. Don't push him until he snaps and makes the same mistakes you did. Let him break the chain. That might not feel fair to you, but it's what a good father—a loving father would do."

Jared's father nodded once in a move that was oddly familiar to me. "I don't want to pull you down, Jared."

In a guttural tone, Jared said, "Then stop. You can control yourself and the demons within you. We all can."

I linked my hand with Jared's then gasped when a red

light appeared on his father's forehead. Jared took out his phone. I read the text as he did.

Your call.

I looked around but saw no one then whispered in a hoarse voice, "Don't let this happen, Jared."

Jared turned the phone toward his father then motioned at his head. "All I'd have to say is yes and you'd be dead."

"And you'd go to prison, like I did."

"Or not," Jared countered. "No one would look for you and I have friends who could make sure if they did no one would ever find you."

I closed my eyes briefly then said, "Your father was already leaving. He's going to find a church or a therapist or both and he's going to work on himself. I believe that."

Jared met my gaze. "You really do?"

"Yes."

He turned to his father. "Then go. Don't contact me again, though."

I added, "Let Jared come to you—when he's ready—if he ever is." I hated that some situations didn't have happy endings, but not all of this one was a tragedy. I looked at his father again and said, "Letting you go, believing you can do better and giving you a chance—that's love."

After a long moment, during which the red dot remained square in the middle of Jared's father's forehead, he said, "I am more than my mistakes."

Jared nodded once in acknowledgement that he might be

as well. After one more long, tense moment, his father turned and walked away.

Another text came in. **Yes or no.**

Jared texted back: **Not today.**

I didn't tell Jared to say, "Not ever" as those who'd known me since childhood would have expected me to. I prayed his father got the help he needed and that one day he could tell his son he loved him and Jared would believe him.

But there was also a primal beauty in knowing that I had a man who would protect our family with his very life if necessary. I wrapped my arm around him and hugged him tightly. Heroes came in all different types. Some were easy to spot, some came with so much damage they could have chosen a darker road.

Doing the right thing, if letting a dangerous man go free to possibly come after us again, was right wasn't easy . . . however it was what stopped Jared from becoming his father.

Jared might not have known what love was when he was young, but he'd learned how to do it right along the way. When he buried his face in my hair and told me he loved me, I believed him. He'd proven it by choosing our future over his past.

I craned my neck back so I could look him in the eye and said, "Jared, I love you too. More than you'll ever know. Will you marry me?"

He searched my face with so much love in his eyes it was hard not to cry. "You're not allowed to steal my opportunity to propose to you. So back up your truck, little lady, and wait until you're asked. I want to do this right." He touched my forehead softly next to but not on my cut. "When you're less bloody."

I smiled at his joke, knowing it was his attempt to ease the tension. "You don't think my garage proposal is good enough? Okay, but guess who's not getting post-proposal sex tonight."

Despite how strained his expression was, his eyes lit with interest. "Wait, wait, wait. Is post-proposal sex different than regular sex?"

Against his lips, I murmured, "I suppose you'll have to wait and see. Hope you're not a slow planner."

He took out his phone and started typing. When I tried to peer over his arm to see what he was typing, he moved his phone so I couldn't.

"Who are you texting?" I asked.

"Your mother, Fara, and Bradley."

My eyes rounded and I gripped his forearm. "You're not telling them about what happened, are you?" In a text was not how I wanted anyone to hear about any of this.

He frowned. "No, we're in a group chat about wedding stuff."

"Tracy's wedding?"

As if he couldn't understand how I could be confused, he tipped his head to one side, then said, "Ours."

Whoosh, that put flutters in my chest. "Ours?"

He pocketed his phone and pulled me back into his arms. "I've never asked anyone to marry me before. Their advice has been helpful."

A huge smile spread across my face. "Did you already buy a ring?"

"Maybe."

"Can I see it?"

He looked around. "Here?"

"Just a peek."

A smile pulling at the corners of his mouth, he pulled a velvet box out of his suit pocket. "One quick look."

As soon as the lid lifted and I glimpsed the simplicity of the stone I gasped. "It's beautiful."

With a sigh, he handed me the box. "Press the button inside the box."

I did and the ring rose above the velvet and a flap on the top of the box retracted revealing a digital note that read: **Coupon for one nude sculpture of us crushing grapes.**

The laughter that burst from me was the perfect way to chase the rest of my nervousness away. Life was full of ups and downs, moments of wonder and moments of terror— but I was no longer afraid. I was stronger because of what I'd gone through and so was Jared. "Will it go in a museum?" I asked.

"Depends on how it comes out," he answered with a smile. "And how well they represent my . . . attributes. We could always build a secret room to keep it in."

"I'd love that."

Leaning over me, looking proud of himself, he said, "The message can be changed from my phone so I could update it on our anniversaries."

I closed the box and held it to my chest. "You made my inner child smile."

He bent and kissed my lips gently before retrieving the box and putting it back in his jacket. "That was the goal. I want to fill your life with all the magic you bring to others . . . brought to mine."

I rested my head on his chest and savored the sound of the beat of his heart. "You already do."

My phone binged with a message. Tracy. **Are you still coming today?**

Oh, shit. "Jared, Tracy's dress shopping without me."

He held up a finger then sent another text. "Let's get you cleaned up then to the helipad. We can have you to Tracy in twenty minutes."

"Really?"

He nodded.

I texted Tracy. **On my way. Be there in 20 if you can wait.**

Her answer made me smile. **I'll serve another round of mimosas, but you'd better have a good excuse.**

Oh, I do.

CHAPTER THIRTY-ONE

Jared

A FEW DAYS later, Michawn and I stood in her parents' living room. It was wall-to-wall people, but no one seemed to mind. I could have chosen a larger venue, or one that some people might have found more impressive, but then I wouldn't have seen the look of sheer joy in her parents' eyes when I asked if I could propose to Michawn at their home.

They'd needed something to look forward to after Michawn told them about what had happened with my father. She conveniently left out the part where I'd threatened his life. Her father had cornered me at his first opportunity, though, and asked me how I intended to keep her safe.

"By whatever means necessary," I vowed. Because I knew he needed to hear the story, I explained why I'd allowed my father to leave and what I was prepared to do if he ever came for my family again.

He didn't suggest I try to work things out with my father or that anything I'd implied might be too extreme. No, we both knew he was capable of the same if anyone came for his wife or children.

We talked about our timeline and I explained that our engagement didn't need to be a short one. We could wait to make our union legal until after Tracy and Corey had their big day, but I wanted a ring on Michawn's finger. I needed the world to know she was mine and that I was hers. "Forever," I added in case there was any question as to how long I intended to be part of her life.

The Courters sure got huggy when they were happy.

I didn't hate it.

Taking Michawn by the hand I raised my voice to call everyone's attention to us. The room quieted and I took a moment to look around. Her friends were standing shoulder to shoulder with mine. Multiple generations of the Courters, Wenhams, and Corisis blended seamlessly. Calvin and Bradley stood in the mix, arms linked, looking on with a mix of pride and amusement.

I turned my attention to my reason for gathering everyone. "Michawn, I have a surprise for you."

Her eyes were wide with wonder. "More than this?"

Waving, I motioned to the Livingstons that it was time. They stepped away then returned with Piper and Sadie on leashes. My friend Rick walked beside them with a special communication board I'd had made for this occasion.

When the board was placed before the two dogs I went onto one knee in front of Michawn and took out the ring box. When nothing happened, I looked over to the dogs and said, "Help me out here, guys."

Piper put his paw on the first button. "Will."

Sadie tapped the second button. "You."

Piper hit the third. "Marry."

Sadie laid her paw on the last one. "Me?"

Michawn clapped her hands together. "I can't believe you taught them to do that. That's amazing."

I cleared my throat loudly, opened the ring box, and waved it to regain her attention.

She laughed. "Oh, sorry. Yes. Yes. Oh, my God, yes."

I stood, slid the ring on her finger, and kissed her soundly.

In the background, the message board sounded as the dogs pressed the buttons out of order. "You. Me. You. Me. Marry. Me. You."

"Did the dogs just get engaged too?" Dominic asked and everyone laughed.

Michawn threw her arms around my neck and gave me a deep, passionate kiss before laughing and saying, "What do you think of a double wedding?"

I bent and whispered in her ear, "I'm not thinking about anything beyond tonight and sampling some of that post-proposal loving."

She laughed, blushed, then hugged me.

Yep, like her parents, she got huggy when she was happy, but I didn't hate that at all either.

Not one damn bit.

EPILOGUE

IN A SLIGHTLY musty room in a small church, Dominic adjusted the sleeves of a simple tuxedo. Jared could have secured a multi-million-dollar venue and filled it with the rich and famous. Hell, he owned a yacht nearly the size of the church—one that was impressive even by Dominic's standards but this wedding wasn't about impressing the masses.

Michawn had reconnected with her family and hometown friends and this was as much a celebration of that as it was a wedding. Dominic respected that. Money didn't make a person—the people they surrounded themselves with did.

In the beginning, Dominic had had his doubts about Jared, but no longer.

The man who'd once kept his name change a secret had grown comfortable enough with his journey to invite one of his foster families, the Seacrests, to his wedding. Few would understand how monumental of a move that was.

Jared had faced down his past and chosen to free himself from the shame of it. For that reason, along with many others, Dominic would ensure no harm ever came to Jared or his family. The Seacrests, even if they never knew it, were protected. What would that mean for Jared's father, Dennis Smith? That would rely entirely on the choices Dennis made.

A knock on an open door was followed by the arrival of Dominic's wife in a stunning navy-blue dress. He took a moment to appreciate how even after twenty years she could still take his breath away. "Beautiful as always," he murmured before dipping his head down to give her lips a careful, non-lipstick ruining, kiss. Single Dominic wouldn't have thought to hold back, but Abby was more than just a woman he enjoyed in his bed. She was his best friend, the mother of his children, and someone who inspired him daily to hold back the darkness.

"Thank you." The slight flush to her cheeks meant neither her lipstick nor that dress would stay on her long that night.

Dominic smiled when she straightened his already straight bow tie. Her gentle touch never ceased to warm him to his soul.

"And you're ready," she said. "Which is good because Gavin was looking for you. He said the best man shouldn't make the groom wait."

After a quick glance at his watch confirmed that he wasn't late, Dominic said, "Tell Gavin if he gives me shit I'll have him demoted to flower girl."

Abby shook her head, but looked like she was holding back a smile. "Dominic Corisi, be nice to Gavin. He graciously accepted that you took his spot beside Jared today."

"He didn't have to. I told Jared he wasn't required to choose me, but Gavin wasn't the one who told him how to win Michawn over."

With a chuckle, Abby linked her arm with his. "Once again you're lucky it worked out the way it did."

He spun her in his arms. "Luck has nothing to do with repeated success. Admit that I might know something about what women want."

Eyes bright with desire, she slid her arms up around his neck. "I admit nothing."

"Mmmmhmmm. Maybe not now, but later you will." Her smiling lips were a temptation he decided he could no longer resist.

As he bent to claim them, a male voice interrupted. "Dominic, I need a moment alone."

A tense-looking Jared filled the doorway.

That couldn't be good.

After sharing a quick look with Abby, Dominic released her and said, "Of course."

Abby gave Jared a quick hug before slipping out.

Jared pocketed his hands and inhaled audibly.

Dominic waited.

In an angry tone, Jared demanded, "Why is this hard? I love her. She loves me. This is the happiest day of my life. What the hell is wrong with me?"

There was a time when Dominic would have said he wasn't a medical clinician so he couldn't say, but instead he kindly held his tongue.

Jared paced before him. "I want to marry Michawn."

"I should hope so, although if you've changed your mind, now is as good as any to announce it."

"I haven't changed my mind. Not at all." He made a frustrated sound then met Dominic's gaze. "Tell me I won't fuck this up, Dominic. I need to know I can make Michawn as happy as you've made Abby. Not just today . . . but forever . . ."

This was something Dominic understood. He'd also feared he would one day repeat the sins of his father, but he hadn't. It was possible to break a generational pattern of abuse, but it wasn't easy. Unwilling to lie to Jared, Dominic said, "You'll fuck up in a thousand different ways, again and again."

Jared's eyes narrowed.

Dominic continued, "So will she. You'll disagree, disappoint, argue . . . that's marriage. But you're stronger than what anyone ever did to you. You don't have to be perfect to be the right man for Michawn. Be kind. Be honest. Listen to her and forgive her when she's the one who isn't perfect. Respect and friendship—that's also marriage."

Nodding slowly, Jared seemed to relax. "And we have that already. I just want to make her happy."

Dominic added, "That's an impossible goal. Happiness is

an individual choice. All you can do is be good to them and encourage them to be good to themselves. Also, bringing home chocolates and bags of chips during strategic times each month doesn't hurt."

That made Jared smile. "Dominic, I don't have many friends but those I do let close become my family. I'm honored to have you at my side today. Thank you for your friendship as well as your advice."

In a thick voice, Dominic said, "You and I have a lot in common—the good and the bad. Now let's get you down that aisle."

Shoulder to shoulder with Dominic they made their way down the hallway to where the groomsmen were standing. Michawn's brothers greeted Jared with jokes and smiles. Dominic nodded in approval. These were good people.

Gavin stepped away from the group to speak to Dominic. "I didn't know Judy was bringing a date. Who is he?"

Dominic tensed, his smile little more than a baring of his teeth. "Nice try."

Gavin's eyebrows rose and fell. "She didn't tell you? Well, this should be interesting."

THE END

Look for scenes from Jared and Michawn's wedding in upcoming books set in this world.

Made in United States
Orlando, FL
19 March 2023

31185708R00183